ESCAPE FROM AMBERGRIS CAYE

JOAN MAUCH

Copyright © 2016 by Joan Mauch
Cover © 2016 by Akira007/fiverr

All rights reserved.

Warning: The unauthorized reproduction or distribution of this copyrighted work is illegal. Criminal copyright infringement, including infringement without monetary gain, is investigated by the FBI and is punishable by up to 5 (five) years in federal prison and a fine of $250,000.

Names, characters and incidents depicted in this book are products of the author's imagination and are used fictitiously. Any resemblance to actual events, locales, organizations or persons, living or dead, is entirely coincidental and beyond the intent of the author or the publishers.

No part of this book may be reproduced or transmitted in any form or by any means, electronic or mechanical, including photocopying, recording, or by any information storage and retrieval system, without permission in writing from the publisher.

ISBN: 978-1523726868

Printed in the United States of America

ACKNOWLEDGEMENT

While there were countless sources of information that I accessed during the course of researching and writing "Escape from Ambergris", the following were especially helpful and include: the Polaris Project; Cathy O'Keefe, executive director of Braking Traffik; Tina Frundt, trafficking survivor and founder of Courtney's House; *Human Trafficking Documentary* by MOTFT (YouTube); *The Slave across the Street* by Theresa Flores (Ampelon Publishing, 2010); *Human Trafficking, Human Misery: The Global Trade in Human Beings* by Alexis A Aronowitz (Praeger Publishers, 2009); and hours of online research on Belize and Ambergris Caye.

Thank you also to my friend, former TV producer, Beth Paul, for keeping me on the right track with respect to TV news production and police procedure; to members of the Iron Pen critique group, Kristal Shaff, Wayne Sapp and Rich Miller for their tireless page reviews; and to my family for their continuing support. As has been repeated many times, it takes a village to raise a child—the same can be said for writing and publishing a novel. Without the assistance of everyone listed here as well as many who are not, this book would not have become a reality. I would also like to acknowledge the encouragement I have received from my readers. Without you, it would all be for naught. Thank you all so very much.

Dedication

For my family—with all my love

Chapter 1

The weight of the gun surprised Hester. It was cold, meat-locker cold—a dead thing. Oil stained the paper bag she'd hid it in. She abhorred the mechanical stink of it. Tears filled her dark brown eyes, making the weapon appear wavy, as though underwater. She began to sob.

Her free hand made its way behind her ear where she traced a circle of rough skin. Almost without realizing it, she pinched and scratched the hated thing, as if she could somehow obliterate it.

Looking out the window at a cement-grey sky, she breathed a long heavy sigh. The rainy weather made her despair even more palpable. Never had she imagined life would serve up such a cruel helping. For her, things wouldn't get better, no matter what she did or how hard she tried.

Taking in a lungful of air, she wiped her cheek on the sleeve of her thin yellow blouse. What she had to do was clear. There was only one path available and much as she would have liked to go a different way, there simply was no other.

She had been fondling the small revolver for several minutes. It felt warm, having absorbed heat from her sweaty palm. It seemed to reach out to her, beckoning almost seductively. It won't be that hard, it seemed to say.

The shabby room was barely nine by nine with a single curtainless window to which ornamental security bars were attached. A metal frame bed sporting a lumpy mattress and a three-drawer bureau populated it. Carved out of the wall was a minuscule closet scarcely large enough for her few articles of clothing.

Hester wouldn't miss the place, for damn sure. Unable to tolerate life any longer, she knew without a doubt only she could change it—and for her the change-agent was this gun.

The odor of yet another greasy supper wafted its way up the stairs and beneath her bedroom door. Rather than stimulate her appetite, it made her nauseous. The damned dog as barking again. That was another thing Hester wouldn't miss.

She swallowed, tried to push down the lump in her throat and then glanced at the cheap watch encircling her wrist. A faint smile played on her lips as she recalled the joy she'd felt upon receiving it. It had been a gift from her mother the last Christmas she was home.

Remembering that caused Hester the same exquisite pain it had countless times before. Intense longing for her family overwhelmed her, nearly threatening her resolve. Tears came in swift moving torrents, overflowing her cheeks and dripping onto her lap. Annoyed with herself, she shouldered them away and returned to her plan.

It was time. If she delayed or lost her nerve, the opportunity may never present itself again and she'd be trapped. For the rest of her life, however short or long it might be, she'd be stuck—like a pig in mud, she'd be up to her ears in it, incapable of changing a thing. Hester understood this with deadly certainty.

The revolver drooped in her hand, its barrel pointing to the floor. Hester had never handled a weapon before but had watched countless TV shows in which they were used. The shooter "cocked" something before firing. She located a knobby thing on top and pulled it back.

Her hands trembled. *Geez, get a grip girl*, she counseled herself, there's only one chance to get this right. If she screwed up, she knew without a doubt the consequences would be dire.

Taking in several mouthfuls of air, as if preparing for a race, Hester hooked her long black hair behind her ear, raised the gun to her right temple—and fired.

Chapter 2

Jackson Taylor panned the street as he filmed B-roll for the story.

"C'mon, let's go. We've been at this long enough," Izzie, his reporter whined. "I'm sick of this stupid festival." She gave her photographer a hard look. "It doesn't have to be perfect, ya' know."

Ignoring her disparaging comment, Jackson continued videotaping. New to Tampa, this was his first experience with Gasparilla and he was more than a little intrigued.

"So, what's it about?" He stopped recording and glanced at his reporter who tapped her foot on the sidewalk, her arms folded tightly across her chest.

She sighed. "It supposedly celebrates a Spanish pirate who operated around here a long time ago. The festival starts with the landing of a ship in the bay. Then the city's invaded by pirates and the mayor turns over the key to the city. That marks the beginning of the festival. It's kinda stupid if you ask me."

Jackson wrinkled his forehead. "So, what's a Gasparilla? Some sort of drink?"

"Not *what*, silly, *who*. It's that pirate, Jose Gaspar."

"And the festival lasts how long?"

"Seems like forever.' Letting out another sigh, she said, "It starts with the children's parade—which was last week, goes into the Pirate Festival and merges into the Sant'yago Illuminated Knight Parade. There's even the Gasparilla Distance Classic races; the Bay Area Renaissance Festival; Strawberry Festival; the Gasparilla Festival of the Arts; the Gasparilla Music Festival and the GIFF."

Before Jackson could ask what GIFF stood for, she added, "GIFF's the Gasparilla International Film Festival. I wish they'd just call the whole thing, "All Things Gasparilla" and be done with it. The whole thing's one big bore."

"Brings in lots of tourists though, right?"

"Yeah, something like four hundred thousand people—and, as you know, traffic's tied up like nobody's business." Her face flushed, Izzie seemed about to lose her temper. "If you don't have any more questions, can we go now?"

Normally slow to anger, Jackson swallowed and bit his lip. "Sure, give me a minute to wrap this up."

"I'm not standing around waiting for you all day." When he didn't respond, she added, "I'm going back to the van."

Jackson watched as she turned her back on him and walked down the block. Then he touched the keys in his pocket and grinned. She wasn't going anywhere.

Chapter 3

Jennifer stood on the balcony, watching the crowd and listening to the cacophony of sound that seemed to envelope her. People laughed, music blared and the crowd cheered as the parade passed by. Beads, coins and candy were being tossed from floats.

She wanted so much to be a part of it—a part of anything for that matter. She draped her thin frame over the banister to get a better look.

"What the hell're you doing out here?" Leon's gruff voice startled her, for a second she thought she'd lose her balance and go crashing two stories to the street below. She almost wished she had.

Grabbing her by the shoulders, he growled, "Get inside".

Jennifer knew better than to sass him. What Leon wanted, Leon got. She went into the hall off the balcony and headed to her room.

"I catch you out there again, and you get to go you know where. Understand?"

Jennifer nodded, "Yes, I'm sorry. I just wanted to see what was going on."

"I don' wanna hear your shit. By now you should know all's that's important round here is *what I want*. Got it?" When she didn't respond, he cuffed her and repeated, "Got it?"

"Uh, uh, yes, I got it."

"Yes, what?"

"Yes, Leon."

"Who loves you?"

"You do."

"Who feeds you, gives you a warm place to sleep and clothes to wear? Who?"

"You do."

"Damn right. And what'll happen if I decide to stop?"

"I'll starve."

Jennifer knew the routine by heart and was careful to make the correct response to his questions. The results of a wrong answer or a sullen expression would mean either a beating or another week in what Leon referred to as the bunker. She headed back to the place she called "her room". A tiny hole-in-the-wall kind of place, it held an iron bedstead with its lumpy mattress and threadbare blanket, and a three drawer bureau—a far cry from the sunny room she'd had growing up.

Startled from her thoughts upon hearing footsteps coming down the hall, she turned around as the bedroom door swung back and hit the wall with a loud thunk.

Leon stood there looking at her, a strange expression on his face. Then without a word, he pushed her down onto the bed.

Jennifer started to protest, but he put his hand over her mouth, "Don't even try. There's no one here to help you—unless you count the dog."

With one quick yank, he pulled her shorts and underpants down. His knee holding her firmly in place, he slipped his trousers off and positioned himself on top of her. He made what to Jennifer sounded almost like the groans of an animal as the metal bed creaked rhythmically up and down.

Tears streaming down her cheeks, she took refuge inside her brain. How long had it been since she got here and where was she anyway? This was certainly not the Midwest. She could tell by the palm trees outside her window, it was someplace down south.

Why hadn't she obeyed her mom? She'd said to stay home and do her homework. But, no-o-o, she just had to hang out at the mall. Her mother wouldn't be any the wiser. She worked all day, while Jennifer went to school. That day, however, school was closed for teacher conferences and at fourteen she was too old for a baby sitter.

So she'd walked the two miles to the shopping center. Despite their parents and teachers' disapproval, that's where all the kids hung out. What was the big deal? She now knew what the big deal was, and it was too late. How would she ever get back home? And what was Leon planning to do with her?

"Now, wasn't that fun," Leon said pulling up his pants. "There's no need to make a fuss. Besides, we have to start getting you ready. You can't live off me forever, you know."

Jennifer's dark eyes widened, "What do you mean? Get me ready for what?"

There was pain between her legs from Leon's forcible intrusion into her body. She tried to ignore it, but it hurt. Gingerly, she propped herself up on the side of the bed.

"Don't act so innocent, you know exactly what I'm talking about."

A wiry man, around five ten, Leon had a swarthy complexion, thick black hair and a day-old beard he seemed to think looked sexy. His piercing black eyes were the first thing most people noticed. They were almost hypnotic, seeming to hold the promise of violence.

Jennifer began to tear up, "No, no, I really don't. Leon, why can't I go home?"

"Let's not start that again. I told you your ma don't want you. You hung around the mall spending her money. She couldn't afford it, so she gave you to me. Remember? I explained how I took you off her hands. You have nowhere to go."

Jennifer trembled. "I don't believe you. Mom would never do a thing like that."

"Calling me a liar, you little bitch?" With one swoop of his muscular arm, Leon hit her across the face, making a sharp cracking sound. Jennifer's head snapped back. She involuntarily gasped and let out a small cry. He grabbed her arm and dragged her down the hall.

"Please Leon, don't, I'll be good," Jennifer said. "Don't make me go down there." The bunker was stifling and smelly. "Please."

"Then shut the hell up and do what you're told." Leon shoved her toward the bedroom. "I'll be back later to begin your lessons."

Downstairs, the dog was barking again.

Chapter 4

Invigorated by his session with the girl, Leon Donatello headed downstairs to get some coffee. Aside from Tiny, his rottweiler, the only one in the house right now was Jennifer, pretty, scared little Jennifer. She'd fetch a good buck for sure. Seymour'd be pleased.

That messy business with the other one was unfortunate. There'd been no need for all that drama. Shooting herself like that? What a goddamned mess. It'd taken hours to clean it up. How she'd managed to get hold of his gun in the first place was beyond him. He'd have to be more careful from now on.

He rubbed his left wrist. He always knew rain was on the way when that twinge of pain began. The injury was a souvenir left over from his childhood and the beatings he received from his screw-up older brothers. Well, look where they were now: one was six feet under, compliments of a shotgun blast from a rival gang and the other was doing twenty- to-life in Statesville.

He touched the scar on his left cheek compliments of another youthful altercation. The odd-shaped mark gave him a bad-boy look, making him appear tough—at least that's what the girls in class used to say—that is when he bothered to go. As he'd passed from middle school to high school he went less and less often and then dropped out. That's when he joined the South Side Vipers thinking they'd provide what was lacking in his life. What that something was, he didn't know. He'd felt a longing for family connections other kids took for granted, but it hadn't worked. The Vipers simply replaced his brothers with their own brand of brutality.

Leon poured scalding water over the instant-coffee crystals. The distinct smell wafted up his nose. He blew on the cup, then took a sip, burning the roof of his mouth. He didn't care. Caffeine was his drug of choice; it energized him, giving him an instant pickup. Oh yeah, he'd experimented with drugs. There was cocaine, weed and the occasional bit of ecstasy, but even though he'd sold the stuff, he didn't care that much about it. No, coffee would do him just fine.

Tiny whined, hoping for a morsel of food. Leon kicked him in the ribs, no sense spoiling the mutt. He was here for one reason and one reason only—to control the product and keep nosy neighbors away. The rot had been Seymour's idea. Leon wasn't a "dog" kinda guy and would just as soon have done without one. Damned dog barked at all hours, course the neighbors don't say much, just gave him the evil eye. Guess they finally got the message: if they knew what was good for them they'd keep their pie-holes shut. So, maybe Seymour was right. The damned dog was good for something after all.

Boss never came around. Wouldn't want to get his carefully manicured nails dirty. He wasn't like that when they were both in the Vipers. How'd he get so high and mighty anyhow? Now the man just "directs and collects". Makes Leon take all the risks. And if he got caught? Seymour wouldn't be around to catch his back, that's for damned sure.

Leon sat by the window and looked out. It was a pleasant enough house. At forty, he was glad to have a roof over his head even if it didn't belong to him. But he couldn't help wondering how long Seymour planned on keeping him around.

A few weeks back Leon had confronted his boss with the fact that his risk was far greater than Seymour's, and that he should get a bigger cut. After all, he controlled the "product"—young girls and women intimidated through beatings and rape. And managed sales with the customers Seymour sent his way.

His boss' reaction hadn't been at all what he'd expected. Said guys like Leon were a dime a dozen and totally expendable. He'd pointed out that the girl's suicide had jeopardized the whole operation, implying it was Leon's fault—which it really was, since it was his gun the girl used to kill herself. Leon shuddered realizing Seymour'd retire him—permanently, if it served his purpose. He knew only too well what happened when someone failed to deliver.

Wonder how the press'd react if they knew Mr. Seymour Cottingham, the respected mortgage broker and philanthropist was not only a former gangbanger, but a money launderer and one of the powers behind the biggest human-trafficking rings in the country. It was worth considering.

Leon finished his coffee, yawned and stretched. *Got to brand the product before the customer arrives. Let me see now, guess it'll be I-4.* He chuckled. *Cops'll go nuts trying to figure out what the mark on that dead girl means, that is if they ever find her body.*

Branding the product was his way of tracking sales. It was like the bar codes stores use. He kept a ledger hidden under a loose floorboard in which he recorded the dates of the product acquisition and sale; the product's code number: state of origin and number and the buyer's name and address. That way he had a complete history of the transaction. Sounded cold, but after all—business was business. How else would he know if Seymour was being straight with him? Leon knew the ledger had to be kept out of the wrong hands, but then who would ever figure out what it meant anyway? It looked perfectly legitimate.

Too bad he'd never made it through school. He had a good brain and a nose for business. If it had been a legitimate product, he could've started his own company, even offered shares on Wall Street. He would've been an entrepreneur.

Leon sighed. Instead of high society, he was forced to live on the seamy side of life, staying in the shadows, carefully hidden by the hypocritical bastard whose bidding he did. He was only a puppet. It wasn't much different from life in the gangs or at home with his brothers, for that matter. Seems like he was always under somebody's thumb.

Chapter 5

Jackson sat in the edit bay; his hand cupped his chin as he stared at the monitor. The tape was paused at the point in his Gasparilla coverage where he'd panned down the street and zoomed in on a girl watching the parade from a balcony. He stared intently trying to figure out what he was looking at. Was that girl simply a recalcitrant teen being disciplined by her dad, or was it something more sinister?

Recently he'd been reading about human trafficking—mostly women from third world countries lured to wealthy nations on the promise of better lives, only to be forced into slavery—everything from prostitution to sweatshops—even servitude in private homes.

Surely that wasn't happening here, not in front of his very eyes. That girl seemed young, couldn't be more than thirteen or so. He took a closer look. His imagination was probably running wild as usual. He told himself to forget about it. Nothing unsavory was going on. Not in a beautiful place like Tampa.

He took a final bite of his cheese and baloney sandwich and a swig from a bottle of ice water. Several stray drops fell onto his blue standard-issue shirt with the station's logo on the front. He wore khaki pants and jogging shoes.

Izzie poked her head around the corner. "Hey Jackson, I'm headin' out for lunch. Want something?"

Jackson shook his head and gestured to the half-empty sack on his desk. "I brought my lunch, thanks." A baggie with three chocolate chip cookies and an apple were all that remained. He was disappointed not to be able to take his reporter up on her rare display of kindness,

Izzie Campbell was attractive in that annoying "Aren't I just the prettiest thing" way many beautiful women have. Intelligent and stuck-up, she apparently thought a year of broadcast journalism made her an authority. Her slim, five foot five figure, sapphire-blue eyes, long blond hair, milky white skin and a generous smile—the rare times she chose to use it—resulted in Miss America quality beauty, a fact upon which she too-often capitalized.

Self-absorbed and overconfident, Izzie didn't seem to realize cameramen like Jackson, made her look good. She often treated him as though he was little more than a mule, schlepping heavy equipment around for her benefit. Jackson sighed. Working alongside people like that came with the territory.

"So what 'cha looking at?"

Jackson looked up, surprised to find she was still there. "Just something I caught on the shoot yesterday."

"What?" Uninvited, Izzie leaned over, touching Jackson's shoulder. She wore a short blue skirt, a crisp white blouse with a gold pendant and gold hoop earrings. Her black heels were low, styled for comfort. Jackson got a whiff of her perfume. It was the same stuff his mom often wore.

She squinted, sending vertical lines between her eyes.

"See that girl," Jackson put his finger on the screen and pointed at the balcony. "Now watch." He advanced the tape a frame at a time. They watched as a man came out and forced the girl inside.

"So? Maybe he's her dad and she was s'posed to do chores or homework and disobeyed him."

Jackson faced his partner. "You notice the look she gave him?"

"Play it again," Izzie said.

He cued the tape and they watched, their faces close to the screen so they could catch every nuance of the unwitting performance being played out before them.

"I see what you mean. She looks scared."

Jackson didn't know if she really thought he'd caught a crime in progress or was merely humoring him. "So what do we do?" he said.

"Do? I don't know," Izzie shrugged her shoulders. "What can we do?"

When Jackson didn't reply, she added, "Let me grab some lunch and I'll think about it. Our next shoot's not till two. We'll talk about it then. I'm starving."

Jackson turned back to the screen and decided to dub a copy to VHS. He'd review it at home. Maybe there was nothing amiss. It wouldn't be the first time he'd let his imagination run away with him. It had gotten him in trouble before, so he didn't want to go off half-cocked yet again.

He finished his package and had a few moments to relax before his next assignment, so he decided to go online and see what more he could find out about human trafficking.

After twenty minutes, what he learned sickened him. According the Polaris project website, modern-day slavery run by multinational crime networks is the second largest and fastest growing illegal trade in the world. As many as nine hundred thousand victims a year are enslaved through fraud or coercion. And the United States is a major destination country for as many as fifty thousand.

My God, it's happening under our very noses. The problem's so hidden we don't even know it's happening. Victims are broken down, "groomed" by beatings and rape, and imprisoned in dog cages, even kept in the trunks of cars. They're forced to work as laborers, sex slaves, even beggars and are so intimidated they fear reporting it. People around them aren't even aware that it's going on.

Could that young girl be the victim of such a hideous crime? The prospect horrified Jackson. He couldn't get it off his mind. He simply had to make certain she wasn't a slaver's victim. *But how to find out?* His mind began to churn out ideas: most of them bizarre and some downright illegal.

Chapter 6

Lifting his tripod and camera from the back of the station jeep, Jackson set up as close to the scene as the cops allowed. He leveled his lens and hit the "record" button. It was obvious something had died and not recently either. The area stank like rotting meat and spoiled eggs. He had to cover his nose and mouth to keep from gagging.

He tuned back in to hear Izzie report the corpse was a female, who apparently died from a gunshot wound to the head. The body was partially decomposed and bloated. A faded yellow blouse, shredded plaid skirt and some underclothes were the only evidence police reported. The victim had a tattoo behind her right earlobe, but they didn't know what, if any, significance it carried.

Izzie concluded with a plea to the public to contact police if anyone knew the identity of the victim or the circumstances surrounding her death.

On the way back to the station Jackson tried to shrug off the tragic story, but a voice inside his head wouldn't let it go. *A woman was dead—and no one missed her? How could that be?* His thoughts went back to that girl on the balcony. *What if? No, don't go there.*

For a change, Izzie was quiet, for which Jackson was grateful. His mind wandered back to stories he'd covered in the past few weeks: A triple-fatal—three people dead at the scene of an accident; a beauty pageant with the typical gorgeous girls vying for a crown of fake diamonds; a bank robber threatening to kill hostages and the discovery of a dead body—like today.

Similar to first responders, news crews often developed their own cryptic language and gallows' humor to help them cope with the mayhem they saw all too often. Jackson hadn't been working long enough to develop an indifference to the tragic stories he covered, but, if only to preserve his own sanity, he was getting there.

Operating the live truck was a part of the job Jackson both liked and feared. A remote studio utilized by TV stations to broadcast stories at the scene, the live truck was a two-edged sword providing a jump on the competition, but also presenting a danger to those involved.

When the truck's fifty-foot microwave mast was extended, if lightning was in the area or the operator got distracted, the results could be fatal. Not long before Jackson was hired, an inexperienced photographer drove off with the boom raised. It collided with high tension wires sending 8000 volts of electricity through his reporter's body. The woman died instantly.

Chapter 7

Leon waited for the microwave to signal that his frozen spaghetti and meatball dinner was ready. With two minutes to go, he walked into the adjoining family room, found the TV remote and pushed the power button. Then he pressed thirty-nine. For some reason, he preferred watching that station's newscast, he really didn't know why. Maybe the reporters were prettier or the weather reports shorter, who knew?

Hearing the oven beep, he went back to the kitchen and retrieved his supper. He sprinkled it with salt and pepper, snagged a can of beer and a fork, then returned to the family room and settled into his aging rocker-recliner to eat and watch the day's news.

He was swallowing his last bite when a story came that nearly caused him to choke. It was a piece covering the burial of the body found at the beach. A woman was making a speech over the coffin. And she was crying, for God's sake.

"I never met you," she began, "but I just know you were awesome. Growing up you must have had such promise. I'm positive your mom and dad were crazy about you and I know if they were here now, they'd tell you how much they love and miss you. Your passing has created an enormous hole in their hearts that never will be filled. They long for the day when they will be with you again. God bless you, little darling, may you rest in peace."

When she finished, the camera panned the cemetery. The woman stood alone at the gravesite.

"What the hell's she doing?" Leon startled Tiny, who lay on the floor next to the recliner.

His alarm made its way from the pit of his stomach through his chest and up to his throat, where it parked itself in a knot, making it difficult to swallow.

Leon leaned forward, spilling the last ounce of beer down the front of his pants. *Damn it all.* He stood up to retrieve a cloth from the kitchen. *Who the hell was that?*

His question was answered a few seconds later as a pretty reporter began the interview.

The lady's name was Martha Simpson from Lutz, a city about sixteen miles north of Tampa. She'd come to experience Gasparilla and visit her son, daughter-in-law and grandchildren. When she heard about the unidentified woman found off Clearwater Beach, it touched her heart and she couldn't bear the thought of someone going to their grave unmourned. So she appointed herself the unofficial representative of the girl's family and attended the burial on their behalf. It was as simple as that.

Leon was dismayed. The woman had succeeded in making an obscure girl's death into a tearjerker.

"Make me cry why don't ya," Leon muttered, disgusted. "Just my luck the network'll notice and run the story on national television. All's I need is for Seymour to see it. Or worse, for the parents to find out what happened to their precious daughter. They'll put pressure on the cops for sure, then here we go.

Seymour'll go ape-shit and who knows what'll happen. Why the hell don't people mind their own business?"

To be on the safe side, he jotted her name and city down in his ledger next to the information on I-3. Now if things got out of hand, he'd know where to find her.

Tiny stood in front of him, whining and trying to make eye contact. The dog was hungry and he hadn't fed I-4 yet either. *Chores, chores, where does the time go?* He also had to get the girl ready for viewing by a customer coming later. Leon hoped the buyer liked I-4. Hanging onto the merchandise too long was risky. Not only that, but he was getting used to having her around. No, better to keep the product moving.

Chapter 8

On their lunch break, which was neither really lunch nor a break, Izzie and Jackson sat by the side of the road in the news van inhaling pizza they'd been able to grab at a local convenience store. With nothing else to talk about, Jackson raised the issue of the girl on the balcony.

"You still obsessing over that?" Izzie snorted.

Izzie's lack of interest annoyed Jackson, who usually managed to keep his opinion to himself. This time the words popped out before his self-censoring mechanism kicked in. "I guess if it's not about you, then it's not important."

"Excuse me?" Izzie's eyebrows shot up along with the tone in her voice.

Jackson felt his ears heat up as blood rushed to his face. "It's just that you don't seem to give a lick about anybody but yourself, let alone those young girls. One either committed suicide or was murdered and the other has some kind of issue going on with that man who yanked her off the balcony. Couldn't you at least pretend to give a flying fig?"

He hadn't meant to go on like that, but the door was open and he'd gone through it. He knew there'd be a price to pay, but it was too late to back out.

Izzie threw him a look that said it all: He was a stupid jerk not worth a response. She looked at her watch and said, "We'd better get going or we'll be late."

Those were the last words she said to him for the rest of the day.

Chapter 9

It was Friday night and Jackson had trouble sleeping. Throbbing pain from balancing the camera on his shoulder was more intense than usual. It was his constant companion these days. *If that was the price he had to pay for pursuing his dream job, then so be it.* To Jackson, a little discomfort was more than worth it.

He got up, took two Advils and then switched his laptop on. After making silly comments to a high school buddy on Facebook and watching some videos on YouTube, he checked his email. That was a big mistake. Izzie had posted a message that sent shivers down his spine:

Okay, Mr. Hotshot Cameraman. U think you no me? Like, what U no don't scratch the surface. Just 'cause I'm a reporter and have looks, don't mean I don't care 'bout people. That girl they buried other day? The one nobody but that woman cared enough to stand at her grave? For your information, Smartypants, I felt real bad bout her. She made me think about the girl on the balcony UR so worried bout. I been going over there to see if I can find out what's going on. Been back several times. That guy in the video started to notice. The last time he waved and asked me to go for a drink. I said no, but if he does it again, I'll take him up on it. If I can get him to invite me in, I'll check on that girl. So, see, Jackson, UR not the only one with a heart. I have one too, even if I don't wear it on my sleeve like U do. See you at work. Izzie

Jackson's heart pounded as he typed, his fingers moving furiously over the keyboard:

No, no, Izzie, don't do that. As you said it was probably only a father disciplining his daughter. If something's going on, you could end up in the middle of it. Please, leave it alone. **DON'T GO BACK THERE!!!!** *I'm sorry for the rude comment. I didn't mean it. My shoulder was hurting and I overreacted. Let's talk about it Monday and see what we can come up with. In the meantime, I'm begging you—don't go anywhere near that guy!!! Jackson*

The next morning, Jackson couldn't shake an uneasy feeling. Izzie's email stayed with him. *What if she'd gone back there? What if the man was a trafficker, had noticed her hanging around and grabbed her? Where was she now?*

Whoa, man, get hold of yourself. You're always letting your imagination get the best of you. *There is no trafficker*—just a guy who noticed a pretty girl and invited her out for a drink. That's all there was to it. Who was he to interfere? Besides, he'd emailed Izzie and told her to stay out of it. She might be a bit stuck on herself and think she knows it all, but she's not stupid. She'll be all right. We'll talk about it Monday. There's no need to get all crazy over this.

Jackson had to fight the urge to call Izzie and make sure she was all right. She'd gotten his email, he told himself. The woman was all but surgically attached to her computer. There was no way she didn't get that message. He'd made it clear she'd be putting herself at risk if she went back there. Besides, she was an adult, more than capable of making her own decisions.

Jackson touched the tender spot on his shoulder and glanced around the apartment: The fridge was almost empty. Dirty dishes filled the sink, an empty pizza box peeked from the overflowing garbage can and a basket burdened with a profusion of smelly clothes begged to be laundered. Collecting empty beer cans that populated his living room like unwanted guests, he decided he'd gotten worked up over nothing. Taking another look at the disaster his living space had become, he headed out the door to buy groceries. The dishes and laundry could wait.

Chapter 10

The weekend went by too fast for Jackson's taste. Seemed like he'd barely got caught up with his chores when it was Monday and time to start the routine all over again. He wasn't looking forward to another week with Izzie. She knew exactly which buttons to push to aggravate him. Well, not today. He'd do his assignments and keep his mouth shut. If she wanted to bitch about people or her personal life, she'd have to find another shoulder to cry on. Speaking of shoulders, he rubbed his. It was still sore.

After picking up his equipment and checking to make sure everything was working, Jackson glanced around, absently listening to the ebb and flow of newsroom activity. Fingers clicked across computer keyboards reflecting the typists' urgency. Reporters and photographers headed out to cover assigned stories. One of the newer photogs gleefully proclaimed he'd gotten a "shot of the blood stains…"

Jackson didn't hear the rest. He didn't have to. Those first days on the job were one big adrenaline rush. He sighed. Was the honeymoon over? He still liked the work, but somehow the excitement was beginning to slip away. It had become something of a grind. Well, what did he expect? Life wasn't one big thrill ride, no matter how much he wished it was.

He checked the time again. It was well after eight. *Where the hell was that woman?* They'd have to get a move on if they were going to make it to the news conference. It was true they had plenty of time, since it was only a few miles away, but Jackson liked to arrive early to get a good spot. Izzie didn't seem to understand his part of the job.

Yes, she had to stand in front of the camera, look good, write the stories and report them without getting her words garbled. Jackson knew that wasn't easy. He'd seen plenty of reporters crack up, then have to repeat it over and over before they nailed it.

But if he understood how difficult reporters' jobs were, why couldn't they understand that photographers worked equally hard? He'd personally taken a workshop on lighting at his own expense to improve the quality of his work. Instead of appreciating it, people like Izzie got annoyed because, in her words, "he's too fussy and should just point, shoot and get it over with."

He'd even overheard her call him a prima donna. Well, maybe he was, who knew? He rubbed his shoulder again and looked at his watch. *Where was that girl?* He'd lost his lead time and would be lucky to even get set up before the news conference began.

Glancing around the room again, he headed over to the assignment editor's desk.

"Why're you still here? Aren't you supposed to be at the convention center by now?" Morris Stone, the chief photographer, had just joined them. "What the hell's going on?"

"I know," Jackson said, "but Izzie's not here yet. She call in sick or something?"

"If she had, you would've been told. Right?" The assignment editor was clearly flustered. "Go on over there and get set up. When she shows up, I'll tell her where to go—literally."

They guffawed at the reference to what happens when someone let the team down.

Jackson headed out the door toward the news van. Now he'd really have to hustle. He didn't have time to worry about a truant reporter.

Chapter 11

Jackson had managed to land a spot to the far left of his preferred position when Izzie pushed her way through the gaggle of reporters and photogs. Generally unflappable, she appeared nervous, her hair less than perfect, her face an odd shade of red.

"Hey," she said.

Jackson glanced up from the camera and nodded. Because of Izzie his tape would no doubt be subpar. And who'd catch flak for it? Not her for damned sure. He took a deep breath, muttered "S'up?" and turned his attention back to the camera.

"Sorry. You have a lousy position because of me."

Izzie never apologized for anything—ever, even when she made an obvious blunder. She always—always turned things around to make it appear as though the mistake was her photographer's fault—in this case, Jackson's. So when the word, "sorry" dribbled from her mouth, however softly, he had a hard time suppressing his surprise.

"No problem," he said, as though arriving forty-five minutes late for an assignment was an everyday occurrence. He was about to ask what happened, when the news conference began. Izzie and her excuse would have to wait.

Half an hour later on their way to the next shoot, Jackson addressed the issue.

"So, what happened this morning? You oversleep?"

"Uh, nothing, it was nothing."

Her expression said it was a whole lot more than nothing, but if she didn't want to talk about something there was no use trying to pry it from her. He tried another tack. "Morrie give you hell?"

She nodded. "You could say that."

"What'd he say?" Jackson knew it was none of his business, but curiosity got the better of him.

"He called me into his office and said if I pulled another stunt like that, not to bother showing up again—period, that I'd be canned."

Jackson knew his boss was something of a hardass, but that seemed harsh even for him.

"He really said you'd be canned?"

"Not his exact words, but his meaning was clear. Man, he doesn't mess around, does he?"

"Guess not. I'd prefer not finding out."

He turned his attention to the latest disaster he had to film. A sinkhole had swallowed a house. Fortunately the family wasn't home at the time. Still, all their possessions had disappeared. From the looks of it, they weren't very well off to begin with. Having to witness so much misery was beginning to get to him.

Afterward, in an effort to get his mind off that newly homeless family, Jackson asked Izzie if she got his email.

"What email?" she said.

"The one telling you to stay away from where we spotted that girl on the balcony."

"And who put you in charge all of a sudden?" Izzie barked, "Since when do I need your permission to check something out if I feel like it?"

"It's not that, Izzie, but when you said the man spotted you, well, I was concerned, that's all."

Izzie turned in the seat to face him. "So you're all concerned about me, are ya? Well, I don't need your so-called concern or your protection neither. I'm a grown woman. I can take care of myself. If I want to do a little investigative reporting on my own time, I'll bloody well do it whether you like it or not. Got it?"

"I'm not trying to tell you what to do." Jackson's heart drummed in his ears. "It's just that I've been reading about human trafficking and…"

"Human trafficking again? That's what got your shorts in a bunch? God, Jackson, get real. This is Tampa, Florida not Malaysia or Thailand. Women here aren't trying to leave the country or escape poverty by falling for whatever dumb story some guy tells them." As she spoke, she became more animated, her eyebrows raising and lowering, emphasizing each point she made.

"I know. That's what I thought too till I started looking into it. Izzie, according to a report by the National Human Trafficking Center, it's happening all over the world—including in the United States. It's going on right in front of us, and we don't realize it."

The skeptical look on Izzie's face said it all. She didn't believe a word he said. "You always blow things out of proportion. Babe, you need to get a life. Find a girlfriend. Go bowling. Do whatever you want, but stop seeing bogeymen behind every tree. Or at least don't keep trying to 'save' me. It's exhausting."

Jackson lifted his hands from the steering wheel in surrender. "I got the message, Iz, what you do on your own time is your business. I'll stay the hell out of it. You want to get yourself in trouble, have at it. Just don't say you weren't warned." With that he pulled into the parking lot, grabbed his gear and walked away, leaving her to follow in his wake.

Chapter 12

Leon opened the back door and let Tiny out. That was another reason he hadn't wanted a dog. The mutt had to go out several times a day. And remembering was a royal pain in the ass. If he waited too long or was away taking care of business, the damned thing pooped in the house. One time, Leon even stepped in it. Almost beat the dog to death for that. They'd both learned something that day: Leon remembered to let him out and Tiny held it until he did.

The house was quiet now. Jennifer was gone. Seymour's client picked her up Friday night. The transaction had gone down smoothly enough despite the unpleasant scene: she'd kicked and screamed, begged him to let her stay. Little bitch even bit the client when he tried to take her. In the end, they'd shot her up with drugs. That calmed her down long enough for them to get her out of the house.

Yes, it was quiet now, a little too quiet for Leon's taste. Well, not for long. Seymour'd be sending another shipment soon. In the meantime, he had some rare free time. Maybe he'd go to Clearwater Beach for some well-earned R&R. Pick up a chick or two.

How about the one he'd noticed hanging around the other day? A real looker she was. Reminded him of somebody, but he couldn't put his finger on exactly who. He'd waved at her from the balcony and invited her to go for a drink. She'd declined, but gave him a flirty smile, then turned and left, her hips in those tight jeans swaying in the most inviting fashion. He told himself she wanted him, that she was playing hard to get. She'd be back, oh yeah. And when she came, he'd be waiting. He had all the time in the world.

Chapter 13

Hi Mom.

Jackson's fingers clicked rapidly over the computer keyboard. He much preferred texting, but she hadn't managed to get the hang of it so he was left to either call or email. With his limited resources, email was cheaper. Besides, he kind of liked getting his thoughts out with no interruption. It had only been a few hours since he and Izzie had had "words" and he was still smarting from her retort.

How're you and Dad doing? Is he feeling better? I know it's hard on you when he's sick—he can be such a baby. Not that me or Zac're any better. Truth is, you're the strongest member of the Taylor family, whether we want to admit it or not

Life in Florida's pretty good though I'm still getting used to it. Tampa's beautiful, but the traffic is bad. I can't wait till you guys come for a visit. There's so much to do and see. I know money's tight so it'll have to wait, still it's something to look forward to.

The job is everything I'd hoped and more. I love being a news photographer. You get to see and do exciting things most every day. When I was in school, I never thought someone would actually hire me. It seemed so impossible, like trying to become a movie star—something you dream about, but never really think will happen. And now, here I am. Mom, I know you worry about me, but I'm fine, really. Eating good. Doing my laundry. Even keeping my apartment clean."

Jackson stopped typing and glanced around his filthy apartment. Only this morning he'd taken the trash out, so it wasn't a total lie. He'd do the laundry tomorrow.

Right now my only problem is my reporter, Izzie. I've told you about her: pretty girl, a year out of college; thinks she knows it all. Comes from money so she thinks she's entitled. Never, ever admits she's wrong or realizes her partner's a professional too. It can be frustrating. Most times I just write it off to her being young and stupid. But lately it's getting a whole lot harder to do that—especially when she does things that could get her in trouble.

Like today, for instance, I found out she's hanging around an apartment where I suspect a young girl may be a trafficking victim. Since I have no proof, there isn't anything I can do about it and reporting it to the police will alert the trafficker that someone's on to him. I planned to keep my eye on the place. Then I found out Izzie was doing the same thing, but that the guy spotted her. When I found out, I told her to be careful, that if the guy is, in fact, involved in trafficking, she's putting herself in danger.

I only told her that because I genuinely care what happens to her. You know what she said? 'Mind your own business. Who are you to tell me what to do? I'm a grown woman and can take care of myself. I don't need you to protect me.' Or something to that effect.

I wasn't trying to boss her around or anything. But she's a beautiful young woman, just the kind a trafficker would love to get his hands on. She thinks I'm making it up when I tell her what I've read about human trafficking going on all over the country, including here in Tampa. Mom, right now I feel like if something happens to her, it'll serve her right. On the other hand, I hope it doesn't and I'm probably overreacting because of everything I've read.

You always said I had an active imagination and that's probably what makes me a good news photographer. I see beyond the obvious. But that can also be a two-edged sword, getting me in trouble. Plus people don't take me seriously because they think I overreact, which I admit I sometimes do.

Then something comes along like this and my own partner refuses to listen. I guess I have no choice but to wash my hands of the whole thing and let whatever happens, happen.

Well, it's getting late and I've had a hard day. Say hey to Zac and Dad for me.

Love, Jackson

Chapter 14

My dear darling boy. I'm glad to hear you love your job. We're all proud of you. Every time I go to the store, people ask how you're doing. I know it's a sin, but I swell up with pride when I see the envy in their faces. I know it's nothing I've done, that you worked hard to be where you are, but I just can't help myself. Now, if only your brother would stop smoking marijuana and finish his education, your father and I could stop worrying and rest easy. I guess I should be grateful at least one of my boys has turned out so well.

Your father's ailing, but try not to worry about it. I'm sure he'll pull out of it as he's done in the past. It's just that the drinking has affected his liver, and I doubt he can get a transplant. I don't think they put people with drinking problems on the list unless they can prove they've stopped and he hasn't, so we'll have to wait and see.

I don't want you to worry, dear boy, there's nothing you can do except pray. You could do that. There's nothing more powerful than prayer, you know. So, throw some your father's way.

As far as that girl's concerned, in a way, she's right. She's a grown woman and if she wants to put herself in a dangerous situation, that's her business. It's really stupid of her not to listen to you, but there it is.

It's like your brother. If he's determined to throw his life away by smoking and laying around instead of getting out there and making something of himself, all the nagging in the world won't change a thing. He's got to make up his own mind.

Same thing with Izzie. Don't waste your time fretting over a girl who thinks she's better than you, just because her daddy's rich. As far as I'm concerned you're head and shoulders better than anyone I know, and I'm not saying that because you're my son. It's the truth.

Love, Mom

Amanda Taylor closed the notebook computer and leaned back in her chair. Writing to her youngest still seemed odd, despite the fact he'd been in Tampa over a year. Tears came to her eyes. Her throat constricted as she held back the pain. She missed him, even if she didn't want to admit it. Life wasn't the same without Jackson around. She could still hear echoes of her boys around the house. Sometimes she thought if she looked fast enough, they'd still be there—tussling or arguing over something.

She so wished she could have those days back—have a do-over, as kids would say. She'd made mistakes despite her best efforts, but it was too late: They were grown up and way past needing her. Jackson was pursuing his dream in Tampa and Zac, well, he was—what could she say about her eldest son? That he was trying to find himself? She shrugged. How many years does it take to find oneself? It didn't appear to her that he was looking very hard. At the moment, the only thing he seemed to be pursuing was his next drink, another drag on a marijuana cigarette, or some girl.

Then there was Dan. How long could he hold on until his liver gave out altogether? Every day he seemed to look more jaundiced. The doctor had pretty much given up trying to make him stop drinking, said it was only a matter of time; that there was nothing anyone could do to help him since he was unable—or unwilling to help himself.

She sighed. Sometimes life could be so cruel.

Chapter 15

Jackson was restless. He had to get out and do something—anything: take a drive, go to the beach, whatever. Weekends went by too fast. Of course, if he'd get up earlier and didn't stay up half the night, maybe he'd have time for other stuff. Problem was, he liked staying up late and getting up even later. He shrugged. Sooner or later he'd figure it out. Maybe a drive to Clearwater Beach would help.

That email from Mom had upset him. He'd known Dad had health problems and that it was related to his drinking, but he never thought it would become life-threatening. Mom probably hadn't intended to reveal the true extent of his condition; she'd more than likely gotten carried away writing and the truth slipped out. The way it sounded, Dad was going to die; it was only a question of when.

Jackson didn't know what to do or if there was anything he could do. Should he quit his job and return home? Offer to give his father a portion of his liver? Was that even possible? He knew he only had the one liver, so it wasn't like a kidney, where a person had two.

Then there was the question of expense. Since his father had seldom been able to hold a job for more than a few months at a time, he doubted he had medical insurance. Even if Jackson was a match and donated a portion of his liver, how would they pay for it?

Dad had had a drinking problem for as long as he could remember. When he was little, he remembered his father coming home from work drunk. He'd literally drink his paycheck, leaving little or nothing for the family. Thankfully, he wasn't a mean drunk, so at least they were spared that.

Jackson inhaled. It seemed like he'd been worried about either his dad or his brother his whole life. Now he was living his dream—and feeling guilty for leaving his mom to deal with the situation. What should he do?

Clearwater Beach was calling. Grabbing his car keys, he headed out the door.

****

Traffic across Courtney Campbell Causeway and over to the Gulf was fairly light for a change, no doubt due to the lateness of the hour and the cool temperatures. As a result, Jackson didn't have to spend time driving around in search of parking. While he would have preferred that it was a few degrees warmer, he'd take what he could get and be grateful for it.

His beach towel and a bottle of water in hand, Jackson locked the car and headed toward Pier 60, a popular spot known for live music, spectacular sunsets over the Gulf and, yes, action—if you managed to get lucky, which he seldom ever did.

Removing his shoes to let sand flow through his toes, he marveled again at the beauty of the Gulf of Mexico and the blindingly white sand. More accustomed to cornfields and the rolling hills of Iowa, Jackson didn't think he'd ever get used to it even if he stayed in Florida the rest of his life.

He spread his towel, turned his face into the sun and took a deep breath as cool air riffled his thick hair. His eyes wandered across the beach to the water which sparkled as it reflected the sun and lapped the shore. Silhouettes of sailboats in the distance added to the charm of the scene.

Jackson had just started to relax, when he saw them up on the pier, leaning over the rail. The man pointed, his arm on her shoulder guiding her to whatever it was he wanted her to see below. It was most likely a porpoise or dolphin as they often were seen in these waters. But it wasn't the creature in the water that caught his attention—it was the woman. *Was that Izzie?*

He squinted, then stood to get a closer look. It *was* her. He could tell by the distinctive hair style, the way she stood with one hip thrust out, her head tilted just so as if she was posing for a picture. It had to be her. She stood like that all the time. And Jackson always noticed.

He took several steps forward to get a better look. *Was that the guy from the balcony?* He couldn't be sure, but desperately hoped it wasn't. What should he do? Go over there and pretend he'd been hanging out and came upon them by accident?

Izzie's angry words came back in a sickening rush. *I don't need your so-called concern or your protection either for that matter. I'm a grown woman. I can take care of myself.* Even his mom had told him to let it alone.

Suddenly the beach lost its appeal. He decided to go home by way of the Sunshine Bridge. Maybe that would lift his spirits. It usually did.

The first time Jackson saw it, he and Izzie were covering a suicide. Some mook had climbed over the side and jumped sixty feet into Tampa Bay. He remembered how emotional Izzie had become. The jumper couldn't have been more than sixteen. Izzie told him later that a few years ago, her brother killed himself at about the same age. In his case it was an overdose of sleeping pills, but the tragic outcome was the same.

He shook his head. The drive was meant to make him forget about the damned woman—and he meant to do precisely that. He looked down at the rippling waves glinting like diamonds in the afternoon sun. As many times as he'd gone across the four- mile span, it never failed to ignite a thrill inside.

Being new to the area, he'd done some research and learned the design was inspired by the Brotonne Bridge in France. The Travel Channel ranked the Sunshine Bridge as one of the top bridges in the world. Wow, now that was something worth bragging about.

However, it'd take a whole lot more than the view—spectacular though it was—to dispel his concern for Izzie's reckless behavior. His father's deteriorating health only added to his discomfort.

Heading back to his apartment, the double helping of worry wormed its way into Taylor's psyche destroying the modicum of peace he'd managed to achieve. He had decisions to make, very serious ones. But it was Sunday night and there was nothing he could do, at least for now.

Chapter 16

Monday morning came all too soon. Jackson had spent a restless night worrying about his father. When he finally managed to nod off, his dreams became nightmares with Izzie alternately insisting he mind his own business and screaming for help. He'd awakened with blankets in a tangle around his legs as he shivered in the cool morning air.

Spending the day with Izzie at his side was not something he looked forward to, especially after having had so little sleep. He yawned and rubbed his eyes. Although he hadn't had more than a few beers the previous evening, Jackson's head throbbed. He briefly considered calling in sick, but thought better of it. A few aspirins and some breakfast—his stomach lurched at the thought of food. Maybe just aspirin and some black coffee…

****

It was noon and Jackson felt better. His headache was gone and his stomach had settled down to the point that he was starving.

"Wanna grab some lunch?"

They'd just finished covering a story in Ybor City where a tourist had been robbed. A unique area not far from downtown Tampa, it once was the epicenter of cigar manufacturing in the U.S. Now home to specialty shops boasting "only-in-Tampa" wares, it was a favorite stop for tourists and natives alike. But unsavory types also roamed the area—at least they had today. Fortunately the only thing this particular woman lost was her purse. While inconvenient, it could easily be replaced.

Izzie was unusually quiet for a change and that suited Jackson. He not only hadn't been feeling well, but his father's condition weighed heavily on him to the point he couldn't keep his mind on his work. He'd been screwing up all day, but hoped his partner hadn't noticed. She did.

"So, what's the story? You didn't get any this weekend?"

Izzie could be a real bitch sometimes. Jackson ignored her and kept chewing.

"She stand you up?"

Jackson set his Coke on the table a little too hard, splashing brown liquid onto the tabletop.

"Whoa, I hit a nerve, didn't I babe? What's her name?"

"There is no *her*," Jackson said, trying without success to keep the annoyance out of his voice. He picked up the remnants of his sandwich and stuffed it in his mouth hoping to discourage Izzie from engaging in further conversation. It didn't work.

"So what's with you today? You've hardly said a word."

"If you must know, I'm worried about my dad. Mom said he's in bad shape." He took a final gulp of his soft drink. "So, now you know." Then, without meaning to, Jackson added, "How about you? Enjoy watching the dolphins?"

If Jackson had hauled off and punched Izzie in the stomach, the response wouldn't have been any more dramatic.

"How'd you know I went to the beach? You following me now?"

"Hell no. I went to the beach for a little R&R, looked up and there you were with some guy." When Izzie's eyebrows shot up in disbelief, Jackson added, "That's the god's honest truth."

"Then why didn't you come over and say hey? Or did you feel guilty for stalking me?"

"I told you I wasn't spying on you!" Jackson's voice rose. "Trust me, I have better things to do in my spare time than chase after you."

"Fine. I believe you."

"So, isn't he the guy we saw on the balcony?"

"What? That again?" Izzie sounded flustered.

"I just wondered 'cause from where I stood it kinda looked like the same guy."

"You win. I'll tell you if you promise to shut up about the whole trafficking thing. Okay?"

Jackson nodded. Despite the warm temperature outside, a cold chill made its way down his spine.

"It's the same guy. You satisfied? And no, he's not some big trafficker—drug or otherwise. He's just a guy living by himself in what looks like a fairly nice house. The girl we saw on the balcony was his niece, his sister's kid visiting from Chicago. Guess she was on spring break or something. Anyway, she went back home, so it's just him and his dog. That's all there is to it. He's a nice guy and I like him. Satisfied? You can stop worrying now. There's no bogeymen, no traffickers, no nothing. Just sunny Tampa—beaches, festivals and lots of work for us news-media types. Which, by the way," she tapped her watch, "we'd better get a move on or we'll be late."

Jackson was still digesting the part where Izzie had revealed she'd been inside the man's house, that she liked him and, while she didn't explicitly say so, that she planned on continuing to see him. He shrugged, gathered up the leavings of their lunch and tossed them in the trash. She and Mom were right. Izzie was a grown woman, free to make her own choices—and like the rest of the adult world, would have to live with the consequences.

****

That afternoon as Jackson sat in the edit bay, reviewing his day's work, his boss stopped by.

"Hey Jackson."

"Hi Morrie." Jackson tried to hide how startled he was. The chief photographer didn't usually stop by in the middle of a shift for no reason.

"Stop by my office when you're done here."

Jackson nodded. "You got it. I'll be finished in about half an hour."

"That works for me."

What could the man possibly want with him? Had he done something wrong? Offended someone? Jackson mentally reran the events of the past several days but could think of nothing that might warrant the attention of his supervisor. Well, he'd find out soon enough.

Thirty minutes later, Jackson popped into the chief photographer's office. "This a good time?"

Morris Stone looked up from a document he was scrutinizing. "Sure, c'mon in and close the door."

The trepidation Jackson felt went up several notches. *What was this about? Was he going to be fired?* It wouldn't be the first time a photographer was let go. He just didn't think he'd be joining their ranks.

"Pull up a chair and stop looking so scared." The man appeared to be trying to lighten the mood.

Jackson slid into a guest chair across from his boss and folded his hands, resting them on his thighs. They were slippery with sweat.

"So, how're you doing?" Morris Stone leaned forward, his weight shifting in his chair.

"Uh, fine," Jackson cleared his throat and sat up a little straighter. He didn't know what Morrie was getting at, but was fairly certain he hadn't asked him to come in simply to see "how he was doing".

"I can see you're puzzled, so I'll get right to the point."

Getting to the point was Morris Stone's specialty. Everyone knew the man didn't mince words. Jackson braced himself for the blow he knew was coming—he was getting canned.

"You've been here, what? Nearly a year?"

Jackson nodded and tried to breathe. His chest felt tight. His throat was constricted, making speech difficult.

"I realize your annual review is a few weeks off, but wanted you to know we've been pleased with your work so far. Plus you get on well with the rest of the staff, have a consistently good attitude and appear willing to step up when something happens—even when it's not your shift. Those are the kinds of things we look for—someone who's a real team player."

So he wasn't being fired? The man had called him in to compliment him? Jackson inhaled. His muscles which had tensed up began to relax. He smiled. "Thank you."

But Morris Stone's expression didn't match his complimentary words. Something wasn't quite right. He fiddled with his ballpoint, letting it roll from one hand to the other. Then he stopped. His hazel eyes searched Jackson.

"So, I'm wondering what's going on? I mean I thought we had a solid photographer in you and now I'm hearing there are problems. The quality of your work has slipped. You're late in filing and you've been making mistakes, the kind someone new on the job might make. So, Jackson, what the hell's going on with you?"

Unprepared for the dressing down he'd just received, Jackson was momentarily speechless. "Uh, well, I, uh, what do you mean?"

"I thought I made myself perfectly clear," Morris said. "The work you turned in today is not representative of the cameraman I hired. Surely you recognize that."

Slowly nodding his head up and down, Jackson said, "You're right. It's not my best work. I'm sorry. I'll do better from now on."

"Jackson, I didn't call you into my office for an apology. I want to know what's happening that has you so distracted you can't keep your mind on what you're doing." When Jackson didn't respond, he continued, "I've been doing this for over twenty years and I think I know a little about human nature. You didn't come in here talented and enthusiastic then all of a sudden shut down for no reason. I want to know what that reason is and I want to know now." He folded his arms, leaned back and drilled Jackson with his eyes.

Jackson breathed in a lungful of air. "It's my dad. Over the weekend my mom called and said he's in a bad way. It's liver failure. He may even be…" He cleared his throat and blinked his eyes several time. "She said he may die if he doesn't get a transplant and…he can't get one because, well, he's an alcoholic and they won't even put him on the list since he's still drinking. I keep thinking I should quit my job, go home and find out if I'm a match so I can offer him part of my liver." The words tumbled out so fast, Jackson was breathless. "I'm sorry this has affected my work, Morrie, I really am. It's just that I'm stuck between a rock and a hard place. Even if I go home, I'm not sure we can come up with the money for the operation."

Empathy for his young photographer was painted on Morris Stone's face. "God, Jackson, I had no idea. I thought it was just some girl who'd blown you off and I was prepared to tell you to suck it up and take it like a man."

He tapped his fingers on the desktop. Jackson could hear the murmur of newsroom activity through the closed door. The situation was hopeless and he knew it.

"Tell you what. I don't want to lose you, but family comes first. So this is what we'll do. You go home and find out if you're a match. If you are, maybe you can have some fundraisers to come up with the money. Take as much time as you need. Just keep us posted so we know what's going on, okay?"

In spite of his best efforts to control himself, tears flooded Jackson's eyes and spilled down his cheeks. Morrie's kindness was so unexpected it left him grasping for words to express his gratitude.

"Now, how're you going to get home? Fly?"

"Uh, well, I don't have the money for that. I'll have to drive."

Morris shook his head. "In *your* car? I don't think so. You'll break down halfway home, then what? No, you'll fly and I'll pay for it. Just don't tell anybody or they'll expect me to do the same for them. Deal?" He stood up and shook Jackson's hand.

"Deal." Jackson's entire body shook with emotion and gratitude as he left the office and headed home.

Chapter 17

Tiny let out a low growl as Leon yanked the shoe from his mouth. "Oh yeah? You gonna bite me? That what this is about? You chew on my new shoes, then threaten *me*? I'll show you who's boss!" Picking the dog up, he threw him with a sickening thud against the wall, knocking a vase of plastic flowers from a shelf. Tiny's yelp was followed with a swift kick to the ribs.

Then he folded his arms across his chest and stared till the rottweiler lowered his head and sank to his belly in a show of submission. "That's more like it."

He turned back to the task at hand: getting ready to go out with that hot Izzie girl. To say he was surprised such a nice piece of ass would give him the time of day let alone go out with him was putting it mildly. When he noticed her outside the house, he'd taken a chance and invited her to go for a drink.

Being turned down was nothing new for Leon; he expected it. Besides, it wasn't as if he was hurting for sex. He could have it whenever he wanted as long as there was "product" in the house.

When he saw her the following week looking toward the house as though she expected something or someone, he decided to take action. With the place to himself for a few days, there had been no risk of discovery, so he'd decided to chance it. What did he have to lose? Besides, with Jen gone, that old feeling of emptiness had set in accompanied by depression. Sometimes it was so debilitating he could scarcely get out of bed. Maybe he could stave it off by distracting himself with a beautiful woman. It was worth a try.

"Hey there Babe," he'd called from the balcony. "You lookin' for me?" *If only.* But then the most surprising thing happened. She'd smiled and waved. As she started to walk away, he'd called after her, "Why don't you make a lonely guy happy and join me for a drink?"

As if he'd said the magic words, she stopped abruptly and retraced her steps. Looking up at him with eyes as big as saucers, she nodded and said, "All right. I'll have a drink with you, but not in there." She'd gestured with her head. "You come out here."

Emotion, like an electric current spiked through Leon's body. "Really? You'll really go?" He could've kicked himself. What a pathetic thing to say. Maybe she hadn't noticed. "Don't move," he'd called, "I'll be right down."

That was a week ago. Since then they'd met for drinks several times, gone to the beach together—he'd even let her come inside the house. It was taking a risk, that's for darn sure, but there was no product around. So what could she discover?

It's true she'd asked about the girl she saw several weeks back. She'd seen him yank Jennifer off the balcony during that parade, but he'd explained it away. Said his niece was visiting from up north and that she'd been something of a pain in the ass, wouldn't do what she was told.

Said he'd had to get tough with her; that he was afraid she might do something crazy and then how would he explain it to his sister? Remember the girl in

Aruba that disappeared over spring break? Well, he didn't want something like that happening to his sister's kid. No siree, not while she was under *his* roof.

He'd been so smooth, the way he'd explained it that she bought it. You could tell by the way she nodded and looked at him with something like respect. Nobody'd ever looked at him like that.

Seymour'd be so proud. Not that he'd tell the sonofabitch. If he did, the man would go off on him for striking up a friendship with anyone—let alone someone like Izzie. And if he ever found out she'd been inside the house, well, there'd be a bullet with Leon's name on it—no doubt about it.

Chapter 18

Jackson stood next to his mom and brother as the priest said a final prayer over the casket. He'd arrived too late. His dad had died two hours before the plane landed.

Now, having helped with the wake and funeral, he felt numb, and somewhat conflicted. On the one hand, he'd truly wanted to help his father, even if it meant donating a portion of his liver. On the other, he was relieved it hadn't gone that far.

He loved his dad, but watching him kill himself a little with every drink wore him down. Not to mention the guilt for having abandoned his mom to deal with it all. The effects were written like a map across her face, making her look older than her years.

As the casket was lowered into the ground, he wondered if, with Dad gone, she'd be able to find some peace. Or would Zac replace him as yet another burden for her to carry? Resolving to speak to her about it before returning to Tampa, Jackson went back to the car and got inside.

****

It was after six when the last of the neighbors finally departed. Every available space in the kitchen was covered with leftovers: casseroles, salads, sliced ham, chicken breasts, deviled eggs, soups and a variety of baked goods. There was more than enough food to feed them for a week, maybe longer.

Grief, in combination with the sickening array of food, nauseated Jackson. "What a mess."

His mother, looking spent, started to pick up a dish.

"Mom, lie down. Me and Zac'll clean up." Jackson gave his brother a meaningful look.

Zac's plate was piled high, his cheeks bulged. Unable to speak, he nodded, although his expression said he was none too pleased.

"You sure? Three sets of hands would make the work go faster."

"We can handle it, Mom. You go lie down," Jackson assured her. After she'd gone upstairs, he got to work wrapping leftovers and piling the dishes while his brother continued to stuff his face.

"How about you start washing dishes while I find some place to store this stuff?" Jackson said over his shoulder, as he pulled the refrigerator door open.

"When did you become the boss of me?" Zac swallowed his last bite of chicken.

"What? No. I didn't mean to…" Jackson knew it was hopeless. Zac had been itching for a fight since he arrived. This was the first opportunity he had and it was clear he wasn't about to let it pass.

"I know. You're the hotshot cameraman, working for a big Florida TV station while I'm a loser. You don't have to say it. I've heard every day from Mom and Dad how I, as the older brother, should've made something of myself and what an embarrassment I am. Oh really? What about Dad?"

When Jackson didn't take the bait, Zac thumped him on the back causing him to spill a bowl of baked beans on the floor.

"Watta slob. Didn't they teach you nothing down in Flor-ee-day, lil' bro?" He took another pull on the beer bottle and let out a loud belch. "Well, sonny boy, you offered to clean up this pigsty, so have at it. I've gonna take me a little nap." With that he left the room.

While there was a lot of cleaning to do, Jackson was relieved. A big fight with Zac was the last thing he wanted. Grabbing a roll of paper towels and the trash can, he began cleaning up the gooey mess.

****

"Mom, how about going back to Tampa with me?" Jackson sat in the family room watching the news with his mother. Zac had gone out—whereabouts unknown.

After a few moments of silence, she said, "Oh honey, how thoughtful of you to ask, but as much as I'd dearly love to go, I can't. There's too much to do here, plus I have my job and all." She paused, then added, "Say, I have an idea. Why don't you ask Zac? He could use a change of scenery, and it'd give the two of you a chance to spend some time together. What do you think?"

She hadn't come right out and said it, but Jackson could read between the lines: It would give her a badly needed break.

Before he had a chance to protest that he couldn't afford to pay his brother's airfare, she interjected, "I have some money saved up—enough for his airline ticket, food and a little left over for fun. What do you say?"

What *could* he say? Jackson nodded with a sense of dread that nearly choked him.

"I can't wait till your brother gets home." She fairly bubbled over with excitement. "He'll be thrilled."

Chapter 19

"Son of a bitch! Why'd she have to go and ruin everything?" Leon slammed his fist on the table, making dishes jump and splashing coffee onto his clean shirt. "Damnit," he shouted, glancing furtively around the room for Tiny, who'd wisely made himself scarce. "Now what'm I gonna do?"

Leon couldn't say he hadn't been warned. Seymour'd told him more than once not to go messing with the "locals"; that considering the "business" they were in, it was too risky. And had he listened? No-o-o, Leon knew better than his scumbag of a boss. Sure he did—and look where it'd gotten him—in a big fat mess, that's where.

Everything had been going along just fine. He and Izzie were hitting it off. He couldn't believe his good fortune: Walking on the beach with a beautiful girl at his side made him feel like a real man—not just some hood who'd spent his life doing things he was ashamed of.

Izzie was a woman who made you want to straighten up and fly right, as his old man used to say. She made him want things other people took for granted: a home, maybe even some rug rats running around. How about that? Well, why not? It wasn't so farfetched. Guys with less going for them managed to do that. Yes, he had to admit he'd begun to dream of a future for himself, even started trying to figure out how to get out from under Seymour and his cronies. It wouldn't be easy, but it was possible—or so he'd begun to think, until the next shipment arrived and Izzie began to ask questions.

At first he'd simply changed the subject and kept her away from the house. That worked until the day she showed up unexpectedly and saw the latest product—a young girl from out west who was in the middle of a meltdown. Tiny was barking and the brat was demanding that he let her go. He had his hands full trying to control the situation. Then Izzie had put in an appearance and all hell broke loose.

Chapter 20

Zac was sprawled out on the couch watching a NASCAR race when Jackson walked in, balancing several bags of groceries in his arms.

"Oh, hey bro," Zac said, his eyes still glued to the screen.

"Hey," Jackson grunted. He set the bags on the pass-through counter and went back to the car to retrieve the rest. Annoyance wormed its way into his psyche. So this is what he had to look forward to for the next few weeks: his brother lying around while he did all the work. No surprise there. Mom had put up with Zac for years.

By now Jackson's anger had reached a boiling point. Mom had paid for Zac's trip, even giving him money for food. Jackson provided a place for him to stay. And Zac? He just lay there like a damned lump.

When he got back to the third-floor apartment and saw that the grocery bags remained on the counter with Zac glued to the TV, Jackson could no longer contain his anger.

Setting the remaining sacks down, he turned and said, "So I guess it didn't occur to you to put the food away?"

Zac looked up as if awaking from a dream. "I'm sorry bro. If you wanted me to do that you should have asked." With that he leapt to his feet and began to pull items from the bags, setting them down willy-nilly. "Wanna tell me where you want this stuff or should I just guess?"

The kitchen in Jackson's apartment was galley-style leaving little room for more than one person in the space at a time. With Zac next to him, neither could move, much less carry cans and boxes of food from the counter to its intended spot.

Zac stared Jackson in the face awaiting his answer.

"That's all right," Jackson said. "I'll do it."

"No, you wanted help, so I'm helping."

Jackson could see the determination in his brother's face. He knew that expression: It said, "You wanna rumble? Let's have at it."

Chapter 21

Monday morning couldn't come fast enough for Jackson. Three days of Zac's laying around and complaining was three too many as far as he was concerned.

"So you're gonna leave me stranded with no way to get around?"

Zac's voice startled him. He'd assumed his brother was still asleep on the couch.

"What do you mean?"

"What do you think I mean? What am I supposed to do around here all day with no wheels?"

"I don't know, Zac. Maybe watch TV?" Hoping Zac wouldn't hear, he added under his breath, "Like you've been doing since you got here."

"Seriously, how about you let me use your car? I'll drop you off and you can get a ride home with one of your fancy reporter friends."

Jackson's blood began to boil. Was there no end to Zac's demands? He comes here on Mom's dime, lays around doing absolutely nothing, gets argumentative if he's asked to do even the slightest thing and now has the nerve to suggest Jackson loan him his car and find his own way home from work.

"Look, buses will take you most anywhere you want to go, or, hey, I have an idea: walk. The exercise'll do you good."

Zac threw his arms up. "Fine. You don't have to go all postal. I'll figure it out myself."

Jackson looked at the wall clock. "I gotta get going or I'll be late. See you tonight."

****

"Oh, good, you're back." Morris Stone looked up from a document he was reading. "Sorry about your dad. How's your mom holding up?"

Jackson nodded and swallowed as emotion unexpectedly surged, making speech difficult. "She'll be all right." He was going to add that Zac had come back with him, but thought better of it. The man didn't look especially interested in his personal life.

"By the way, you'll be on your own today."

Jackson's forehead crinkled. *On his own?* "Izzie taking the day off?"

"Days off, you mean. We haven't seen or heard from her since the middle of last week. It's a damned shame. That girl had potential, if she coulda got her mouth under control."

At first, Morris' words confused Jackson. As he took in their meaning, he was stunned. "Are you saying Izzie's been fired?"

"Well, duh. What do you suppose we *should* do with a reporter who fails to report for work? Doesn't even give us the courtesy of a phone call to tell us whether she's sick or quit. We're not running a day-care center here, you know, and it's not too much to expect our people to act like professionals. Wouldn't you agree?" He squinted at Jackson.

"Yes, but did anyone check to see if she's all right?"

"Of course. Look, don't worry about it. Snotty girl like that? Thinks the world owes her a living. I see it all the time. Pretty girl thinks she's going to be a movie star or a news anchor. Never occurs to her she's a dime a dozen. I'm not wasting any tears on her—and neither should you. Now get to work. The stories are pretty routine. All we really need is some footage. I'll pair you up with somebody in a few days. Oh, and Jackson, glad to have you back."

Chapter 22

Dragging his feet as though attached to a fifty-pound weight, Jackson inserted his key in the door and heaved a sigh of relief. The day was over and he could kick back with a cold beer. Then he remembered: he wasn't alone. Zac was staying with him and it had been like pulling teeth from the get-go. Oh well, maybe he'd go out for the evening.

"Well, hey, bro. You're home." Zac's voice boomed out.

No such luck. The man was back from wherever he'd spent the day. Feeling like he'd been punched in the gut, Jackson managed a wan smile.

"Oh, hey, Zac. How was your day?" From the look of the apartment his brother had spent a fair amount of it parked right where he was. Clothes were strewn about, dirty dishes piled on the cocktail table amidst partially empty beer cans. The place reeked of garbage and body odor. Swallowing the urge to snap at him, Jackson said. "What'd you do?" As if it wasn't obvious.

"Not a whole hell of a lot. I gotta get the lay of the land before I venture forth," Zac grinned as if his choice of words would make up for having trashed Jackson's place. "You look bushed. Have a hard day chasing the bad guys with your little camera?"

When Jackson didn't pull a face or throw a sarcastic retort in his direction, Zac followed up with, "Seriously, is something the matter? I mean besides all this? I'll clean it up, in fact, sit down and I'll cook supper, how's that?"

It sounded great. "Okay, I'll shower and have a quick nap." No one had cooked a meal for Jackson since he'd left home. *It might be exactly the thing to snap me out of my funk.*

He'd asked around and no one seemed to know—or care—what had become of Izzie. He'd called her cell and emailed her, all to no avail. She seemed to have simply vanished. Did it have anything to do with the guy she'd been seeing? Had something happened to her?

His co-workers weren't aware of her relationship with a man who may or may not be dangerous. At least he didn't think she'd told anyone. Besides, as far as he knew, she didn't have any close friends at the station. She'd been so rude no one liked her.

He stepped into the shower and, with hot water splashing over him, his muscles began to relax despite the hold Izzie continued to have on his thoughts. Why couldn't he get her off his mind? She'd lost her job and that was that. There was nothing he could do. Still, he should check to make sure she was all right. Tomorrow if he was still without a reporter, he'd swing by her apartment, then when he was satisfied she was all right, he'd put her out of his mind once and for all.

Jackson had to admit Zac had done a yeoman's job of fixing dinner. They had stuffed pork chops, baked potatoes, a green bean casserole and apple pie for dessert. The kitchen was a mess, but the food was so delicious, he hardly noticed.

"Wow. Where'd you learn to cook like that?"

Zac's face brightened. "I took some cooking classes a couple years back. Thought I'd be a chef." The hint of a smile faded. "That was until Dad… Never mind, so you really liked it?"

"Liked it? Oh my gosh, yes, it was terrific." Jackson's eyes fell on the disaster in the kitchen. It appeared that every pan he owned had been used. With the food now caked and drying, it'd take hours to clean up. Having grown up with Zac, he knew the drill, there was no point getting into a fight over it: whenever Zac cooked—which wasn't all that often—Jackson cleaned up, that's just the way it was. It seemed fair enough until you consider most cooks clean up as they go, so at the end, there isn't much to do.

Jackson stood up and started to clear the table.

"I've got it," Zac said. "You go in and take it easy."

If you'd told Jackson that he won the lottery he couldn't have been more surprised—or pleased. He went into the living room, switched on the television and ten minutes later was sound asleep.

Chapter 23

After work the following day, Jackson drove by Izzie's place in the off chance that she was home. She lived in a gated community off Bay Pointe Drive. It pissed off Jackson to realize that despite being younger and far less experienced, she obviously made more money than he did.

Today he was less concerned about salaries than he was about her safety. Since the gate was open, he drove in and glanced around the parking lot. Her car, a hot red Mazda, was there, covered in leaves and bird poop.

Jackson knew how proud Izzie was of that car. It had been a graduation gift from her parents. She took it to the car wash weekly; kept it in pristine condition. Parking his old car next to hers, he got out to have a closer look.

As he expected, the car was locked. Putting his hands up to the driver's side window, he looked inside. Everything seemed fine. In fact, there was nothing to be seen at all—no fast-food wrappers or pop cans, nothing. Unlike his car, it was immaculate.

With a queasy feeling in the pit of his stomach, Jackson headed toward Izzie's apartment. It was a second floor walkup. Taking the steps two at a time, he rang the bell, then when no one answered, he began pounding on the door and finally shouting, "Izzie. Izzie. It's Jackson. Open up."

A few seconds later, a woman next door poked her head out and said, "She's not home. Haven't seen her for about a week."

"Do you know where she's gone?" Jackson said.

When the woman hesitated, he added, "We work together and she hasn't shown up for several days, I'm beginning to worry. Do you have any idea where she is?"

Scrutinizing him with her dark eyes, the woman shook her head. "I'm sorry but we keep pretty much to ourselves around here. Why don't you go over to the office and see if they know anything?" She started to go back into her apartment, then turned and said, "I hope she's all right. I enjoy watching her on the news. She's so pretty."

"That she is. Thanks for your help."

Ten minutes later, a grumpy apartment manager asked him to tell "that girl to pick up her mail. Her box is overflowing and UPS dropped off several packages. Tell her that despite her impressions to the contrary, we are not—I emphasize *not*—her secretaries. Besides, you're not the first person to come looking for her, you know. Several people have been around asking for her. Well, lemme tell you this: She might have servants at that TV station but I assure you she doesn't have them here. And you can tell her that Mavis said so." When she'd finished her tirade, her face was crimson, her hands twisting a tissue.

"So, you haven't seen her then?" Jackson said, deliberately keeping his cool. *Stupid bitch!* There was nothing to be gained losing his temper with the only person who might know where to find Izzie.

"You got that right."

"If you happen to see her, would you mind having her call me?" He offered his card.

"No, I'd be mighty happy to hold onto your card and ask her to give you a call if and when I see her next. With only two hundred residents, I don't have another damned thing on my mind except to watch out for her." With that she took Jackson's card, tossed it in the wastebasket and went back to her desk.

Not knowing where else to look for his partner, Jackson headed home, a prickle of dread in the back of his throat.

****

"So, you have a tough day?" Zac threw the question at Jackson over a supper of fried chicken, pasta, mixed peas and carrots and a tossed salad.

"Not especially. Why?"

"You're so quiet. I thought maybe something was wrong. Wanna talk about it?"

Jackson was surprised at Zac's concern. Maybe Mom was right, the change of scenery seemed to actually be doing his brother some good. Not wanting to interrupt the good vibes between them, Jackson decided to share.

"It's probably nothing, but while I was back home, my reporter seems to have disappeared off the face of the earth. She hasn't been at work for over a week now and nobody knows where she is. What's worse, at least in my opinion, is that no one but me seems concerned. I mean, what if she's sick or something happened to her?"

He stopped talking and waited for his brother to make some kind of sarcastic remark, reminding him how he always jumped to conclusions which invariably turned out to be wrong.

Much to his surprise, Zac listened intently, then leaned in and said, "Anyone report it to the police?"

Jackson thought for a moment. "Now that you mention it, I don't think so. My boss assumed she walked off the job. Said it happens all the time and not to worry about it, but I don't think Izzie would do that. She loves the job. Besides if she's gone, why's her car still in the parking lot outside her apartment?"

"I don't know." Zac scratched the stubble on his face. "You said neither a neighbor nor the apartment manager have seen her and that her mail's piling up?"

Jackson nodded.

"Then something's not right, bro. Let's drive over and see what we can find out."

****

An hour later they were at the police station filling out a "missing person's" report. There was little information Jackson could provide other than what Izzie had told him about herself. Leaving Morris Stone's phone number and asking to be notified if they learned anything, they returned home no wiser than before.

Chapter 24

The next morning at the TV station, Jackson was about to head out the door, camera in hand, when the unmistakable sound of Morris Stone's gravelly voice stopped him.

"Taylor. Over here." The man didn't sound pleased.

Mentally ticking off the stories he'd covered the previous day, Jackson couldn't imagine what the problem was. It wasn't unusual for someone to call in complaining. They'd expected to be in a story that hadn't run. The photographer—in this case, Jackson, made them look bad, or didn't get the story right, or misquoted them or…you name it. Usually management blew it off saying complaints came with the territory. But Stone's tone of voice said the mistake was significant. With a sinking feeling, Jackson set the camera down and headed for his boss' office.

"You wanted me?" Jackson summoned up his most innocent expression, hoping to minimize the damage.

"Close the door."

Whatever it was, Jackson was certain it wouldn't end with a compliment like the last time. He'd scarcely managed to sit down when he was pummeled with the gruff tone his boss used when he was angry.

"The police came to see me this morning," he began. Before Jackson had a chance to react, he added, "Wanna know who gave them my phone number? Oh, yeah, that would be you."

Since there seemed to be no question involved, Jackson thought it best to keep his mouth shut.

"So, now, I gotta ask why my photographer goes out and reports one of my employees missing and makes it look like I don't give a crap. Can you answer me that?"

Jackson was about to respond, when Morris Stone continued. "They questioned me for half an hour, like I was somehow responsible for her. How am I supposed to know why some ditsy broad quits? For all I know she met the man of her dreams and went riding off into the sunset."

The longer he talked, the more animated he became until Jackson feared the man would strike him. He clutched the sides of the chair and waited.

"Now I ask you, Jackson, why would you deliberately go out and do something like that? Tell me that 'cause I gotta say, I don't understand."

Jackson's mouth was bone dry making speech difficult. He licked his lips. "I'm sorry if I caused you any trouble, it wasn't my intention."

"*If?* The man says—*if he caused me any trouble*. The police treated me like I was some kind of damned suspect. We don't even know if the girl's missing or holed up somewhere with her latest squeeze."

When Jackson didn't say anything, he continued, "Well, we don't know, do we? Or is there something you're aware of—and if so, speak up."

"Uh, well, it's just that things don't add up, that's all." Jackson said.

"What *things* would that be?"

"Well, for instance, her car's in the parking lot of her apartment and it's covered with leaves and bird droppings."

"So?"

"So, Izzie loves that car. She'd never allow it to be in that condition. I know for a fact she wouldn't."

Morris Stone heaved a sigh. "That's all you've got? A car covered with bird shit? You filled out a missing person's report because of that?"

"Not only that. Her apartment manager said her mail hasn't been picked up for over a week, said it's piling up. If she was leaving town, wouldn't she have put a hold on her mail?"

"Not necessarily. I would, but young people don't always think about stuff like mail and notifying bosses when they leave town." His tone of voice softened a bit as he leaned in toward Jackson.

"Look, I know you mean well. You're concerned about your partner. You come back from your father's funeral and she's not around. Anyone in your shoes would be concerned. We were too. We did everything we could: called her apartment, checked the contacts on her emergency-call list, left messages on her cell, everything.

"No, we didn't contact the police and maybe we shoulda. It just didn't seem warranted. Even the police admitted that if someone wants to walk off the job and disappear, they have every right to do so. There's no law that says they have to give their employer proper notice. Last I checked it was still a free country and people can come and go as they like."

Jackson listened intently, nodding in agreement, but in his mind he kept hearing Izzie tell him how she'd started seeing that guy from the balcony. Should he tell his boss about that or keep it to himself?

Morris Stone was wrapping up his tirade. "Now unless you have something more to tell me, I'd advise you to put Isabelle Campbell out of your mind for once and for all. The girl has moved on, and if you value your job, you should too. Capisce?" He stood up signally the discussion was over. There was nothing more to be said.

Chapter 25

It was after three in the morning and despite his best efforts Leon Donatello was still awake. Even Tiny's rhythmic snoring from his corner on the floor hadn't made him the least bit drowsy the way it usually did.

Having spent the day working to ensure the products' enclosures were secure, he was dog-tired, but simply couldn't get Izzie off his mind. The harder he tried, the more wide awake he became. Finally, with the red numbers on the clock approaching four, he decided to get up and start his day.

Measuring grounds into the coffeemaker, he wondered for what seemed like the hundredth time why Izzie couldn't have just stayed out of his business: why she had to start asking questions and showing up like that. He had grown to care for her, damn it. Had let himself become vulnerable for maybe the first time in his life. Why'd she have to go and ruin it?

Grounds overran the top of the filter as he'd continued to obsess over his ruined relationship.

"Son of a bitch!" he shouted to the empty room, adding two more swearwords for good measure.

Then the oddest thing happened: Leon Donatello, the tough guy who wasn't afraid of anybody or anything—except maybe Seymour Cottingham—

began to bawl. It wasn't a brief emotion-filled breakdown either; it was the real thing.

Leon's torrent of heart-wrenching sobs left his face awash in tears which poured down his cheeks and onto his boxers. Unable or unwilling to exercise control over his imagination, the love of his life appeared before him looking every bit as lovely as the last time he saw her. That evening her skin had seemed almost translucent in the moonlight; her smile dazzled him. It never occurred to him their relationship would end the way it did. His mournful lament was that of a grief-stricken man who would not be comforted.

"Izzie," he cried, "Why'd you have to go and be so damned stupid? I miss you." he buried his face in his hands and wept until he had no tears left. Only then did he become aware of Tiny at his side, nuzzling his foot with his nose.

Baffled and angered by vulnerable feelings with which he had no experience, Leon picked up a plate from the counter and threw it as hard as he could at the nearest wall. The violent sound of shattering china startled Tiny who tore from the room and took shelter under the nearest bed.

Chapter 26

Zac listened intently as Jackson recounted the dressing-down he'd received earlier that day. "So your boss isn't the least bit concerned about your reporter? That what you're saying?" The incredulous expression on the older brother's face said it all. How could it be that one's employer would be so dismissive of what might be the disappearance of a member of his staff?

Jackson shrugged. "I don't know, but that's the way it looks. He said they'd done everything to contact her and then just assumed she'd quit. I guess it never occurred to them she might've met with foul play."

They were sitting in the living room waiting for supper to finish cooking.

"Is that what you think—that something bad happened to her?" Zac leaned in, his body language took on a more serious posture together with his uncharacteristically somber expression.

Jackson hesitated a few seconds as if reluctant to state what to him was obvious. He realized his reputation for jumping to conclusions was as well-known at work as it was among his family and friends. It made him all the more hesitant to raise concerns like this. But Zac seemed open to the possibility that something had indeed happened to Izzie. Besides, at this point, he could turn to no one else.

"Okay, yes, I think she's in serious trouble—maybe even dead." The word "dead" came out in a near whisper as emotion surged inside him.

Zac took a pull on his beer bottle, swallowed and then said, "What makes you think that?"

"Two things: from the research I did on human trafficking, I found out it's going on here in Tampa—right under the noses of law enforcement and little or nothing's being done about it. During a shoot we witnessed a young girl being yanked off a balcony by a man she was obviously afraid of and Izzie, in her misguided desire to become an investigative reporter, first staked out the place and then, of all things, started going out with the guy."

"And you know that how?" Zac's forehead was a mass of wrinkles.

"She told me he'd asked her out for a drink. Then I saw her with him at the beach. She said she'd been to his house and the girl, who he claimed was his niece, was gone. She got furious when I suggested she might be playing with fire; said she was a grown woman and for me to mind my own business."

"Well, there it is. The little shit told you to back off. Whatever happens or happened to her serves her right." Zac leaned back in the chair and put his feet on the cluttered cocktail table. When Jackson remained silent, he added, "You agree?"

"I know you and Stone are right, still I can't help feeling something's really wrong here. Zac, if it was me would you shrug your shoulders and walk away? Well, would you?"

"No, but you're my brother and my job's not on the line. Didn't your boss pretty much say if you didn't let it go you'd be fired?"

Jackson nodded.

"So, what choice do you have? We reported it to the police, so I say let them do their job. Hey, if it'd make you feel any better I'll stop by the police station tomorrow and see if they found out anything. That is," he threw a sly grin in Jackson's direction, "if you loan me that old beater you like to call your car."

Chapter 27

"That girl's not missing," the cop at the desk insisted.

Giving the man a skeptical look, Zac said, "But do you know for a fact nothing happened? I mean, doesn't it seem odd she'd leave without saying a word to her boss, her partner or her apartment manager? Just leave her fancy car to the elements? Not bother to forward her mail? Doesn't any of that sound the least bit suspicious?"

"Happens all the time. Man, if we chased down every person who decided to fly the coup, that's all we'd be doing." The policeman scratched the bald spot on his head. When it became obvious Zac wasn't satisfied, he added, "We checked with the family. They weren't especially concerned; said she's taken off before only to show up in a week or so. Unless you provide us with evidence of foul play, there's nothing to investigate."

Zac reluctantly agreed with the cop. Besides, he knew his brother was prone to jumping to conclusions. He'd been like that ever since he was little.

He recalled the time Jackson was absolutely sure Zac had been "kidnapped" and told his teacher, who went to the principal, who in turn reported it to the police. By the time they were finished, half the town was searching for him.

Imagine the furor when he returned home at the "usual" time, having played hooky. He'd been punished royally and didn't speak to Jackson for a week.

With nothing better to do and in possession of Jackson's old heap of a car, he decided to head over to Ybor City. It was where Jackson had spotted that girl on the balcony. Besides, Ybor was supposedly a tourist attraction. After being cooped up in the apartment for several days, he could use the distraction, even if it meant watching someone roll cigars in a storefront.

Zac turned off Seventh Avenue and found a parking spot. He figured if he walked the area he could check out the house without calling attention to himself. The place wasn't hard to find. Jackson had played the videotape for him so many times he recognized it immediately: There it was—the two-story house with the balcony.

Zac bent down as though to tie a loose shoelace, then glanced around acting nonchalant. The property's front yard with its ankle-high grass and half dead bushes seemed embarrassed to be seen. Shades gave the place an unfriendly vibe, preventing even the slightest peek inside. Security bars, the decorative type, enclosed each and every window. It made the house appear charming—in a European sort of way. Still, if the man inside had something or someone to hide, that would be a perfect way to do it.

Surreptitiously scrutinizing the property, Zac sauntered down the block playing the role of tourist to the hilt for anyone watching. After strolling a little over a block, he glanced at his watch, then turned around. Lil 'ol tourist guy's lost and going back the way he came—at least that's what he hoped nosy neighbors would think. He barely reached the edge of the property when a man came out the front door and headed down the street without giving Zac a second glance.

It couldn't have been more perfect if Zac had scripted it himself. He'd follow the guy and see what he could find out. The man wasn't hard to track. His shabby apparel set him apart from the stylish tourists parading up and down the street. He appeared preoccupied to the point he nearly got hit by a car as he crossed the street and entered a cafe.

The place reminded Zac of the eateries back home where he could afford to dine without having to take out a loan. Its shabby walls were covered with local art—a devil with a hot pink joojoo eyeball; sassy signs suggested customers could "Take it or leave it"; and sculptures that reflected Cuban-American taste.

Booths squatted along one side of the room, a counter with stools on the opposite side with a smattering of tables down the center. Zac hesitated at the door as if waiting to be seated. Nodding when a server said he could "sit anywhere" he drew a breath of relief. The man had parked himself at the counter with two unoccupied stools next to him.

Zac quickly followed before the opportunity was lost. Picking up a menu, he began to scan it, then turning to the man, said, "You eat here often?"

"What if I do? What's it to you?"

Zac had to admit the man wasn't bad looking in a tough-guy sort of way. He had thick black hair, piercing eyes with eyelashes most women would kill for. His most obvious flaw was his teeth. Apart from needing a good cleaning and some whitening, he probably should've worn braces as a kid. They weren't what used to be called "buck teeth" but were crooked, detracting from what was possibly a pleasant smile. With a well-developed set of muscles the man had an attitude that said using them on whoever crossed him would suit him just fine.

"Sorry." Zac'd love to bust the guy across the mouth but since that wouldn't get him anywhere, he put his nice-guy face on and said, "I've never had Cuban food and wondered what someone who eats here often would recommend. Do you?"

"Do I what?"

What's the guy deaf? Digging deep to avoid showing his annoyance, Zac said, "Eat here often?"

A light bulb seemed to go on inside the man's head. His attitude went from rude and sullen to that of a connoisseur.

"Oh, yeah, I s'pose I do at that. Sure. Wadda ya' wanna know?"

"What's good to eat?" Zac figured if he kept his sentences short, maybe the man would understand him.

"Oh, lemme think." He moved one stool over so as to sit next to Zac. "Myself I most always order the 'Real Cuban.' It's so good they got an award for it. Has crusty bread, pork and ham with some kinda mustard-mayo mix, pickle and Swiss cheese. Plus they include a dipping sauce." He stopped for a moment and swallowed as if in anticipation.

Returning to the subject, he added, "But don' let me tell you what to order. Most anything here's real good." He waved his hand as if he owned the place. "I've had it all. But the Cuban's what keeps me coming back whenever I want something special."

Right then the server approached and both men ordered the Cuban with sides of fries and, at the man's suggestion, a Corona. Zac would have preferred a Coke but didn't want to risk offending him. He appeared to be teetering on the edge of some kind of breakdown and Zac didn't want to be the one to push him over.

While they waited for their order, Zac reached out and said, "Thanks for your help. Name's Zac. I'm visiting my brother for a few days."

Half expecting to be rebuffed, he was more than a little surprised when the man grinned, shook his hand and said, "You're welcome. I'm Leon. Welcome to Tampa."

"Thanks," Zac tossed him a smile so big you'd think he'd just met his favorite rock star. "So what's to do around here for fun?"

"Depends on how much ya wanna spend. You can go high-end and do the town with shows, theater, expensive dining and women—or do it on the cheap by going to the beach, the aquarium or a ballgame if the Rays are in town."

"And how about you? What do you do?"

A shadow seemed to fall across Leon's face. His pleasant expression morphed into what Zac took to be pain.

"Sorry, didn't mean to pry," Zac feared he was about to lose the man along with what may well be his only opportunity to get to the bottom of the Izzie situation.

Clearing his throat and putting on what looked like a forced smile, Leon said, "No, it's all right. You weren't sticking your nose in my business or nothin'.

It's just that my girl and I, well, we, uh, sort of broke up and I'm still dealing with it. Know what I mean?" He stopped talking and took a swig of beer.

"You kidding me? Broads can tear your heart out, shred it to pieces and feed it to you on a fork. Been there more than once, believe me."

"You've been dumped? Seriously?" Leon set his beer bottle down on the counter and swung the stool around to face Zac.

"Hasn't everyone? That what happened?" He realized he was pushing the envelope. If he went too far, Leon might shut him out and leave. But he'd opened the door and if the girl he'd broken up with was Izzie, then he might have information on her whereabouts. He had to at least give it a try.

"Not exactly. My girl, man she was perfect, drop-dead gorgeous—had these big blue eyes that just begged you to take her to bed. Know what I mean?"

Zac watched Leon become increasingly animated with every reference to his lost love. His expression alternated between joy and grief as his words brought memories of her to the surface. It was curious how he referred to her in the past tense. Was that merely his way of expressing the death of their relationship?

The conversation lulled as Zac chewed the last bite of his Cuban while Leon stared across the counter at something or someone only he could see.

"So, what happened?" Zac said it carefully hoping he hadn't crossed the line.

Leon appeared startled as if he'd forgotten Zac was still there. "What happened with what?"

"With your girl, uh, what's her name now?" Zac held his breath. If Leon said anything other than Izzie, all bets were off and he'd know he was barking up the wrong tree.

"Isabelle Campbell's her name, Izzie for short. God, I miss her."

"She dump you?"

"What's it to you?" Leon lashed out at Zac and reached for the bill.

Zac put his hand on Leon's and said, "Let me get it. You've been good company for a lonely tourist. I didn't mean to stir up bad memories. I was just interested, that's all. No harm done?"

Leon examined Zac's face as if searching for a hint of duplicity. Apparently finding none, he blew out a sigh of relief. "Well, thanks. I ain't had nobody buy me lunch in like, well, maybe never. 'Preciate it."

"My pleasure." Zac pulled out several bills and, not knowing what else to say, stood up preparing to depart.

"Say," Leon said, as though a light had gone on inside his head. "If you're not doing anything, wanna go over to Clearwater? The pier's a cool place, 'specially if you've never been there."

Zac eagerly agreed. This day was turning out to be damned near perfect. Not only had he connected with the man who may have something to do with Izzie's disappearance, but he'd get to see the Gulf of Mexico for the very first time. How cool was that?

Chapter 28

It was the end of a long day covering stories accompanied by an intern. Morris Stone had said it was the best he could do for the time being. The girl was sweet, but not particularly bright; Jackson'd had to grit his teeth to keep from yelling at her. He knew better than to do something like that. It wouldn't be the first time someone called the station to complain about cameramen "abusing" their reporters. Yeah, right. And who complains about how reporters treat their photogs? No one, that's who.

He sighed and inserted his front-door key into the lock. Now all he had to do was get through an evening without Zac having a meltdown. He'd be glad when his brother's visit was over. After little more than a week, he'd had about all he could stand of him lying around, messing up the place. Cleaning up after himself was hard enough for Jackson without having to do it for two.

He swung the door open, expecting to see his living room in shambles and his brother stretched out on the sofa watching TV. To his surprise, not only was he greeted with a silence so complete he could hear the faint ticking of the living room clock, but the apartment looked pretty much the same as when he'd left for work that morning. Puzzled, Jackson poked his head into his bedroom and then went out on the lanai, expecting to see Zac passed out in an alcoholic stupor.

"Zac," he called out. "I'm home." More silence. *What the hell? Where was he?* Then he remembered he'd loaned him the car and was, no doubt, out living it up. Well that was just fine. After all the man had never been to Florida before and was probably bored silly laying around doing nothing all day. Still, he'd have to start using the bus. If Jackson could do it, then he could too.

It was a little after nine. Jackson had finished eating and was watching television when the door flew open and Zach strolled in.

"Hey," Jackson said, recovering from a sudden start. "Where've you been? I already ate but there're some leftovers if you're hungry."

"I'm good." Zac went to the fridge and got a bottle of beer. "Want one?"

Jackson shook his head.

"So how'd your day go?"

Jackson shrugged. "I still don't have a reporter, so I just did some VOSOTs. Got tied up all day with a new intern who doesn't even know how to attach a video camera to a tripod. Damned near broke a $50,000 piece of equipment. And guess who'd get blamed? Me, that's who. Man, I'm so tired of dealing with people like that." He took a deep breath. "Maybe I'll have that beer after all."

Zac, who'd started into the living room, retraced his steps. "Here you go. Um, what'd you say you did?"

"What? Oh, the VOSOTs. Sorry, sometimes I forget how much jargon we use at work. VOSOTs are voice-over sounds on tape. It refers to a story read by the anchor in which the viewer sees video over part of it, for example a car accident, followed by a sound bite say, from a witness. We use them when there's no reporter available."

"Oh, I get it." Zac took a pull from his beer and leaned back in the swivel rocker. "Cool."

"How 'bout you? What'd you do? Looks like you're sunburned. Go to the beach?"

"Well, yeah, actually I did, but that's not the half of it." Zac's leg bounced rapidly. He began to twist the beer bottle around and around.

"So?" Jackson reached out and put his hand on the bottle.

"Well, like we agreed I went to see if the police found out anything and, of course, they hadn't. Said they'd checked with the family and were told Izzie takes off sometimes, but shows up eventually. So unless we come up with evidence of foul play, there's nothing they can do."

Jackson nodded. "Yeah, but…"

Zac raised his hand to stop him. "So, I decided to check out the house with the balcony."

"You did *what*?"

"I went over there to see what I could find out. I gotta say it's kinda creepy what with the grates over the windows, the shades pulled down and all. Well, I walked past then as I turned around, this guy comes outta the house, so I followed him."

Jackson leaned in toward Zac. "You didn't."

"Yeah, I did. Followed the guy into a little dump of a restaurant, sat right next to him at the counter too."

Jackson's mouth dropped, his eyes fairly bulged as Zac related the details of his encounter with Leon.

Several times he started to interrupt, only to be tamped down.

"Lemme finish, then you can ask all the questions you want." Zac told him the whole story, ending with the fact Leon's girlfriend was named Isabelle Campbell.

The expression on Jackson's face was a mix of hope and alarm. "I *knew* it. That guy has something to do with Izzie's disappearance."

"Well, maybe he does and maybe he doesn't. He seemed genuinely upset by their breakup. Said he loved her and was having a hard time dealing with it. Didn't you say she was a stuck-up bitch? Maybe she went out with him a few times, led him to believe they had something going and then dumped him. That's what it sounds like."

"I don't know, Zac, I just have a feeling there's more to it than that."

"Well, the guy does come off tough, like he wouldn't mind kicking your teeth in if you looked at him wrong. Anyway, I'm going to tell the cops what I found out and suggest I get to know Leon better. He said he was in the 'import' business and I want to see what he means by that. When I asked him about it, he was evasive, which makes me think he's hiding something. On the other hand, with Izzie out of the picture I figure he's lonely and might welcome someone he can trust."

Zac leaned back and took a final gulp of beer. "So, what do you think?"

If he'd stuck his finger in an electric outlet, Jackson could not have been more shocked. His brother, Zac, the deadbeat who'd spent the past ten years smoking weed, drinking and carousing, planned to literally put his life on the line for a woman he'd never met.

"I think the police better be in on this from the get-go or you could end up either the victim of a trafficker or accused of being one." *What if Zac up and disappeared like Izzie had?* "And bro," his voice wavered, "be careful."

Chapter 29

"Just so I'm clear. You want to make friends with a guy who not only may have something to do with that girl's disappearance, but also may be involved in human trafficking? Is that what you're proposing?" If Detective Richard Anders' eyebrows rose any higher, they'd go clear off his forehead.

Zac nodded with the enthusiasm of a six-year old. "Exactly. I know for a fact he was seeing Izzie. He told me so. Said he loved her. No question about it. I don't know what happened. He got defensive when I ask why they broke up. Maybe she dumped him and he doesn't know where she went after that. But if that's the case, why not say so? Anyhow, there's something fishy going on, know what I mean?"

Zac sat across from the detective in one of the interview rooms. He wasn't a stranger to the setup, having found himself at the wrong end of the law on more than one occasion, mostly getting caught driving drunk or buying marijuana. He knew that big "mirror" on the wall was one of those two-way things equipped with a listening devise.

The detective was a thoughtful man whose face reflected concern. "I know the guy you're talking about; name's Leon, right?"

"Right."

"We've actually had our eye on him for awhile. From time to time, neighbors have complained about noise and the condition of the place, but we could never get anything to justify a warrant."

"So, what about my idea? I could buddy up to him, make him think I'm his friend. Get him to invite me inside and take me into his confidence. Who knows, maybe he really is just a poor sap mooning over a breakup, but I have a feeling there's more to it."

The detective took a sip from his Styrofoam cup, leaned back and cleared his throat. "So you're asking me to take you on as an informant?"

"Exactly."

The detective scrutinized Zac to the point he felt as though the man had reached not only inside his head but into his very soul. Finally he said, "I'll have to talk to my commander, but I think we can do that. Before I do, I want to make sure you know what you're getting yourself into. Human traffickers are the absolute worst; they're the scum of the earth. They'll stop at nothing to avoid detection—and that includes murder. You up for that?"

The serious expression on the Anders' face gave Zac pause. Was he willing to take that big of a risk for someone he'd never met? Did he really give a damn what became of her? If Leon actually was a trafficker, where did that leave Zac? His head began to spin.

"Maybe you'd better think it over before you give me an answer."

Hesitating for the slightest second, Zac came to a decision. To this point he'd lived a life devoid of concern for anyone but himself. He'd misused every relationship he'd had from as far back as he could remember. Maybe it was time he grew up and put someone ahead of himself for a change. It was true he'd never met the girl, but his brother was concerned about her and that was good enough for him.

"I have thought it over, Detective. I'm up for it," he said and hoped he hadn't just made the biggest mistake of his life.

Chapter 30

Leon leaned back in what passed for his favorite chair—a broken-down rocker recliner left behind by the former owners of the place. He closed his eyes and let the strains of Beethoven's Fifth wash over him, flooding his mind with memories of a distant past.

Classical music had been his secret passion ever since he'd first heard it in Miss Krause's music-appreciation class. He couldn't risk telling anyone for fear of being labeled a sissy. After all, his friends—if you could call them that—had been into gangsta' rap. He'd have gotten beat up every day if they found out.

So he'd kept it a secret from everyone, including his family—no, especially from them. If they'd ever discovered his one record, his brothers would've smashed it into tiny pieces, just to see him cry. Somehow Leon had managed to keep it a secret to this very day.

Although it was badly scratched, the music still came through, soothing him and bringing him sorely needed comfort. It crossed his mind that he could replace it with a CD, but then he'd have to go out and buy a CD player. He had a birthday coming in a few weeks. Maybe he'd treat himself to one, instead of ignoring the day as he usually did.

Leon poured more bourbon into his glass and sat back down, twisting the antique ring his grandmother had given him when he turned sixteen. She'd told him to always wear it, that it'd bring him luck. Now it was wedged so tight on his left pinkie finger he'd never get it off. *Some luck!*

That guy he'd met earlier, what was his name? Jack? No, it was unusual. Leon was bad with names. He never forgot a face, but names, he always had a hard time with them. Zac, that's right. His name was Zac. He hadn't bothered asking his last name. *Who names their kid Zac?* Playground bullies must've had a ball with that.

Leon took another gulp and closed his eyes. It was nice being alone for a change. There was so much drama whenever the product was around. He had to deal with their needs and get them ready to sell. Sometimes Leon wondered if it was worth it. Oh, the money was good, especially since he wasn't qualified to do anything, but, as his painful experience with Izzie proved, he couldn't have a normal life.

It hadn't bothered him until he met her, then everything changed. He'd fallen so hard, so quickly. In such a short time she'd made him see that life held possibilities he'd never dreamed of, then, just like that, it all went up in smoke and he was listening to music by himself…again.

He'd enjoyed this afternoon on the beach with Zac. The guy seemed all right. Said he was visiting his brother. Maybe, if he was careful, he could meet up with him for a drink before he left town. Leon was in between product and had time on his hands. He'd learned his lesson with Izzie, but surely meeting the guy for drinks and a few laughs would be all right. He'd just have to be careful. That shouldn't be too hard. All he had to do was remember what happened with Izzie. He couldn't make that mistake again.

Chapter 31

Zac was sitting in the car trying to figure out what to do next when his cellphone rang. He didn't have caller ID, so he had no idea who it might be. Maybe it was Mom checking to see if he and Jackson had killed each other yet.

"Yes?" he said. He'd never kicked the habit of refusing to identify himself when answering the phone for fear of who might be on the other end.

"Zac?"

"Yeah, who's this?"

"Leon. You know, from yesterday—at the beach and uh, the restaurant?"

Zac laughed. "Leon, you old dog. How're ya doin'?" He hoped he wasn't putting the old-boy routine on too thick.

"Fine. Hey, if you're not doing anything, wanna grab a bite? Then I'll show you around Tampa, unless you have something better to do."

"Me? Like what?"

"I don' know, like maybe hangin' with your brother?"

"Naw, he's workin'. So yeah, I'm in. See you around twelve."

Zac smiled. Problem solved. How about that? Now he could stop turning himself into knots trying to come up with an excuse to get in touch with the guy.

Shortly before noon, Zac sauntered into the restaurant and spotted Leon at the bar in almost the exact same spot as the previous day. *Bet he's been here at least half an hour. Like an overeager girl on her first date.* Zac chuckled. *Pathetic. And this loser's dangerous? Please.*

Slipping onto the barstool, Zac said, "Hey Leon, what's up?"

For the next forty-five minutes or so, the two men made small talk between bites of Cubans and swigs of beer. Then it was time for that tour.

****

Although the afternoon was turning out to be pleasant, Zac had deep misgivings. He'd never been picky about his choice of companions, but having to cultivate Leon's friendship hit a new low—even for him. Of course, he could be wrong. Maybe the man was simply lonely. Somehow Zac had to get Leon to open up. It wouldn't be easy.

They were downtown, walking past the Port of Tampa. "Cruise ships like that leave from here all the time," Leon pointed in the direction of an ocean liner docked nearby. "I'd like to do that someday. It'd be a blast, don'cha think?"

Zac nodded. "So, go for it. What's stopping you?"

Leon shrugged. "Now's not the time. I got responsibilities."

"What kind of responsibilities? Looks to me like you pretty much come and go as you please." Zac held his breath. Maybe he'd finally got his foot in the door.

"Oh, you know, the usual."

When Leon didn't elaborate, Zac decided to push a little farther.

"Like the import business you're in?" He clamped his mouth shut and waited for what would come next.

Leon hesitated as if trying to decide whether or not Zac could be trusted. "Yeah, that. If I'm not here, I lose money. How 'bout you? What do you do?"

Zac gave him a sheepish grin. "Not a whole hell of a lot. Back home I live with my mom and mostly just hang out. She's always on my case to make something of myself, but I think she finally saw the writing on the wall and gave up. That's why I'm visiting my little brother."

He gave Leon a long look. "I know the big brother's the one who's supposed to be successful. Well, in my case it's just the reverse. All my life, I've heard how smart and handsome he is. Got to the point I hated the sight of him." He stopped talking as the truth of what he said sank in. It wasn't Jackson's fault he was a failure.

Leon appeared to listen with his heart instead of his ears. "I had older brothers who bullied me from the time I could walk. I don't mean just the usual kid stuff either. I ended up with broken bones—cracked ribs and such."

"So, what'd ya do to make them stop?"

"Joined a street gang, what else?"

"So you traded one bunch of bullies for another?"

"Got that right. But I toughened up to the point where I became the bully. Trust me it's a lot more fun on that side of the fence." They both chuckled.

Resuming his role of tour guide, Leon said, "We're in the Channel District. That's the Tampa Bay Times Forum where the Republican National Convention was held several years ago."

Zac realized the moment had passed; he wouldn't be getting any more information today. Might as well relax. Weaseling his way into the man's confidence would be a long drawn-out affair. He just hoped Izzie wouldn't run out of time before he got there.

Chapter 32

That night, Zac was uncharacteristically quiet, which made Jackson more than a little nervous. When his brother kept his mouth shut for any length of time, it generally meant he was up to no good.

"So, you get things squared away with the police?"

Zac nodded. "Yep, I'm a bona fide snitch. They're even gonna toss a few bucks my way every now and then. How about that?"

"Seriously?"

"That's what they said. I'll believe it when I get the cash, but that's not what this is about. I just want to find out what Leon's up to and if he did anything to Izzie."

"Really?" Jackson was having a hard time believing his brother had transformed from a layabout into an upstanding citizen practically overnight. What if this was all a ruse? What if his brother was really interested in Leon so he could get in on the action?

An involuntary shudder passed through his body. God, he hoped that wasn't the case. This could turn out to be a disaster of monumental proportions. His mother would never forgive him; hell, he'd never forgive himself if Zac ended up in prison—or dead.

"What?" Zac scrutinized his younger brother. "Is it so hard to believe I'd do something worthwhile? You really think that little of me?" He got up and left the apartment, slamming the door behind him.

****

Jackson was getting worried. Several hours had past and Zac hadn't returned. Finally, just before midnight, the key turned in the lock. His brother was home, hopefully not as angry as before.

"Hey," Jackson said, looking up from a book he hadn't really been reading.

"Hey back at 'cha." Zac mumbled and plopped into the closest chair.

Neither spoke for several minutes. "Listen," Jackson began. "I'm sorry if I upset you earlier. I didn't mean…"

"I know *'xactly* what you meant. Ya don' have to pretend. *I know*," Zach hiccupped, then continued, "I know what everone thinks a' me. Think I don'?"

Several hours of serious drinking made itself known with the difficulty his brother had expressing himself. Not wanting to make things worse, Jackson bit his lip.

"Tha's right, be the same good lil' boy who sucked up to Mom 'n Dad while I was the screw-up. Well, lemme tell you sumpin' kiddo: 'fore they went out and got you, I was the golden boy. Far as they were concerned, I was damn near perfec. Then they jus hadda get a brother fer me 'n ever thing change. It was 'careful don' wake the *baby*;' 'that new toy's for *the baby*;' 'isn' he jus' the sweetes' thing?' *Yeah right*."

Jackson was still focused on Zac's remark about his parents going out and *'getting'* him. Odd. Even in his drunken state, wouldn't he have said something like, 'when you were born'?

"What did you mean they went out and got me?" Leaning in toward his brother, Jackson could smell liquor on his breath.

Zac laughed in only the way someone who's had too much to drink would. "You don' know, do you? They never got 'round to telling their *very* spechul child—one who's *so-o* smart, *so-o* handsome, so-o 'complished; th' one they love more 'n me—that he's not really a Taylor uh t'all. That he was," he let out a loud belch, "you know—adopted."

The news crashed in on Jackson like a cement block to the head. The thought never entered his mind. Oh, from time to time, a neighbor had remarked on how very different the Taylor boys were from each other, but that was often the case in families. One child might be blond with blue eyes while another's eyes and hair were dark; one short, the other tall enough to play professional basketball. Now, Zac was saying he'd been adopted. All these years he'd known and kept it a secret.

Unable to respond, Jackson just sat there staring at his older brother. Finally, he said, "That's not true. You're jealous, always have been. Well, this time you've hit a new low. It's one thing to say something like that, but to suggest Mom and Dad lied all these years, it's despicable, that's what it is."

Zac stood up and leaned over him, putting his hands on the back of Jackson's chair for support. "Oh it is, is it? Call Mom and ask her, why don' ya'? She might tell her precious baby boy the truth now that he's all grow'd up." Weaving uncertainly, Zac fell back into the chair.

By this time, anger had bubbled up inside Jackson to the point he had a choice between popping his brother in the chops and going to his room without another word. Not wanting to destroy his apartment, especially in a fistfight he was sure to lose, Jackson went to his room and locked the door. Then, going over to his desk, he began to compose an email:

> *Dear Mom,*
> *How're you doing? Me and Zac are…*

Jackson fumbled around for several minutes. He didn't want to worry her by giving the impression they weren't getting along, even if that was the case. Still, for the most part, things had been relatively peaceful, especially after Zac had sunk his teeth into the whole Izzie/Leon situation. Finally he began typing again.

> *Zac told me something odd a while ago. Admittedly, he'd had too much to drink and probably won't remember telling me tomorrow, but I wanted to check it out with you all the same. He said I was adopted. Is that true? I mean, I have a hard time believing you and Dad would keep something like that from me all these years.*
>
> *I love you, Mom, regardless of the truth nothing will change that. Despite Dad's drinking, it's been a privilege to be part of the Taylor family. But I have to know the truth.*

Jackson hesitated a long moment as tears clouded his vision.

Are you my birth mother? And if you're not, can you tell me who is?

I'm truly sorry if this email comes as a shock. Please don't get mad at Zac. As I said, he was drunk when he told me and I'm sure didn't do it out of spite.

Jackson bit his lip; he was pretty sure Zac fully intended to hurt him with that revelation despite being inebriated.

All I want to know is the truth and I'll never mention it again.
Your loving and grateful son,
Jackson

After finishing the message, Jackson's hand hovered over the "send" button, then, almost involuntarily, moved it to the right and pressed "delete". No matter the truth of his birth, he couldn't hurt the woman who'd shown him nothing but love all his life. When the time was right, he'd bring it up, but that time was not now, and most certainly not by means of an email.

The camaraderie he and his brother had cultivated over the past week was gone. In the morning he'd tell him to get out. Zac could go back home to his drinking buddies or stay in Tampa, Jackson didn't care. As far as Izzie was concerned, he'd somehow manage to find her on his own.

After a sleepless night obsessing over how to tell his brother he was no longer welcome, Jackson got up and left his room expecting to see Zac asleep on the couch. He walked down the hall debating whether to wake him and demand that he leave immediately, or wait until he got home from work. His resolve weakening along with his anger, Jackson went into the living room to an unexpected sight: Zac, along with his belongings, was gone.

Chapter 33

Leon had finished his second cup of coffee when he heard a tapping on the door. *Who the hell is that?* His question was directed at Tiny, who had been reclining on the cool tile floor. At the sound of the knock, the dog sprang to his feet, began to bark and growl, and then dashed across the room toward the front of the house. No one ever came around except for a pickup or drop off, making Leon that much more concerned.

Was it the police? Had they finally caught up with me? Will I be hauled into court to face those whiny bitches? Sweat poured in rivulets down his face and back, making dark circles under his arms. The breakfast he so recently enjoyed now sat like a lump in the pit of his stomach. Whoever it was, rapped again.

Should he answer it—or follow his impulse and hightail it out the back? Glancing around, he concluded there was nothing lying around. There had been no deliveries for several weeks now. What the hell, might as well open the door and see what whoever it was wanted.

Squelching the urge to greet his visitor with a bullet through the door, Leon swallowed hard and joined his spastic watchdog. He opened the door a crack—just enough to see who it was that had so rudely disrupted his morning.

There, standing on the stoop, his arms folded over his chest, foot tapping as if waiting for a bus, stood his newfound friend, Zac. *What the hell was he doing here?* Had Leon forgotten he'd agreed to do something with him? How did Zac even know where he lived? Oh yeah, the other day he'd made the mistake of pointing the house out when he went to get the car. When would he learn?

"Zac," he exclaimed, grabbing hold of Tiny's collar as he opened the door. "How ya' doin'?" He put on his most welcoming expression, which wasn't all that much of a stretch. He really did like the guy.

"Hey, Leon." Zac appeared bedraggled: He wore a badly wrinkled shirt; there were dark circles under his eyes; his strong body odor broadcast the need for a shower.

For a moment neither one spoke, each waiting for the other to begin. Finally, Zac said, "I didn't mean to just show up like this, but me and my brother had this big fight, see, and he kicked me out. You're the only one I know around here."

He stopped talking and gave Leon a lost puppy-dog look, then added, "I wondered if you'd let me stay with you a few days 'till I figure out what to do?"

Leon, who'd never had someone to hang with let alone a friend who needed him, was momentarily speechless. Here's this guy he barely knew asking if he could move in with him. What should he do? The guy was obviously in a bind: no money, no place to stay, no food. Boy could Leon relate to that. He'd been in the same spot more than once and knew what sleeping on a park bench was like. Not only was it cold and often wet, but next to impossible to sleep for fear of being mugged or even murdered.

"C'mon in," he said.

For the next hour the two men sat around the kitchen table drinking coffee and sorting out their options.

"The other day you said you were in the import business, right? I wondered if there was any way I could get in on the action."

Leon, who'd grown weary of shouldering the responsibility for this part of the operation, perked up at the suggestion. Then he realized what it was the man suggested: let him in on a situation so dangerous that any revelation to the wrong people could result in their being arrested—or murdered. That's what he dealt with on a daily basis.

But this here guy might be the key to a better life. Hell, look at him: family turned their backs on him, no job. Couldn't be more perfect. He was a short step up from the product they snatched off the street.

Leon scratched the day-old stubble on his chin. "Well, I don't know about that," he said and cleared his throat as if pondering Zac's suggestion. "The business I'm in tends to be dangerous. You up for that?"

"Danger's my middle name," Zac said and leaned in toward Leon with a hopeful look.

"Yeah, well, there's danger and then there's danger, if you get my drift." Was this guy for real? Did he have any idea what he was dealing with? "I mean, you look like an upstanding kinda guy. You ever find yourself on the wrong side of the law?"

Zac guffawed. "Hell yes, all the time. Back home the cops'd come get me the minute there was any trouble. Figured one way or another I was behind it." He leaned back in the chair and folded his arms.

"I'm not talking 'bout small-town crap teenage boys pull, drunk driving or getting busted for drugs, that's not what this is about."

"So whyn't you tell me what it's about, then we'll decide if I'm up for it or not."

When Leon didn't respond to Zac's suggestion, he added, "Look man, I'm desperate here. Got no money, no job, no place to stay. Don't even have enough dough to go back home. If you'd let me in on the action—just till I get on my feet, it'd be a big help. Besides, seems like you could use someone to share the load."

Scrutinizing Zac as he made his pitch, Leon became convinced the man was for real. But how did he know he could be trusted? What if he was an undercover cop? Then what? Hadn't Seymour drilled into him time and time again that no one—absolutely no one—was to be trusted? Look what happened with Izzie.

As he deliberated, Leon chewed on a bothersome hangnail. *What to do. What to do.* On the one hand it was a huge risk, one that could cost him not only his freedom, but his life, if things went south. On the other, Zac appeared to be a savvy sorta guy who knew his way around the block. He wasn't some choirboy who'd never been in trouble. Best of all, he needed Leon more than Leon needed him. And if it didn't work out, Leon would take care of it. Taking care of problems was his specialty.

"Oh, what the hell. Why not?" he said at last. "But lemme warn you, this is a tough business. We help people get in the country and find them jobs, hence the import label. But ya gotta be careful; can't trust anyone…see what I'm sayin'?" Leon saw Zac's forehead contract into a mass of wrinkles.

"What's illegal about that? Sounds like you provide a service."

"Right. That's exactly what it is…a service." Leon scratched the stubble on his chin and slapped the table. "Actually we should get an award for what we do, but," he heaved a sigh and gave an exaggerated shrug, "It is what it is. So…you on board?"

"Sure, man, count me in."

"But now, ya gotta understand, all this is on the QT. If word gets out, we could land in jail…or dead."

"I get the jail part," Zac said. "Authorities enforce laws even when they don't make sense, but who'd wanna kill us?"

"Competitors. We're not the only ones in this business, ya know. It's a dog-eat-dog world out there. Just make sure you're not the one that's eaten."

Zac nodded and reached out to shake his hand. "Thanks for giving me a chance. You won't be disappointed. I promise."

"I better not be." Leon reinforced the implied threat with a long, penetrating look. *I really like this guy. Hope he doesn't screw up. I'd hate to have to drop him off the Sunshine Bridge.* "Here's what we'll do…"

Chapter 34

Jackson was glad his brother was gone. It relieved him of having to demand he leave. He'd no doubt go back home and resume sponging off their mother. It was unfortunate, but he'd done what he could and it hadn't worked out. At least she'd had a little over a week of peace without him and that was something.

He sighed and locked the door behind him. Today would be another day of worrying about what happened to Izzie and dealing with a clueless intern. Oh what a glamorous life he led.

Jackson chuckled as he recalled the looks on people's faces whenever he told them what he did for a living. A TV news cameraman? Or even better, when he used the word "photojournalist" he might as well have said he was an astronaut. They wanted to hear all about it and seemed surprised to learn all the education and training it took.

He was tired. The whole Zac-Izzie thing wore on him. God, what he'd give to go back in time a few weeks before Dad died, when Izzie was just his annoying reporter. If only he hadn't noticed the girl on the balcony. That's what really started it all. If he could manage to control his over-active imagination maybe he wouldn't keep getting into these god-awful situations. Sure, and he might as well take an axe to his brain 'cause that what it'd take for him to stop.

As the day wore on, Jackson went about his assignments with the enthusiasm of a robot. Even his intern noticed. "So, Jackson, you have a fight with your girlfriend?"

"I don't have one of those." Jackson's response was curt to the point of being rude, but really, he hardly knew the girl. What business of it was hers to ask a question like that?

"I didn't mean to pry, it's just that it seems like something's bothering you. If you want to talk about it, I'm a good listener."

Jackson realized the intern meant well and hadn't deserved his brusque treatment of her. "I'm sorry. I just have a lot on my mind."

"Anything I can help you with?"

Jackson shrugged. The girl was persistent, he'd give her that. They were on their way back to the station to edit footage. It was mostly VOSOTs, but that's probably what he'd be doing till they hired a reporter to replace Izzie.

The thought of Izzie renewed the twin pain of fear and regret he felt at her ongoing absence. By now she'd been gone a little over a week. With no word as to her whereabouts, it was like she'd simply dropped off the face of the earth.

And the fight with his brother, how had that happened? The same way so many fights with Zac had over the years. He didn't even remember who it started. Something set him off and he'd stalked out of the apartment. When he came back, that's when they'd nearly come to blows over, oh yeah, Zac dropping the bomb that he was adopted.

The intern stared at him.

"Uh, no, it's nothing. I'm just tired that's all." He gave her a weak smile and pulled into the parking lot.

Later at home, Jackson got to thinking. Maybe he should check to make sure Zac made it home or at least warn Mom he was on the way. He dreaded making the call. What if he ended up asking her about being adopted? The wound was still too fresh for him to be able to handle the subject in casual conversation: Oh, yeah, Mom, when were you going to tell me I'm not really part of the Taylor family? Didn't you think maybe I had a right to know?

Threads of anger shot through his body; his sore shoulder tensed up. Without thinking he massaged it, trying to ease the pain. It helped, but not much. Maybe he'd put off calling for the time being. He flicked on the TV, grabbed a beer from the fridge and settled back on the sofa. It was good to have the place to himself again.

Chapter 35

Wow, that was easy. Zac put his feet on the bed, leaned back and reflected on the morning's accomplishment. He'd anticipated encountering resistance to his suggestion that Leon make him part of the operation. It was almost too easy. Was the man really that gullible? Or was he playing the lonely ol' boy routine in order to find out what Zac was up to?

He'd have to be careful; his life may depend on it. It was a good thing he'd baited Jackson like that. At the time he'd felt guilty, but now he realized it'd been the right thing to do. Jackson was so angry he wouldn't give a damn whether Zac went back to Iowa or not so long as he didn't show his face at the apartment. And that was good for them both. It'd keep Jackson away from Leon's house and prevent him from giving Zac away. He took a deep drag on his cigarette. But if it was so good, why did he feel like crap?

He glanced around the shabby room. It was barely more than a good-sized walk-in closet. The bed and dresser occupied the lion's share of the space. He stood and looked out the grimy window to the scrubby front yard and street below. He remembered the decorative security bars from when he first saw the house. It gave him the creeps. While he was free to come and go, the former occupants of this room were not. Sweeping the windowsill with his finger, some kind of indentations drew his attention. Bending down to take a closer look, he realized graffiti was scratched into the woodwork. With great difficulty he made out what seemed to be part of a name: "HEST..., followed by numbers: 5633597 ... He couldn't make out all of them.

Getting out his wallet, he jotted down the information. Maybe Detective Anders could decipher it. He'd have to figure out a way to report in without getting caught.

How long would he be able to act as though he believed the bullshit about it being an import business? He'd had a hard time keeping a straight face when Leon said that. It would've felt good to smash the asshole right in the face and make him admit he was not only *not* providing a "service", but forcing unsuspecting women and children into slavery. The very word made him shudder.

For a few minutes, Zac wavered, wondering what he'd gotten himself into and how—or if—he would manage to get out alive. Guilt seeped inside him on a number of levels: He regretted the shabby way he'd treated his family over the years—especially Jackson, who only ever wanted a big brother he could look up to; he felt remorse for never having made anything of his life; and now he began to wonder about the whole Leon business. It was probably the only unselfish thing he'd ever done and, as he sat back down on the uncomfortable bed in the tiny room, he began to try and conjure up ways to get out of this mess.

He could tell Leon he'd changed his mind, that his mother was sick and needed him. Yeah, that'd go over big; especially since the man practically admitted he was a criminal and more or less threatened him with serious bodily harm if he ever crossed him. Well, he hadn't come right out and said as much, but Zac assumed that's what he meant. Or he could simply leave without telling the miserable bastard anything; maybe go back to Jackson's place and apologize. After the things he'd said though, he very much doubted that was an option. But Jackson tended to be softhearted and had that live- and let-live philosophy going for him, so maybe he *would* take him back, who knew?

Then Zac thought about Izzie. Jackson had shown him a photograph of the young woman in an unguarded moment. She was a real looker in a vulnerable sort of way. He obviously cared about her, probably more than he even realized.

She must've gotten in over her head with Leon. Whatever it was, she must've paid a very high price for it. Realizing he'd just referred to Izzie in the past tense, he corrected himself. She was probably alive. He just didn't know if they would find her in time—or what would be left of her when they did.

The little Zac knew of Leon told him the man had a mean streak and could be vicious if crossed. Maybe he'd discovered Izzie was stringing him along, doing her "investigative reporter" thing. According to Jackson, she was almost obsessed with breaking a big story so it'd end up on the networks and make her famous. He said being an anchor on one of the major news shows was her dream and that she was determined to make it happen.

If that was the case, and Jackson, who had worked with her for nearly a year, would surely know—then he was probably right—she was in serious trouble.

The question confronting Zac was whether she was worth risking *his* life for. Maybe she was, maybe not—but he knew one thing for damned sure: Jackson was willing to stick his neck out to save her, and that being the case maybe it was time he stepped up. Regardless how things turned out: whether Izzie was dead or alive, whether he managed to rescue her from some trafficker or died trying, at least he will have done something worthwhile for a change.

Having made what was the biggest decision of his life and hoping it wouldn't turn out to be fatal, Zac stretched, got up and went downstairs to see if Leon wanted to go out for a Cuban.

Chapter 36

Jackson's hand hovered over his cellphone. He needed to find out if Zac had gone home but wanted to neither disturb his mother's newfound peace nor speak to his brother. He was still angry and hurt by what had transpired. The more he thought about it, the more baffled he became.

He couldn't recall having done anything to set Zac off like that. Maybe it was Jackson's surprised expression when he'd announced his plans to work with the police that did it.

Jackson tapped his mouth as he realized that must have been it. Zac always could read him and must've become offended when he saw Jackson's astonishment at his generosity. It was a momentary flash of doubt, but obviously long enough for Zac to have seen it.

No wonder he was upset. Here he'd arranged to work with the police at his peril to locate a woman he'd never met and cared nothing about and how was his decision received by the one person who should've been thrilled? By skepticism, that's how. He must've felt insulted, maybe even humiliated.

As he slowly worked out the reason for Zac's sudden explosion, Jackson realized it was all his fault. But then there was the thing about him being adopted. *What was that all about? Was it even true?* Had Zac, in his drunken stupor, made it up out of spite—or had the alcohol lowered his inhibitions to the point of revealing a secret he'd kept far too long?

Jackson shrugged. There was no way to find out without confronting his brother, his mother—or them both. And right now locating Zac was uppermost in his mind. The adoption thing would have to wait.

He pressed number "one: on his speed dial and listened: It rang once, twice, three times. At the fourth, he was about to hang up when his dead father's voice came over the wire: "You've reached the Taylor residence. We're not available to answer your call…"

Jackson was so startled he dropped the phone. The recording continued while he picked it up and then snapped it closed. He felt sick with grief. Even in death the old man had managed to insert himself into his affairs. Brushing away several tears that overran his eyelids, Jackson realized for the first time how sorely he missed and loved his father in spite of his monumental failings.

His mother must be out with friends—or maybe she'd gone to the airport to pick up Zac. He'd call back later. Maybe by then Jackson would be in a better frame of mind and willing to let bygones be bygones.

Chapter 37

Furtively looking around to make certain his new "roomy" hadn't come downstairs, Leon headed down the hall toward the back of the house, where a built-in bookcase took up part of the wall. He pressed a hidden latch, then pulled causing it to rotate forward, revealing a staircase which descended into a bunker. Designed to keep the home's original occupants safe in case of a nuclear attack or a violent hurricane, it was perfect for Leon's purpose.

The bottom of the stairs melted into a space around twelve feet wide by twenty feet long. It smelled musty, but the product was generally only held there a short time. He looked around. There were several beds, a table with two chairs and a bookshelf. Product down there no doubt got bored, but the way he looked at it, that was the least of their problems.

He noticed mice droppings in the corner. He'd sprinkle some D-Con around later. He glanced at the bucket they used to do their business. Damn, using this room would be like having to remember to let Tiny out. It was easier before he took Zac in.

Other than the product coming and departing, he'd always been alone in the house, so he'd only used the bunker to discipline rebellious ones. It was amazing how fast their attitudes changed after a few hours in the "hole".

Leon sighed. Better get upstairs; don't want his "trainee" to discover the secret room. For now, he'd be limited to contact with the "imports". They couldn't speak English and had no idea what was happening. He'd tell him about the "domestic" product later—after he was sure the man was onboard and could be trusted.

He chuckled. If this worked out, life would be a whole lot easier. Zac could do the stuff he was tired of doing—which was most everything. To keep him happy, he'd even throw a few bucks his way. The guy wasn't the sharpest knife in the drawer. He obviously had no idea how lucrative this business could be.

He'd just made it up the stairs and closed the bookcase when Zac appeared in the doorway. "Hey, Leon, I'm starving. Wanna go get a Cuban?"

Chapter 38

"Hi Mom, how're you doing?" Jackson finally made the call he'd been putting off for several days.

As his mother caught him up on the latest problems at work, he wondered when she'd ask why Zac had returned home so soon. After several minutes of small talk, Jackson said, "So, Zac make it home all right?"

"Home? Zac? Why no, isn't he with you?"

The news that his brother hadn't gone back to Iowa hit Jackson like a blow to the back of the head. He didn't know how to respond. Should he tell his mother the truth or make up a story to keep her from getting all worked up. He chose the latter. There was no point upsetting her when Zac would probably come back in a day or so, his tail between his legs.

"No, I mean, yes, he's here, he just took off for a few days. Probably wanted to do some sightseeing while he's down here. You know Zac, he'll show up in a couple days with some real whoppers; probably say he was hangin' with Brad Pitt or something."

Even as he soothed his mother with lies, Jackson's heart sank. *Since Zac hadn't gone home, where was he?*

After exchanging pleasantries for a few more minutes, his mom ended the conversation with, "Well, dear, I love talking to you but I have to run. The church ladies have a meeting tonight to plan the bazaar and I promised to attend. Give Zac a kiss for me when he gets back. I'm glad the two of you are spending time together. I love you, Sweetie. Stay safe."

"I love you too, Mom." There was a lump in Jackson's throat the size of a grapefruit. He could scarcely breathe, let alone swallow as he put his cellphone down. He'd just led his mother to believe all was well, that he and Zac were actually getting along like brothers should when nothing could be farther from the truth.

Then Jackson remembered something that made his earlier concern seem almost silly. The night they'd fought Zac said he'd volunteered to get closer to Leon so he could find out what happened to Izzie and that police had agreed to let him become an informant. That's probably where he'd gone.

Jackson's heart sank. Volunteering to partner up with the worst kind of criminals put a target on Zac's back if they discovered what he was doing. Plus he had no experience with this type of thing. Yes, he'd done stupid things that got him in trouble from time to time, but something of this magnitude? He couldn't possibly realize the danger he was in. Somehow Jackson had to find him, warn him, extricate him. It was his fault Zac had taken an interest in Izzie's welfare and he'd have to do something—anything—to get him out before it was too late.

The following morning, Jackson called in sick. Holding his nose and coughing into the phone, he said, "I came down with some kinda bug."

Thankfully except for going home to help with his dad, Jackson hadn't taken any sick days, so it wasn't hard to convince the assignment desk editor that he really was sick. He'd called early to avoid talking to Morris Stone.

"Yes, I'll get plenty of rest and drink lots of fluids. I'll try to make it in tomorrow. Thanks. Bye."

As soon as he hung up, Jackson began trying to figure out what to do next.

Chapter 39

"Exactly who was it you wanted to see?" The police officer's face was flushed with what Jackson assumed was exasperation. He obviously had more important things to do than chat with some idiot who didn't seem to know what he wanted.

"I, er, uh, well, see I don't know who it was my brother spoke to. He just said…" Jackson looked around to make sure he wasn't being overheard. The room was empty except for the cop behind a glass partition and the drunk sitting on one of the chairs bolted to the wall.

"…I think he said he talked to a detective about becoming an informant."

The officer sighed. "Do you have any idea which detective it was? It might interest you to know that we have more than one."

"I'm sorry he didn't mention his name," Jackson said, feeling like a lost six year old.

The officer shook his head, mumbled to himself, then said, "Have a chair. I'll see what I can find out."

Jackson walked across the room and sat at the opposite end of where the intoxicated man snored. He didn't want to end up having the guy use him for a pillow—or worse yet—a vomit bag. The digital wall clock seemed frozen in time. How could a minute go by so slowly? Guess when you're anxious about something, time stands still.

He crossed and uncrossed his legs then his arms and shifted in his seat. With nothing to read and nowhere pleasant to park his thoughts, he began to watch people as they walked into the station with their stories of woe. He managed to overhear the louder ones, those whose distress had overridden their need for privacy:

"I haven't seen him for two days now," a woman declared. "It's just not like him to…" Jackson couldn't hear the rest. He hadn't learned whether the missing was a child or adult, husband or boyfriend. He was left to fill in the blanks himself.

The next person had been held up at gunpoint and relieved of his wallet. He was more indignant than frightened: "What the hell's this city coming to when a guy can't leave his house without getting held up?" In both cases, the desk sergeant took down some notes and handed them off to what Jackson assumed were detectives.

He yawned, shifted in his seat again and glanced at the clock. Although it seemed longer, only fifteen minutes had passed. He started to think the man had forgotten him when his name was called.

"Mr. Taylor."

Jackson was led to an interview room by an officer. "The detective will be with you shortly."

Yeah, sure he would. This was a stalling tactic if he ever saw one. They'd let him stew for another twenty minutes, then tell him they'd never heard of Zac. Just watch. That's what they'll do. Then what? Jackson drummed his fingers on the table and tapped his foot. He glanced at the wall mirror. *So watch, why don't ya?* He didn't give a flying fig what they thought.

Looking at the wall clock again, he folded his arms across his chest and let out a sigh. It'd been exactly three minutes. The door opened and in walked a man he'd never seen before.

"I'm Detective Anders. I believe you have some concerns about the whereabouts of your brother?"

Jackson was nearly speechless. He assumed they'd blow him off. But here was a guy who appeared to take him seriously. About six feet tall, the detective had salt and pepper hair with a receding hairline, a kind smile and tired blue eyes that said he'd seen more than his share of tragedy.

"Yes, Officer, er, Detective." Jackson fumbled for the right words; he didn't want to offend him. "See, my older brother Zac is visiting from up north and is—was—staying with me. We had a fight the other night and when I got up he'd left with his belongings. I think he might be in trouble."

"And what makes you think that?" The detective took out a notepad and began to write, looking up between words.

"Well, the night he left he said he came here with information about a guy named Leon who he said he'd struck up a conversation with and the guy mentioned a woman who we reported missing. Said he offered to get close to him and be a police informant."

"Then what happened?"

"What do you mean?"

"Did the police accept his offer?"

"He said they did."

"And you believed him?"

"Of course, why wouldn't I"

The detective tried to take another sip, but the cup was empty. "Maybe he was yanking your chain. I don't know your brother. Only you can say whether he'd tell you something that wasn't true. Would he?"

"What? Lie? What on earth for?"

"Maybe to impress you. You said he's your older brother? He working?"

"N-no," Jackson stuttered in frustration. "What's that got to do with anything?"

"Humor me a minute. What do you do?"

"I'm a TV news photographer."

"Impressive."

"Not really. It's hard work."

"You make good money?"

"Not now, but I will eventually." Jackson's patience was wearing thin. "What's this have to do with my brother?"

"Maybe nothing. But don't you see, he probably feels humiliated that you've been able to land what most people would consider an exciting job. You've got a whole career ahead of you if you play your cards right. And your brother—your *older* brother, what's he done with his life?"

Jackson stared at the badly scratched tabletop. He noticed the name Carly and idly wondered if it was someone's girlfriend.

"Well?"

"Well, what?"

"What's your brother accomplished so far compared with what you've done?"

Answering the detective in a voice barely above a whisper, Jackson said, "Nothing."

"So, now he wants to do something important. You said he wanted to be some kind of police informant and catch the guy responsible for your friend's disappearance. Right?"

Jackson nodded. "But, Detective, the guy might be dangerous. I'm worried something might happen to him."

"Look, if he's an informant and does as he's told, he'll be in touch with his handler. He's not totally on his own out there."

"So you're saying he's one of yours?"

"I'm not saying anything one way or the other. What I'm telling you is that it sounds like your brother wants to do something he considers important. That being said, you should get out of his way and let him do it." The detective's steel-blue eyes drilled a hole right through Jackson. "I know you're worried about him, but he'll be all right. Trust me."

"Can I at least check in with you from time to time to find out what's happening?"

"Sure, you do that." The detective stood up, shook Jackson's hand and walked him to the door. "Catch you later," he said.

He was gone before Jackson realized he hadn't learned a damned thing.

Chapter 40

Izzie blinked, trying to figure out where she was and how she got there. It was dark, so dark she could scarcely see her hand as she brought it to her face. Had she been buried alive? A surge of fear coursed through her. Dear God, was she going to die like this with no one knowing what happened to her?

A dull pain throbbed in the back of her skull. She was groggy—thirsty—her tongue so dry it fairly stuck to the roof of her mouth. *Where the hell was she?*

The last she remembered Leon had erupted in fury when she'd walked in on him. She'd knocked, of course, but he mustn't have heard, so she'd turned the knob. Discovering the door unlocked, she went inside. After all, it wasn't as if they were strangers. They'd gone out several times; once he'd even invited her in.

In the beginning, she'd been suspicious. After what Jackson had told her, who wouldn't be? And she'd seen the video, oh yeah, she'd seen that video. Over and over he'd shown her the damned video. But Leon's explanation made sense. Besides he'd been a perfect gentleman. He seemed to really care about her. So why not surprise him with a six pack of Coronas? He'd be thrilled.

But that wasn't what happened. She had opened the door quietly and tiptoed down the hall to the kitchen where she'd heard voices. He was probably listening to one of those police dramas he loved. The girl on the show screamed; the guy shouted. She was nearly to the kitchen when she realized the man doing the yelling was Leon. *Who was with him and why was she screaming?*

Whatever was happening, Izzie realized she'd better get out of there—and fast. Trembling to the point she could scarcely move, she turned around. The beer slipped from her hand, splashing broken glass and liquid across the hardwood floor. Izzie panicked, covering her mouth with her hand. Tiny barreled through the door, barking furiously and knocking her down—right into the puddle of beer.

"Who's there?" Leon shouted, following several steps behind the rottweiler, a pistol in his hand.

"Me, it's just me," Izzie managed to call out over the din. She'd cut her finger on a piece of glass. The blood made a zigzag pattern down the front of her pale green skirt. Popping the wound in her mouth to staunch the bleeding, she sucked on it a second, then added, "I knocked, but I guess you didn't hear me. This," she gestured at the mess on the floor, "was supposed to be a surprise."

Leon's face transformed from a scowl to a smile. "Tiny, pipe down." He was about to add something when a young girl tore out of the kitchen.

"Help. Help. You got to help me," she screamed. Her eyes were swollen and bloodshot, her face flushed. There seemed to be the start of a bruise on her cheek. She appeared to be around twelve. The terror on face cried out even louder than her words. Grabbing onto Izzie, she cowered behind her.

Tiny lunged at the child—growling, barking and leaping. Izzie, afraid of the large black dog anyway, shuddered violently.

Amidst the barking and screaming, Leon raised his gun and shot into the air, making a hole in the ceiling and adding a shower of plaster to the mix.

"Everybody, shut the hell up!" he yelled. "And clean up this mess."

Izzie stared at Leon, her body stiffened in indignation. *Who does he think he is, ordering me around?* She didn't take crap like that—not from anyone—and most certainly not from the likes of him.

She cleared her throat and took a deep breath. "Is this the niece you told me about? I thought she went home."

The girl peeked from behind her and shouted, "I ain't his niece, lady. I been kidnapped. You gotta get me outta here."

Izzie looked from the frightened child clinging to her, to the man she had begun to trust. "Leon?" she demanded. "What's she talking about?"

Leon angrily shook his head. "Izzie, why the hell'd you hafta go do something like this? You've ruined everything."

After that all she could remember was the look on his face. It was an odd mix of regret and rage. Then amidst the escalating racket emanating from the girl and the dog, he'd punched her and everything went black.

Now here she was—wherever that might be. Her head aching, she could neither hear nor see a thing. All she could do was wait for what was yet to come.

Chapter 41

Zac forced an awkward laugh. Leon's coarse joke wasn't remotely amusing. He wasn't a prude, but this guy seemed to think the more obscene the story, the funnier. The man was disgusting. Well, at least the Cuban tasted good. He wiped his mouth on a paper napkin and pushed his chair back from the table. Hoping to get away from the man for a few hours, he said, "I'll see you after awhile."

"Whoa, what're you talking about? When you work for me, you don't take off whenever you feel like it." Leon's harsh glare delivered his message in no uncertain terms.

"All right. Whatever." Zac said, surprised by Leon's scolding. Clearing his throat, he said, "So…it's like a regular job?"

"Well, duh. Did you think you'd just come and go whenever?"

"To be honest I didn't think about it one way or the other," Zac said. "If I have working hours, what are they?"

"They're when I *say* they are." Leon's eyes fairly bulged out of their sockets. "That work for you?"

Zac was about to say, "Don't get your shorts in a bunch," but knew he'd better cool it. He had to remember why he'd hooked up with the sonofabitch in the first place. He'd have to hold his tongue—and his temper—till he figured out what happened to Izzie. He knew Jackson wouldn't be satisfied until he did—and truthfully, neither would he. So he gave Leon a shit-eating grin and said, "Whatever you say, Boss."

"That's more like it. Now let's go home and figure out exactly what you'll be doing."

****

Back at the house, Leon gestured for Zac to sit down. "Okay, here's the deal. Every so often, I get a shipment that has to be held till the distributor or buyers come. Could be only a few hours, or even days. In the meantime, it's our job—yours now—to keep things under control."

Zac nodded, then wrinkled his forehead. "Now, this shipment...what is it exactly? I mean, is it meth, smack or what?"

"Like I told you, it's people—illegal immigrants, that's what we deal in. People from poor countries looking for a better life. We help them find that." He paused as if to allow Zac a minute to take it in. "So you in? If you're not, speak up now."

Zac knew what his answer was, what it had to be, that he really had no choice, but he thought he should appear hesitant—not too eager to get involved in the sordid business. After a few seconds of silence, during which he looked down at the floor, he said, "I'm in. What do I need to do to keep our guests happy while they're here?"

"Not much really, mostly keep them quiet. You'll see what I mean when the next shipment comes in."

"Where do they go after they leave here?"

Leon shrugged. "Wherever cheap labor's needed. Could be south Florida, across the country, most anywhere. Once the distributor picks them up, I'm out of it. The less we know the better."

"Why's that?"

Leon looked a bit agitated. "Let's just say it can be dangerous to know stuff—if you get my drift."

Zac got his "drift" all right but needed to know more. "So, do you also export?"

Leon slowly finished the last of his beer. It seemed to Zac he was stalling, maybe trying to think up an answer. "Not all that much. We mostly act as a middleman for the imports. Far as exports go, that's seldom done and then only on a case-by-case basis."

"Why's that?"

"You're just *full* of questions, aren't you?"

When Zac didn't respond, Leon continued. "The market for our product is in the good ol' U.S. of A. I mean, think about it. Why would poor countries want to import our people when they have more than enough of their own to go around? Americans can afford to pay for the services our imports provide."

Zac nodded. "I never thought of it that way, but it makes sense. So, what industries hire them?"

"You'd be surprised. Massage parlors, factories, hotels, farms, strip joints, rich people—you name it."

Zac noticed he hadn't included whorehouses, but he supposed that was a given. He dreaded what the next few days would bring.

Chapter 42

Zac didn't have to wait long. That night there was a tapping on the back door. It just so happened that he and Leon were in the living room watching television. Tiny alerted them by his sudden barking and the aggressive dance in which he threw himself at the door.

"Tiny." Leon yelled. "Shut the hell up. Sit." His command was so forceful Zac had all he could do not to slink off into a corner himself.

"Who do you think it is?" Zac said.

"It's a delivery. You're about to get your first taste of our import business." Leon grinned.

Zac shuddered. *How could any woman be attracted to a man like that?* He supposed some found the guy appealing with his rugged good looks and bad boy personality. He remembered that Jackson said Izzie was pursuing a story that would catapult her to the top of the news media, so the attraction must have all been in Leon's mind.

"Now let me do the talking. I'll let you know if I want help."

There was a second knock. It sounded like some kind of a signal. There were two short knocks followed by a pause then another knock. With a pistol held behind his back, Leon opened the door a crack, then pulled it back. "Hey Sam, you sonofagun. How ya' doin?"

Sam was a stocky, muscular man of about six feet. He wasn't someone Zac would care to tangle with—he'd get the short end of the stick or more likely no stick at all.

"Got somethin' for me?"

"Sure do." The man nodded and pulled out some kind of document. "Just sign here and we'll get them inside."

As Leon took the paper and signed his name, Zac was reminded of how much their exchange mimicked a business transaction. Of course, in their minds that's precisely what it was.

"Let's get 'em inside and I'll be on my way." He shook hands with Leon and nodded at Zac. "Seymour finally sent you a helper, I see. About time."

For a second Leon seemed at a loss for words. "Yeah, this here's Zac. He came onboard yesterday."

Zac nodded.

"Well, I gotta go. Catch ya' next time."

Zac stayed inside as the two men went out to the alley where a van was parked. A moment later, he heard a shuffling of feet on the back steps. The screen door opened and he came face to face with a group of young women. It was worse than he imagined. The only sound as the bedraggled group filed into the room past him was feet hitting the linoleum, and an occasional cough or clearing of the throat. Even Tiny knew better than to make a ruckus.

"All right, now," Leon directed his comment at Zac. "Take our guests upstairs to the back bedroom. Show them the bathroom and let them use it one at a time. I'll fix some food and bring it up. Don't talk to them and if they talk to each other, let them know to keep still. Got it?"

With his eye on the women, Zac nodded, then gestured for them to follow him.

After they were settled on cots in what Zac assumed had been the master bedroom, he indicated the attached bath, pointed at the nearest girl and gestured. It took a few seconds, then she understood. One by one the women relieved themselves as he stood guard.

In their early- to mid-teens, the women were slim, with long dark hair and olive skin. They wore blue jeans, jogging shoes and low-cut tops with exposed cleavage. Zac wondered exactly what they'd been told to make them so cooperative. None seemed frightened. Actually it was the opposite; their eyes sparkled in anticipation of what Zac assumed they thought was the beginning of a new life. It'd be a new life, all right, only one far different than they dreamed it would be.

It wasn't long before Leon poked his face in, holding a large tray of sandwiches, chips and soft drinks. He set it on a side table and watched as one by one the girls helped themselves and began to eat.

"This'll hold'em for the time being. Buyer's stopping by in about an hour, so we'll get them out of here in no time. Just the way I like it—no fuss, no muss"

Chapter 43

That night Zac had a hard time getting to sleep. He kept seeing the trusting eyes and shy smiles of the young women who were destined for a miserable life. They, no doubt, came from some Third World country. The traffickers most likely had promised their parents they'd go to college or get good jobs and send money home. Whatever lie they'd been fed, these girls were obviously not aware of what was about to happen.

Zac turned over in the uncomfortable bed and punched the lumpy pillow. A glance at the bedside clock said it was three-thirty. If he'd been able to, he would have led those girls right back out and taken them to a shelter. It was too late now. They were on the next leg of their journey and Zac had no doubt this stop would look like Paradise compared with their final destination.

He wasn't sure how long he could keep up the charade of being an accomplice to Leon's disgusting business—or what the consequences might be when he decided he'd had enough and wanted out, Izzie or no Izzie. With that thought in mind, he fell into a troubled sleep populated by young women screaming for help.

Chapter 44

On his way back from the police station, Jackson couldn't get his brother out of his mind. If he hadn't gone back to Iowa and wasn't a police informant, then where was he? The detective hadn't said one way or the other, and Zac had bragged that he was, as he put it, "a snitch". Was it safe to assume he'd told the truth for a change?

He didn't know what to think, but couldn't lose the uneasy feeling his brother was in danger. Should he take Detective Anders' advice and let it alone? Zac was a grown man and apparently wanted to do this. The detective had said he wasn't in it alone, that if Zac was working for them, he'd stay in touch. That he wouldn't be in any real danger. Still, Jackson had a sick feeling in the pit of his stomach, the kind he got when something was seriously wrong.

He took out his cellphone and pressed the number "three". That was Zac's number on his speed dial. It rang once, twice, three times. Then his brother's familiar voice came through loud and clear.

"Yep, it's me, Zac. You know what to do."

At the sound of the tone, Jackson said, "Hey, where the hell are you? I know you didn't go home cause I talked to Mom. Don't worry about the other night. You were drunk and probably don't remember what you said. Come back to the apartment, okay? Talk to you later."

Yeah, like maybe *he* didn't remember the things he'd said or didn't mean them. Problem was, Jackson remembered and they still stung. He didn't know what to think. Was Zac jealous, as the detective had suggested, or was his spiteful revelation true? Jackson sighed. Eventually he'd learn the truth, but for now he had to find his brother and make sure he was safe—whether Detective Anders liked it or not.

Unwilling to return to his apartment without answers, he headed to Ybor City and the house with the balcony. He didn't have a clue what he'd do when he got there, but he'd figure something out.

Fifteen minutes later, Jackson parked the car and approached the house, trying to think of an excuse for knocking, when the front door opened and two men walked out. One of them was Zac.

Chapter 45

Gingerly stretching her arms out as far as she could, Izzie began to feel her way around whatever it was that held her captive. Was it a casket? It didn't feel like one. No, it wasn't oblong and it wasn't lined in soft material designed to convince people their loved one merely slept.

No, this felt more like a crate of some kind. She sat up halfway, surprised to find it was tall enough for even that. It didn't seem like she was buried alive since she didn't gasp for air. She took a deep breath to be sure. Whatever Leon had done, it wasn't with an eye toward killing her or she'd already be dead. So, then, where was she? Had he locked her in a container and stashed her somewhere in the house?

She put her ear against the side to see if she could hear voices. There was nothing.

"Help. Get me out of here," she called, hoping someone would hear. She didn't really expect a response. As far as she knew, Leon and that young girl were the only two in the house and he'd probably sent the girl on her way by now.

She punched her fist against the enclosure. That's when she realized it was lined in some kind of packing material. Of course, that would serve a double purpose: it'd protect her from injury if it was moved and muffle any sound she made. She could scream her head off and no one would hear.

She felt around the space and found a small box containing chips, energy bars, beef jerky and bottles she assumed contained soda or water. No, Leon didn't want her dead. He just wanted her gone. She opened a bottle and swallowed, easing her parched throat while trying to tamp down growing panic. If she was to survive, she'd have to remain calm—somehow.

Chapter 46

Staying well behind the two men to avoid detection, Jackson followed them to a nearby restaurant. That had to be the one Zac told him about. Deep in conversation as they walked along, they didn't notice him tailing them.

At least he'd managed to find his brother and see for himself that he was all right. But for how long would he be able to continue without Leon catching on?

While Jackson's instinct was to approach his brother and urge him to come back with him, he knew Detective Anders was right. Zac was doing this out of the goodness of his heart. He'd never met Izzie; all he knew about her was what Jackson told him and none of it was flattering. He must be doing this to show Jackson he wasn't a total screw-up; that somewhere beneath that good-for-nothing exterior was a heart of gold. That's what Jackson chose to believe as he returned to his car.

He didn't know where to go next. Back to the police station to report what he'd seen? Back to work and try to act as though nothing was wrong? His only option was to keep his eye on the place. He'd check on it at different times and days in between working. If he was discovered, he'd say he was a reporter covering a story. At least that way he'd have some idea what was going on—and that his brother was still among the living.

Having made a plan of sorts, Jackson headed home for the balance of the day. The last thing he wanted was for his boss to find out what he was up to. That would never do. Considering he'd been ordered to forget all about "that snotty little bitch,"—as Morris put it, the man would take a dim view of what Jackson decided to do. But really, what choice did he have?

Something terrible happened to Izzie and now his brother was knee deep in it. From what little he'd read about human trafficking, he knew these guys didn't mess around. Cross them and you're dead, no two ways about it. For all he knew, Leon may have already killed Izzie and fed her to the sharks. Zac may be risking his life for nothing. Somehow, Jackson didn't think so, but he wasn't really sure. In the meantime, he'd already lost a reporter, he wasn't about to lose a brother as well.

Chapter 47

For the next few days, Zac occupied himself doing badly neglected chores around the place. It was clear Leon placed a low priority on such things. On the other hand, he'd been alone in this endeavor and, no doubt, had more important things on his mind than whether or not the toilet was clean.

Zac didn't like doing housework either, but he had to do something to make himself useful and keep Leon from deciding he didn't need him after all. So, he tried to be as agreeable as possible, but it was a stretch. He wasn't used to going out of his way to be nice. For most of his life he'd done the exact opposite—cultivating something of a bad-boy reputation around town.

"When's the next shipment coming in?" He looked up from the sink full of dirty dishes as Leon came in the room.

"Don't know. They call when they're about to come."

"Doesn't that put a crimp in your social life? I mean, having to be on call at a moment's notice like that?"

Leon nodded, "Sure does. With you here, maybe I can actually have a life. Ya' think?"

"Absolutely," Zac said. "You tell me what to do, and I'll take care of it, no problem."

"Whoa, we're not there yet. You have a lot to learn and I have to make damned sure I can trust you, know what I mean?"

"Of course," Zac said. He finished washing the dishes and began putting them away. Leon appeared to be in a good mood for a change, so it might be a good time to ask for some time off. "I'm done here. Think I could take off for a few hours?" He gave Leon his most self-effacing look, the one that said he knew who was in charge.

"Well, things seem to be in good shape. You've been a big help. The place hasn't looked this good in a long time. Go on, but be back around five."

Zac was about to go out the front door when Leon came up behind him, causing him to jump. "I scare you?" He laughed then said, "So, where're you headed?"

"I'm going to take the trolley and wander around downtown a bit. Wanna come?"

"Trolley? You mean the streetcar?"

"Trolley, streetcar, what's the difference?"

"I guess a country bumpkin like you wouldn't know, but if you're gonna stick around Tampa, you probably oughta find out what things here are called."

Surprised at Leon's U-turn from being mellow to snarky, Zac masked his annoyance and struggled to control himself. Under normal circumstances, he would've told the sonofabitch where he could put his *streetcar*, but these were definitely not normal circumstances and backtalk would only make things worse.

"You're right; I'll keep that in mind." He turned the doorknob, anxious to leave before Leon found something else to bitch about. "See you around five."

****

As he waited for the streetcar, Zac glanced around before making the call to make sure he wasn't overheard.

"Detective Anders? It's Zac. I'm fine, well, as fine as you can be living with that scumbag. You're right. They're running illegal immigrants through there. A group came in last night. I'm not sure where they're from, but they're not Mexicans, so I don't know how they get in."

Zac listened as the detective suggested several possible points of entry, including Tampa International Airport and the Port of Tampa.

"Really, I never thought of that. I thought they came across the border or by boat from places like Cuba. How do they do it? They don't look like tourists and if they're illegal, I doubt they have passports."

"Oh, but that's where you're wrong. Trafficked victims are given forged documents that are confiscated when they arrive at their final destination," Detective Anders said. "Most think they'll be going to school or given jobs so they can earn money to send back home." He went on to explain that trafficking was facilitated by corrupt border patrol agents and customs officials who were bribed to look the other way.

"And get this: while thousands of foreigners are trafficked into the U.S. each year—over a hundred thousand Americans are trafficked within our *own* borders. Most are underage girls."

A car horn beeped repeatedly. Someone was apparently on the verge of major road-rage. Zac had trouble hearing Anders. Readjusting his cellphone, he said, "Seriously? American citizens are being forced into slavery? Right here?"

"That's right."

Just then a very attractive blonde walked right in front of him. She was so close he could smell her perfume. It was familiar—the kind his last girlfriend wore. For a second, recalling their final romantic encounter, her face flashed before his mind's eye. He cleared his throat and struggled to pick up a thread of the conversation.

"How can that be?" He paused, then went on. "I mean, if people from poor countries are duped into thinking they're going to hit the jackpot coming here, really what've they got to lose? But you're saying Americans in *our own country* are also likely to get sucked in?"

"That's exactly what I'm saying."

"Could you have it wrong?" He hoped that was the case.

"Nope. I have it on good authority and—get this: the numbers could be higher. We can't exactly survey these folks to get an accurate count, now can we?"

Zac sighed. He had no words to express his disgust. All those people. It was hopeless. "Oh yeah, by the way, I found what looked like a name and some kind of number scratched on the windowsill in the bedroom." He pulled the scrap of paper from his wallet and read it off to Anders. "Maybe you can figure out what it means."

"I'll check it out. Anything else?"

"No, that's it. Hey, I gotta go. The '*streetcar*'" he emphasized the word to prove he was hip to Tampa, "just pulled in."

"Good work. Stay in touch and—Zac, be careful."

"Will do."

Before turning off his phone, Zac listened to Jackson's message then deleted it. No use getting him involved. It'd be better if he thought Zac was still angry. He'd been hard on his brother, but it was the only way to get him out of the picture. He just hoped Jackson didn't get it in his head to go after Leon on his own. That'd be a real disaster.

His hand hovered over the "two" on his speed dial. Call him? Don't call him. He dithered a few moments then decided to let it go. After all, Jackson had a job to keep him occupied and both his boss and the police had told him Izzie was most likely off with some guy having the time of her life. Zac just hoped Jackson's overactive imagination didn't land him in deep shit with those traffickers—in which case, there was no way to save him.

Chapter 48

That night Jackson sat in his car in the alley several doors from Leon's place. He was scrunched down in the seat to avoid detection. It was dark out and he'd worn black, so it was unlikely anyone would notice. Still he didn't want to take a chance.

From his vantage point he had a clear shot past Leon's backyard. With the tall fence, he couldn't see inside, but if people came or left he'd be able to spot them. *And if so, what would he do about it?* That was the flaw in his plan. Should he call the police? If he could see them arrive, that'd be his best shot at catching Leon in the act.

He glanced out the window. Only one light illuminated the alley. Still, if a truck or van pulled up carrying its illegal cargo, he'd see the headlights.

Jackson's back and shoulder hurt like crazy. A photographer was on vacation, so his day had been busier than usual. And sitting in the car in a cramped position didn't help. What he needed right now was a good session with a chiropractor.

It was after ten and he had a hard time staying awake. He sat up just as a car caught him in its headlights.

"Shit," he muttered and slumped down so his head was level with the dashboard. A few seconds later, his car lit up like a Christmas tree and there was a tapping on the window. Red and blue lights strobed across the alley reminding Jackson of a carnival ride. The only things missing were music, screaming fans and, of course—the ride. A beam of light flashed directly into his eyes temporarily blinding him.

"Is there a problem officer?" he said, lowering the window.

"License and registration," a voice behind the flashlight said.

"Why? Is it against the law to sit here?" Jackson wasn't accustomed to challenging law enforcement officers, but it had been a long day and he was not only tired, but grumpy.

"Let me see your license and registration. Now," the voice repeated with determination.

Jackson knew he had to do as he was told or spend the night in jail. It was his choice. He reached across the seat and pulled the documents from the glove compartment. Making a concerted effort to keep the annoyance he felt out of his voice, he said, "Here you go."

The cop turned his flashlight on the driver's license, turned it on him and then went back to the squad car. Jackson drummed his fingers on the dashboard while he waited. Lights in apartments began to switch on as neighbors apparently noticed the police car's lights flashing against their buildings. Exposure was the last thing Jackson needed.

A few minutes later, the man returned. "So, why're you sitting all alone in the dark?"

"No reason. I'm just sitting here. Thinking. There a law against that?"

"You a wise guy?"

"No sir."

"Then answer my question."

"All right. I work for a TV station. We have reason to believe illegal activity is going on inside that house." He pointed at Leon's place "I'm on a stakeout."

"Seriously? Let me see your press badge."

With some trepidation, Jackson produced his credentials. If Morris Stone found out what he was doing, he'd get canned for sure.

"What kind of illegal activity you talking about?"

"Human trafficking."

"Human trafficking? Why not report it to the police and let them take care of it?"

"I already did. They said they suspected as much for some time, but haven't been able to catch them in the act. Without proof, there's nothing they can do."

"And you're trying to catch them in the act, that it?"

"Yes sir."

"Leave it to the police. They'll catch them eventually."

"But by then it'll be too late," Jackson said.

"Too late for what? Is there something you're not telling me?"

Jackson hesitated. A train whistled in the distance, emphasizing his isolation. His dad was dead, Izzie had gone missing and now Zac was in the process of making himself a target.

"My reporter's missing and I have good reason to believe the dirtbag that lives there knows something about it. I tried to get the police involved, but they say she's probably shacked up with her boyfriend somewhere. They won't do anything till I can prove a law's been broken or that she met with foul play." He didn't add that his brother was inside that house and he was worried sick about him. The cop didn't have to know that.

"And you can do neither, I assume?"

"Right"

"And that's why you're sitting alone in a dark alley?"

The policeman removed his hat, scratched his scalp and then replaced it. "Well, you're right. You're not breaking the law sitting here, except maybe loitering. I can't prevent you from doing that, but I urge you to leave it to law enforcement. If your friend is really in danger, as you seem to think, it'll do no good for you to get involved. What I'm saying is, it'd be best if you went on home, but I guess that's up to you.

"On the other hand, if we get complaints about you from concerned citizens, then you'll have to leave. As things stand, no one's called. As far as I'm concerned you can sit here as long as you like. Just be careful. Sitting alone in a dark alley isn't the safest thing you can do."

With that, the officer left Jackson to continue his lonely vigil. After noticing a number of porch lights snap on and shades raised, he realized people had taken notice. Fearing one of them might be Leon, he took the cop's advice and went home.

Chapter 49

Izzie finally got her fear under control and had dozed off when the container she was in lurched, knocking her sideways. It was being moved and not with care either. She could hear a faint mumble of voices as the jostling continued.

"Help, get me out of here," she screamed, pounding till her fists were sore. It was useless. She either couldn't be heard, or whoever was doing the moving, didn't care.

She felt around for the bottle, unscrewed the cap and took a swig. The water was tepid but felt good as it went down. Then, locating some kind of food bar, she unwrapped it. What she assumed was chocolate had melted, making a sticky mess on her hand. Eager to assuage her hunger, Izzie licked her fingers and devoured it. Feeling around in the small box, she located several more. She'd have to ration them, taking only small bites now and then. Same thing with the water. Who knew how long she'd be locked up?

The container lurched again, some water spilled from the open bottle. Izzie quickly felt around for the lid. At this point water was more precious than gold, she couldn't afford to lose a single drop. It was so hot and stuffy, she had a hard time breathing. She urgently prayed that God would rescue her before it was too late.

Izzie thought of Jackson and how concerned he'd been over her welfare. She realized now how rude she'd been, acting like she was better than he was. And why? Because he schlepped all that video equipment in and out of the news van every day? Often sweating like a pig?

In retrospect, she realized he worked a lot harder than she did: balancing a fifty-pound camera on his shoulder, even running with it to capture reluctant subjects. She had just never appreciated how difficult his work was or how seriously he took it—trying to get his best shot and making sure the lighting was just right. *How could she have been so stupid?* Now that she could do nothing but lie there and wait for whatever would come next, her mind played back her interactions with him. None of it was good.

Tears streamed down her face as she recalled how he'd tried to keep her away from Leon. And her response? She'd told him to mind his own business— that she didn't need to be protected by the likes of him. Turned out she was wrong. *God, was she ever wrong.* If only she'd listened. It was too late now, and she may spend the rest of her life regretting it.

Chapter 50

Jackson pulled into the station's parking lot and began to unload his equipment. It was unusually warm for this time of year. He hoped that didn't presage what the summer months would bring. He generally preferred Florida's weather to the frigid winters of the Midwest, but when the thermometer rose above one hundred, he had to admit sometimes he longed for the cool weather back home. For the most part, however, he was content to stay where he was.

His mother, having lived in the Midwest all her life, never understood his disdain for cold weather. And how could she? He'd grown up in the Midwest too. But it was just the way he was, he concluded and didn't try to understand. Some people like it hot, some like it cold; there was no rhyme or reason to it.

He was working at the edit bay finishing his footage, when Morris Stone stopped by.

"Come into my office," he said.

Jackson didn't like the sound of that. Stone was usually more genial in his approach. Not this time. It was an order, not a request. He signed off on the computer and made his way down the hall to his boss's office. Before he managed to throw a genial "What's up?" his way, Morris Stone said, "Close the door."

Jackson's heart thumped a sharp staccato in his ears. Had something happened to Zac? Was his mom in an accident? Had they discovered Izzie's body dumped in one of the canals? He sat down and held his left hand with his right to keep them both from shaking. There was no point asking what this was about; he'd find out soon enough.

"Do you like working here?" Stone asked, his face as hard as his name.

"What? Yes, of course. I love my job." *What was this about? Had someone complained?* Jackson mentally ticked off the stories he'd covered over the past several days: The opening of a new Walmart; that child who'd gone missing and then was discovered a mile away at a friend's house; the author who'd written her first novel; the impact of rising gas prices on motorists; the politician running for re-election. Nope. Nothing he could think of. Far as he knew, it had all run smooth as silk. What about his intern? Maybe he'd inadvertently made a comment she'd taken the wrong way? If he had, he didn't recall doing it.

"What's this about?" he said.

"It's about you misrepresenting yourself to law enforcement, that's what *'it's about'*." When Morris Stone got angry, his neck turned bright red and the flush crawled slowly up until it engulfed his face and ears. There was no mistaking the man's emotional state even on the rare instances he tried to hide it.

Jackson's uncomprehending expression only served to further inflame the situation.

"You don't recall telling a police officer you were a reporter staking out a house where suspicious activity was taking place? That you told him the police hadn't taken your report of a colleague's disappearance seriously and you feared she'd fallen prey to a human trafficker? Any of that sound the *least* bit familiar?"

"Oh, that," was all Jackson could think to say. In checking out his story, the officer must have talked to someone at the station who'd reported it to Stone. *Perfect. Just perfect.*

"I'm sorry, Mr. Stone. I needed a cover story and it was the best I could come up with at the time. It won't happen again."

"You're damned right it won't happen again. If it does, you can look for another job. That clear?" The pitch of his voice rose.

Jackson nodded. "Absolutely. I, for sure, won't ever do it again." He felt like a kid being reprimanded.

"I'm assuming this has to do with Izzie?"

"Yes, sir, it does."

"And what'd I tell you about that?"

"That I was to forget her; that she was a stuck-up bitch who probably ran off with her boyfriend."

"And, did you?"

"Did I what?"

"Forget about her?"

Jackson's face fell. "No sir. I didn't. I have it on good authority that she was hanging out with the guy I suspect is a trafficker. My brother had lunch with him and he admitted he'd been seeing her." Jackson couldn't bring himself to tell Stone the whole story.

"So, some guy had the hots for her. That doesn't mean he's a trafficker or that he did anything to harm her. Jackson, you've got to let this go. If you want to keep your job, you'll do as I say. Take this as a fair warning. I'm not telling you again. *Got it?*"

"Yes," Jackson said. "I understand." He stood and left the office, heading for the parking lot on legs as wobbly as Jell-O.

Now it wasn't only Izzie and his brother's lives on the line—but his job as well. As far as Jackson was concerned, if he lost this job—a career he'd trained so hard for; a job he loved and dreamed of having ever since he found out there was such a thing as a TV news cameraman—if he was fired, it'd be akin to losing his life. Without this job, he'd be lost.

Jackson had to figure out which was more important: his dream job or the lives of two people—neither of whom had been especially nice to him

He unlocked his car and sat for a moment, mulling over the situation. He really didn't have a choice. He knew what he had to do. There were no options; none at all. This decision was going to affect his future—and not in a good way.

He shrugged and started the engine. If he complied with Morris Stone's demand and something bad happened to them, would he be able to live with himself?

He slapped his hand on the steering wheel as the realization struck him with the force of a lightning bolt. *Morris Stone be damned.* There was no decision to be made. Jackson knew what he had to do and he would do it. That's all there was to it.

Chapter 51

Zac stood on the pier watching a cruise ship disgorge its passengers. He wondered how many of those well-dressed people arrived under the guise of tourism and were facing a life of unimaginable horror.

Standing there, gazing at the multistoried ocean liner gleaming in the sun, Zac felt like an ant beside a Hummer.

He wandered to the other end of the wharf where cargo was being unloaded: steamer trunks, shipping containers, luggage. There were even animals in special crates. As he watched, the thought occurred to him that this would be an easy way to smuggle someone out of the country.

Is that what Leon had done with Izzie? Surely not. Leon said they imported illegals to help them get a better life. Yeah, sure, if you mean a life of unpaid labor tied to a sewing machine or picking vegetables twelve hours a day. He'd said they weren't in the business of exporting Americans, that it was too dangerous.

Then what had he done with her? *Murdered her?* Zac didn't think so. The man was way too emotionally involved to have done something like that. He would have figured out another way to dispose of her.

For all his bad points, Leon still had a vestige of humanity about him. Zac simply did not believe he'd kill the one person he cared for. Get rid of her to protect himself, yes. Slaughter her? Not a chance. So where the hell was she and how was he going to find her? Good questions, but no answers—at least not yet. He'd find them, or die trying.

As he watched, he began to wonder where those ships went. Perhaps that's where he should begin. As he headed to a nearby travel agent's office, he felt oddly exhilarated. It wasn't so much that he knew what he was doing or had a solid lead; it was that for the first time he was taking a positive step in that direction. And at this point, that's all that mattered.

The woman at the desk was professional looking in a phony, yet attractive way. From his shabby clothes, she had to know he didn't have the money for a trip of any kind. It'd be a waste of time, or as Jackson might say, a goat rope. Still, she treated Zac as though she might actually make a commission off him.

"Good afternoon, sir. How might I be of assistance?" Her smile revealed white—almost too white—teeth, and dimples in both cheeks. Her dark hair was perfectly coifed into a mid-length page. She wore a single strand of pearls with matching dangle earrings. There was a hint of cleavage in the off-white top she wore under a navy blazer. Zac couldn't help but wonder if she was as perky in bed as she was at the moment, or if it was all an act.

He returned her greeting and said, "I wondered where those cruise ships go." He realized he sounded more than a little bit like a hick, but in truth that's what he was.

"Ports of call you mean? It depends on the package and the cruise. Is there anything in particular you're looking for?"

"Not really. Watching the passengers get off the ship got me to wondering. Can you tell me?"

"As I said, it depends on the cruise line and the particular package." As she handed several brochures over the counter, Zac noticed her glossy red nail polish. "These should help. Look them over and let me know if anything interests you."

"Oh, I see something that interests me all right," Zac said, catching her eye and giving her the smile that easily snagged girls back home. It didn't work on this one.

"It was nice talking to you," she said, her perfectly phony smile in place. "You come on back if there's anything more I can do to help plan your trip." Then she picked up the phone and began to dial.

Zac took the hint and left her to make money off real customers.

Chapter 52

"There you are," Leon said making a point of looking at his watch. It was nearly five-thirty. "I thought we agreed you'd be back by five."

"We did. I just didn't count on the trolley, uh, streetcar getting stalled on the tracks for half an hour. Sorry about that."

"Yeah, well, when I say be back by a certain time, I expect to see your butt here, stalled *'trolley'* or not. If you're going to work for me, I gotta know I can depend on you. Otherwise, you might as well get the hell outta here right now."

Zac knew he was late, but didn't think it was all *that* important; in fact he didn't expect Leon to notice. "Hey man, chill. I'm still finding my way around. It's hard when you have to depend on public transportation, know what I mean? It's not as reliable as a car." He thought his broad hint might prod Leon into lending him his car, but no dice.

"Yeah, well, from now on you'll have to take that into consideration, won't you? And don't go telling me to 'chill' either."

Zac could see he wasn't making any headway with his boss and decided to change the subject. "I went to the Port of Tampa and watched a cruise ship unload its passengers. Man, those things are humongous, aren't they?"

"Sure are."

"Ever been on one?"

"What? A cruise?"

"Yeah. You ever go? I mean you're right here where they take off." He pulled out the brochures the travel agent gave him. "Look here, you could go to The Caymans, Costa Rica, Belize—any or all of them. And it doesn't seem like it's all that expensive either, especially since you don't have to pay airfare."

"Yeah, all I need is money—and the time to get away from here."

"Well, I doubt money's a problem for you what with all the business you do and…" Zac was going to add that with him on board now, Leon could easily take off for a few days whenever he liked, but he was interrupted.

"What the hell do you know about my business?" The man had gone from making small talk to being livid in less time that it takes to sneeze.

"Only what you've told me. I just thought…"

"You're not here to think. You're here to do what you're told—unless you think you're too smart for this gig, in which case you can go running back to your brother. Oh, that's right, he kicked you out; you've no place to go. So, maybe you just better keep your trap shut. How's that sound?" Leon was nearly nose to nose with Zac now, his voice getting louder and angrier by the second.

Zac took a step back in a bid to regain his personal space. "Sounds all right by me," he said, and put the brochures in his pocket.

Before leaving the room, Leon said, "A shipment's coming in tonight around ten. Be here."

Chapter 53

Wary after being "outed" by that damned policeman, Jackson decided to do his surveillance on foot. He parked the car close to the tourist area of Ybor City and made his way back to Leon's house, taking a circuitous route to avoid being spotted. He realized he was getting paranoid, but didn't want to take any chances.

It was around nine-thirty and a moonless night made it difficult to see. Jackson squeezed behind an overflowing Dumpster and waited—for what, he wasn't sure. After only ten minutes, he was ready to go home to the comfort of his apartment. The stink of rotting garbage and lingering heat from the sun beating on the concrete all day sank into his pores, making him dizzy and nauseous. The occasional scurrying feet of some four-legged critter only made things worse.

Besides that, mosquitoes were making him their late-night snack. With little success, he waved his hand frantically in front of his face to ward them off. They seemed to return as quickly as they departed.

He was about to call it a night, when a van pulled up and stopped directly behind Leon's backyard. It was the break Jackson had been hoping for. All he had to do now was make sure that van contained the human cargo he suspected it held and then call police, hoping they arrived while the victims were still inside. It shouldn't be that hard.

As he stood up, a startled cat fled, knocking over a pile of beer cans. He quickly stooped behind the Dumpster, lowering his head in an effort to somehow make himself smaller. After a few seconds, hearing nothing, he got on his feet. That's when he felt cold metal press against the back of his neck and heard a voice shout, "Leon, get over here. We got company."

Chapter 54

Waiting for the latest shipment of illegals to come through the back door, Zac sat at the kitchen table perusing his travel brochures. Not only did he suspect Leon may be using cruise ships as a means of "importing" his so-called product, but he wondered if the man used it as a means of the occasional "export" as well. He had no proof, of course, any more than the police did. It was only a gut feeling.

As he looked at the colorful pamphlets, he couldn't help but think how great it would be to go on one of those trips. The flier he held in his hand was for five days starting in Tampa, with stops in the Grand Caymans, Mahogany Bay and Belize—wherever the hell they were. By the looks of the photographs, they were tropical places. How cool would that be?

He was so focused on pictures of the gleaming cruise ship with its festive passengers, placid ocean scenes and endless beaches, complete with scantily-clad beauties, that he didn't hear Leon approach.

"Hey, Zac," he called out, "Look what we found."

Zac glanced up and saw the last thing he expected: Jackson being hauled through the door, a gun at his back. Struggling to keep from acknowledging their relationship, Zac avoided eye contact with his brother.

"Oh yeah? He come in the van with the others?"

"No, stupid. He look like one a them women who don't speak English?"

Zac shrugged and scrutinized Jackson. His brother, shorter than Zac anyway, seemed to have shrunk by several inches.

"Guess not. Where'd he come from?"

"He was hiding in the alley watchin' us unload the van."

"Really? He with the police?"

"Don't know. Didn't have ID. Says not, but why else'd he be out there this time a night?"

Zac shrugged. "What'd he say?"

"Said his old lady kicked him out 'n he wuz searching through the Dumpster for food."

"Maybe it's the truth."

"Yeah, right. Look at him. Way he's dressed? He look like someone who'd have to rummage through garbage to find food? Even if he's telling the truth, wouldn't he just spend the night at a hotel or with a friend?" He thumped Jackson hard on the back.

"You. Sit." Turning to Zac and nodding toward the new arrivals, he said, "Take them upstairs while I sign Sam's papers and figure out what to do with him."

Zac took a hard look at his younger brother. *Why the hell hadn't he stayed away?* As usual he'd stuck his nose in where it didn't belong. But this time he might pay for it with his life.

Chapter 55

The whole time he was upstairs watching the latest "shipment", Zac brooded over what he could possibly do to rescue his brother. No matter which way he looked at it, the endpoint was the same: they'd be found out—and would pay a heavy price for their deception.

Leon was not a forgiving man. He'd consider Zac a traitor. After all, he'd provided a place for Zac to stay when he had nowhere else to turn. If he discovered Zac was a snitch, well, as they say in those old Westerns, his life wouldn't be worth a plugged nickel.

One of the girls nudged him and pointed to the bathroom. He nodded. Why they felt his permission was necessary, he didn't know. A pattern had been established when they entered the room and, one by one, the women sought his approval to go to the toilet. It made him feel like a school teacher. At least he didn't ask if it was for "number one" or "number two."

Leon came up with a tray of rations: some kind of sandwiches, soup, chips and cans of pop. The women were so hungry, they seemed grateful, as though it was a feast—which maybe to them it was. Who knows when they'd eaten last? Zac wondered what would happen when they reached their final destination and realized they'd been duped; there'd be no fancy education or high-paying job—only a slave's life of endless work or sexual exploitation.

One pretty young girl looked particularly hopeful. She smiled at him as she dug into a baloney sandwich and sipped her drink. At the thought of what she faced, a surge of anger tore through Zac. Unable to make eye contact, he swallowed hard and looked away.

Before Jackson's unexpected appearance, Zac had begun to think about dumping this gig. By now Izzie was probably dead or in some Middle-Eastern harem. The police hadn't been able to catch Leon and his cronies in the act. And from what Detective Anders said, human trafficking in the U.S. was so pervasive, catching a few victims or traffickers here or there wouldn't make a dent in the problem. *Why bother?*

That's the frame of mind he'd been in to the point he'd seriously begun to think about taking one of those cruises and then heading back to Iowa. Now with Jackson's arrival, all that changed. What a freaking mess.

Chapter 56

It was after eleven and the "guests" were thankfully gone. When Zac had escorted them downstairs, he expected to see Jackson at the kitchen table under Leon's watchful eye, but the room was empty. *Where was he?*

While Leon was outside finishing up with the distributor, Zac took a quick tour of the first floor, thinking his brother had been stashed in one of the rooms, but there was no trace of him. Sweat erupted on his temples and under his armpits. The temperature in the room seemed to spike. He could scarcely breathe. Did Leon murder Jackson? *Oh God, no, not that.*

He loved his younger brother. Yes, they'd had their differences. If he was honest, Zac had to admit his younger brother's success gnawed at him.

Five years older than Jackson, Zac had always been something of a screw-up, taking the easy way out, never thinking beyond the next drink or hookup. Their parents had tried to "motivate" him by comparing his younger brother's accomplishments to his failures.

To say it didn't work, would be an understatement. It didn't make him want to succeed, or go back to school and get some training. It just made him angry—at his parents, at his brother and at the world. And now? Dad was dead. Mom alone. And his only brother? *What had Leon done with him?*

The back door slammed shut signaling Leon's return. How could he bring up the topic of Jackson? He'd have to be careful.

"So, they're on their way?"

"Yep. Another day, another dollar, so to speak." Leon swept his hands together, a relieved expression on his face. "I'm always glad when we move them out without nosy neighbors causing problems." He stooped down and retrieved Tiny's food bowl. "Feel free to feed him when I'm busy," he said. "I don't gotta do everything around here, ya' know."

"All right. Sorry about that." Zac stretched and yawned. "It's been a long day." He looked around as if checking for something. "Say, where's that guy?"

"What guy?"

"You know, the one you found in the alley. You let him go?"

"Don't worry. I took care of him."

"What do you mean? What'd you do?" Zac knew he shouldn't quiz Leon. The man had a sixth sense and would quickly figure something was up.

"Nothing. What's it to you anyway?"

"I just wondered, that's all. He saw me too, you know and can cause me as much grief as you. If I'm going to be part of this operation, I need to be able to cover my ass."

Leon hesitated, as if trying to decide whether to let Zac in on a secret. Then, he shrugged. "Follow me."

They went into a back room, a kind of office which held a desk and several chairs. A built-in bookcase took up part of the wall.

Zac was puzzled. They'd been talking about what Leon did with Jackson and now the guy was showing off his home office? *What the hell?* He was about to ask Leon about Jackson again, when the man moved the desk, pressed something on the side of the bookcase and pulled. It rotated, revealing a hidden staircase. Zac was astonished. He'd only ever seen such things in movies.

Leon snapped on a wall switch and gestured for him to follow. As they went down the steps, the space opened up into a room. On the bottom step, Zac blinked to accustom his eyes to the dim light. After a few seconds, he could make out several objects. Then what he saw caused his stomach to drop.

Lying on a cot was Jackson. His eyes were closed, his mouth agape. Bruises on his face appeared swollen and bluish-black. Cold fingers of dread coursed through Zac. He took several deep breaths. He couldn't let Leon see how upset he was.

"He dead?" Zac managed to keep fear from overtaking his voice.

"Naw. I drugged him. He'll be out a long time— or at least till we take care of him."

Zac stood over the bed, looking down at his brother. He hadn't a clue what Leon had in mind. Before he had a chance to speak, Leon pointed to a steamer trunk stashed in the corner.

"We'll stuff him in that and send him on his way."

He's going to dump Jackson in the Gulf? Zac's heart drummed in his ears. How could he prevent Leon from killing him? He glanced around the room for something to smash over the man's head. That's when he remembered Izzie. With Leon dead how would they find her? He knew in his gut Jackson would never forgive him if he did something like that.

"How's that?" He managed to say casually, as if asking about dinner plans.

"What?" Leon turned toward Zac, drilling him with his dark eyes.

"I just wondered what the plan was." Zac had to work hard to keep his voice on an even keel. *Tell yourself you're talking about Leon's favorite ball team— the Rays?*

"Oh yeah, you haven't done this before. I keep forgetting you've only been here a few days." Leon slapped Zac on the back. "See how fast I got used to depending on you?"

Surprised at the compliment, Zac forced a grin and wondered how to cash in on it. If Leon had begun to have confidence in him, maybe he'd let *him* "dispose" of his brother.

"That's what I'm here for." He said, drawing on the acting experience he'd learned in high school theater. "So, what d'ya want me to do with him?"

Leon looked from Zac to Jackson and back. "He'll be out a long time. Let's go upstairs and we'll talk about it."

Tiny was asleep in the corner, enjoying the feel of cool cement against his body.

"C'mon boy," Leon nudged the dog with his foot. "Let's go."

Chapter 57

Back upstairs, Leon rotated the bookcase making sure it was securely locked. "Get me a beer."

They sat around the kitchen table drinking the last of the Coronas, Leon's favorite. Zac made a mental note to buy a case the next time he was out. Leon flipped through the brochures Zac left on the table.

"Hey, you wanna go on a cruise?"

He said it as though it occurred to him out of the blue. It was the last thing Zac expected. He thought he'd be ordered to dump Jackson's body in a sugarcane field or a canal somewhere for alligators to find.

"A cruise?" Zac didn't bother keeping the astonishment from his voice.

Leon threw his head back and laughed. "Don't be so shocked. You were talking about it earlier." He spread the brochures out in a fan and waved them in the air. "So, wanna take a cruise or not?"

"Hell, yes," Zac said. This time his enthusiasm was genuine, even if he was still puzzled. Why would Leon be so generous all of a sudden? Only a few hours ago he'd said he had neither the time nor the money for a cruise. "When do we leave?"

"*We're* not going—*you are.*"

Zac was even more confused. What was Leon getting at? "I am?"

"Yes. You are. And you're taking our buddy downstairs with you."

All of a sudden the murky picture came into focus. Leon wanted Zac to spirit Jackson out of the country in a steamer trunk. For a moment he was at a loss for words. What do you say when your boss demands you do something that may very well mean the death of your only brother—and when refusing's not an option?

"I am?" he repeated.

"Yes, you're going to take care of this for me, and here's how."

"Sounds like maybe you've done this before." Zac tried to make it sound like an observation rather than an accusation.

"You could say that." Leon didn't gloat—exactly, but to Zac he seemed proud. *Right.* Delivering people into slavery was an accomplishment all right, but to his way of thinking it wasn't worth bragging about.

"Well, it's not a cruise exactly, but close enough."

"What do you mean?" If it wasn't to be a cruise ship, what did Leon have in mind?

"It's a yacht. Ever been on one a those?"

"A yacht?" Photographs of beautiful people lounging on a gorgeous craft danced before Zac's eyes. "Where're you gonna get something like that?"

A smug expression crossed Leon's face. "I got connections. In this business you got to have 'em or you're dead meat." He spoke as though tutoring a particularly slow child. "First we need to get you—and our friend downstairs—passports. Don't worry about it. I have a guy who takes care of that stuff. Already called him. I took a picture of the guy, so we just need one of you—unless you have a passport. Do you?" He looked hopefully at Zac.

"No. Never needed one of those," Zac said.

"I didn't think so. They'll be ready tomorrow. I also called about the yacht. You leave tomorrow—with the trunk, of course."

"What about customs? Won't it be searched?"

"Naw, they don't usually bother us. They'll think you're just another tourist going deep-sea fishing or riding in a fancy boat."

"But won't he suffocate, I mean being in a trunk like that?" Zac was frantic. How could he possibly rescue Jackson?

Leon snorted. "Dude, I've done this a time or two and haven't lost one yet. If they die, I don't get paid; so ya' think maybe I'm motivated to do it right?"

Zac scratched his chin. "Is that what happened to that Izzie girl? You ship her off some place?" He realized the question was out of line, but he had to at least try.

Leon's face took on a sad mixture of sorrow and rage, then he glared at Zac. "You ever bring up her name again you'll wish you hadn't."

He'd hit a nerve. That must be precisely what Leon did. Izzie'd been carted off in a steamer trunk. Now he had to find out where.

After a few minutes during which Leon got himself under control, he said, "So, your passport'll be ready and the yacht's booked. All you gotta do is get on and keep your eye on the trunk. Here's the key. Give it to the buyer when you get there."

Zac noticed how Leon always used business lingo when referring to his illegal activities. Maybe it was his way of justifying what he did—making it appear to be legitimate.

"When the ship arrives in Belize—"

"Belize? We're going to Belize?"

"Yeah, didn't I tell you that?" Leon seemed amused.

"No, you didn't. How far is it?"

"Around 800 miles. It should take a little over two days, assuming there's no problem with the weather."

"So, the guy—you know, the guy downstairs—he'll be in the trunk the whole time?"

"Yep."

"How? I mean, he's gotta have food, water, be able to use the bathroom. Besides, being all curled up in a trunk for two days, I wouldn't do that to a dog."

"Good thing you're not in charge, then, ain't it?"

The expression on Leon's face said don't mess with me. Zac knew that look only too well.

"If you're not up to the job, I'll take care of it."

The way Leon said it reminded Zac of a parent trying to get their kid to take out the trash. He couldn't risk letting Leon *take care* of Jackson. "I'll do it," he said. "Does the guy who owns the boat know what we're doing?"

"Not in so many words, I mean I think he's figured out we're not exactly Boy Scouts, but he doesn't ask questions long as he gets his money."

He took a final swig of beer and tossed the empty bottle in the garbage. "Once you get to Belize, the buyer'll be waiting for you at the dock. You deliver the trunk and the key; he pays for the merchandise and your job's done. That's all there is to it."

"Do I pay for the boat too?"

"Naw, I take care of that upfront. Anything else?"

"Be okay if I stay a few days? I've never been to Belize. I'd like to look around if it's all right with you. I could fly back." It was the only way Zac could begin to extract Izzie and Jackson from the mess they'd gotten into.

"No problem, but don't stay too long. I want my money, ya know and I need your help around here—now that I've gotten used to it. And, Zac…don't even think of running off. As you probably figured out, I have a big network of contacts. One word from me, and *you'll* get a trunk of your own." Leon's expression said he meant every word he said.

"Hey, you don't need to worry about that." Zac put on his "you can trust me" face and hoped the man bought it.

Leon stared at him, then leaned back in the chair with a satisfied look. "So, think you can get the job done without screwing up?"

"Absolutely," Zac said, trying to sound more confident than he felt. He had to succeed—with his own mission, not Leon's. The consequences of failure were simply too horrible to contemplate.

Chapter 58

"What'd you say?" Morris Stone's face took on the shade of crimson it always did when his blood began to boil.

"I said Jackson didn't show up for work this morning."

Stone looked at the wall clock. It was a little after nine-thirty. "And you're just telling me now? Wasn't he due in an hour ago?"

"Yes. I thought maybe he got caught in traffic or overslept. When it got to be nine, I called. He's not answering his cell. I left several messages, but he hasn't called back. Want me to send someone to his apartment and make sure there's nothing wrong?"

Stone sat back, absently swiveling the chair first one way then the other. He drummed his fingers on the desktop. "Yeah, do that. And he'd better be in a coma if he knows what's good for him."

As he waved his assignment editor out of the room, he thought about the warning he'd given Jackson after hearing about his escapade with the police: Staking out some guy's apartment, then telling a cop some cockamamie story about being a reporter trying to uncover a human trafficking operation. He'd told Jackson if he didn't stop it'd cost him his job.

He realized it was about that reporter. Why the guy couldn't forget about Izzie was more than he could fathom. As far as he knew, they'd only been co-workers, partnered up to cover stories. He didn't think they weren't dating, so why Jackson felt obligated to keep badgering the police and then stick his neck out like that was beyond him.

Well, he'd better be home and so sick he couldn't manage to call in or even answer his phone—or else. Morris Stone knew he'd have to fire the guy. It wouldn't do to let the rest of the crew think they could skip work, not call in and still expect to have jobs. Even if Jackson *was* one of his best cameramen—talented, conscientious to a fault and, until the whole Izzie mess started, the most reliable.

He sighed. Some days his job sucked. The phone rang. Maybe that was Jackson now. Maybe he'd had car trouble or was in some kind of a fender-bender. Honestly hoping that was the case, he picked up the receiver and said, "Stone."

Chapter 59

After what seemed more like years than days, Izzie awoke to what sounded like the rattle of keys. A few seconds later, the top of the container was yanked back. The sudden light blinded her. After such a long time in the tight space with little food and water, she could scarcely move. Every muscle in her body screamed for relief.

As her eyes began to adjust, she made out several men peering down at her. They spoke a language she didn't understand. They held their noses at the obvious stench days without bathing or toilet facilities had produced. One bent down and touched her hair. Then he smiled and nodded.

A man grabbed her around the shoulders and pulled her to her feet. Terrified and weak, Izzie collapsed into his outstretched arms. He laughed, pinched his nose and pushed her away. Where was she and what did they want with her?

One of the men tapped her on the shoulder and pointed to a bathroom. He didn't have to tell her again. She was only too happy to oblige. Maybe this wouldn't be so bad after all. Then she saw the gun.

Chapter 60

Leon and Captain Tom finished up as Zac stood beside the steamer trunk hoping against hope that his brother was all right. Motioning for Zac to join them, Leon said, "This here's my buddy, Zac."

The yacht owner turned. "How're ya doin'?"

Without giving Zac a chance to respond, Leon continued, "When you get to Belize, just leave the trunk on the dock. Zac'll take care of it, then you can be on your way."

"He's not coming back with us?"

"Naw. He's never been to Belize so he wants to check it out. He'll come back when he's sick of all the tourist crap." Both men laughed and shook their heads.

"I hear ya'," the captain said. "There're only so many T-shirts you can buy," He glanced at the horizon. "We better get going. I think a storm's brewing. Hope we can outrun it. I hate like hell being out there during a hurricane."

Zac's ears perked up at the words "storm" and "hurricane". "You expecting one?" That put a whole new slant on things. He'd agreed to the yacht trip, but being on a boat during a storm was something else again.

Captain Tom threw his head back and laughed. He was exactly what you'd expect in a ship's captain: ruddy complexion; dark commanding eyes; a beard compensating for thinning hair up top; and a boisterous manner that seemed quick to find everything hilarious.

"Relax, Zac," he said, and thumped him on the back. "You'll be safe with us." He motioned to his yacht and a man who stood beside it. "This here's my first mate, Charlie. Between the two of us, you're in good hands. I take it you've never been sailing?"

Zac nodded. The whole idea which had intrigued him a few hours earlier quickly lost its appeal. "You're right about that."

"We'll make a sailor out of you by the time we hit Belize, you wait and see." He glanced around, then motioned to his first mate. "Get that trunk on board and we'll be on our way."

Watching Charlie struggle to lift the chest and Captain Tom making no effort to help, Zac picked up the other end. Groaning and bumping their way up the ramp, they managed to get it on the boat. Zac shuddered as he thought about his brother inside. He hoped for his sake the drug was still working.

"Charlie, show this landlubber around and give him a quick lesson on what things're called so I don't hafta toss him overboard." He threw his head back, whooping as though what he'd said was side-splittingly funny.

Zac glanced at Charlie to see if he'd joined in. The man wore a pained expression. He'd only known Captain Tom a few minutes and the man was already getting on his nerves. Imagine having to endure unexpected bursts of laughter all day long. The word "mutiny" came to mind.

Charlie looked from Zac to the trunk. "Want this stashed in your stateroom?"

"My what?"

"It's where you sleep. You want it down there or should I leave it topside?" Before Zac could respond, he said, "Probably best to stow it where you can keep an eye on it, especially if a storm blows. Don't want it to end up in the Gulf."

The thought of his younger brother washed out to sea locked inside a steamer trunk gave Zac the willies. "No, that wouldn't do at all."

"Okay, then let's get her below."

A few moments later Charlie gestured at the space before them. "This here's the "saloon" where we relax. He indicated an L-shaped settee, flat-screen TV and several comfortable looking easy chairs.

Everything appeared to be bolted in place. Zac didn't have to be told why. Anything loose in a storm could become a missile capable of injuring someone.

They took a few steps farther inside. "Here's the kitchen or what's referred to as the 'galley'." A tidy space with cabinets and built-in appliances presented itself. Zac was amazed at how every square inch had been used. There was a stainless steel sink, a refrigerator, range and microwave oven—even a trash compactor. Spotless countertops gleamed.

"Nice," Zac said and thought about his mom's kitchen back home which wasn't nearly as modern.

"Yeah, it is, except when you're on KP."

"That your job?"

"Of course. Captain Tom..." he hesitated as if complaining about his boss might not be wise. Then he added, "Yeah, I'm the chief cook and bottle washer on this vessel." He turned and gestured toward the rear.

"The captain's stateroom's back there and yours is below. Might as well take the trunk with us."

Zac didn't know what he'd expected, but it was nowhere near what he saw. There was a queen-sized platform bed with drawer storage below; lamps for reading and wall lights; cedar-lined lockers adorned one wall; plush carpeting completed the space.

Charlie pointed to a small side room. "That's the bathroom—called the 'head'."

Zac took a quick look and was again surprised at how clean it looked. It didn't even stink.

"This where you sleep?" Sharing the room with the first mate would be a problem.

"Only when there're no paying guests. On trips like this, I sleep on a bunk in the pilothouse." He glanced at Zac, "That's where the boat's…"

"I know," Zac interrupted. "I'm not a total idiot."

Charlie gave him a pained smile. "Never took you for one." As they retraced their steps, he added, "Now, you probably already know this, but…" The engine revved and the boat began to move. "…when you face front, the right side's 'starboard' and the left is 'port'. The front of the boat is the 'bow' and the rear is the 'stern'. I don't mean to insult you, but if you call things by the right names, the captain'll treat you a whole lot better."

Charlie wasn't quite finished. "Upstairs is 'topside' and the rear—where we got on—is the 'transom'." Charlie hesitated, "Oh, and the Bessie Rose is a trawler yacht."

Zac followed Charlie as he retraced his steps, tossing his words over his shoulder. "It resembles a commercial fishing vessel designed to drag nets called 'trawls' behind." As he reached the steps, he said, "Okay, enough of that. Go topside and relax while I fix lunch."

As he went on deck, Zac's head buzzed with the new information: bow, stern, starboard, port, head, galley, stateroom, and, what was the living area called again? Oh yeah, "saloon"—as in a bar. Odd name for a living room, but he guessed that's where they drank. Then there was: topside, transom, pilothouse and that trawler business.

He sat back in a comfortable deck chair and looked out over the water that stretched blue and calm as far as he could see. Seagulls trailed behind, hoping for a handout. A close look at the surface revealed a pod of some kind of large fish. Cool. He stood and leaned over the edge to get a closer look. "Well I'll be a son of a bitch," he said aloud. "They're dolphins." He watched until they disappeared from view, then sat back down.

The sun and rocking motion made him sleepy. Remembering all those odd names shouldn't be that hard, figuring out how to keep Jackson safe and hidden was what mattered. He'd close his eyes just for a moment.

"Hey, Zac." Charlie shook him. "Lunch's ready. Have a good nap?"

Zac blinked then remembered where he was. "Uh, yeah, real good."

"Join the captain."

"Aren't you eating with us?"

"Somebody's gotta be at the helm. Oh, yeah, new word—the 'helm's' the steering gear of a boat. Now go eat while it's still hot."

Zac didn't look forward to sitting across the table from that buffoon, but he had no choice. If the man exploded in laughter one more time, he'd punch him and throw him overboard. Charlie would, no doubt, give him a medal.

"Hey, Captain Tom. How're you doing?"

The captain nodded, his cheeks bulged as he chewed. "Grab a plate and dig in," he said from the side of his mouth. "We don't stand on ceremony around here." He took a swig from what looked to be a mug of beer. "Food's good and there's plenty of it, so don't be shy."

Zac didn't have to be told a second time. His stomach growled as the smell of barbecued beef wafted through the air.

"Charlie teach you a thing or two?"

Zac nodded and swallowed. "He sure knows his stuff, doesn't he?"

"Wouldn't be my first mate if he didn't."

To Zac, the captain's response sounded a tad sharp, as though the compliment he'd paid Charlie annoyed him.

"Now you know the difference between a bulkhead and the ship's hull?"

Bulkhead? Hull? Zac didn't recall hearing those terms. Taking a big bite of bun dripping with sauce so he wouldn't have to respond, he nodded as he reviewed what he'd been taught. Those two words weren't in his lexicon.

"Then tell me, what's a bulkhead?"

The man was nothing if not persistent. Zac cleared his throat, picked up the mug of beer and took a mouthful. The delay didn't help. He still didn't know a bulkhead from a bulwark. The meaning of both escaped him.

"It's another name for the bathroom?" The inflection in his voice gave away his lack of conviction.

The captain leaned back and howled. "No, idiot, that's called a head. Bulkheads are walls separating rooms. They prevent water or fire from spreading. Guess Charlie forgot to tell you that."

"Guess so," Zac's temper was beginning to rise. The man was an asshole.

"And where's a boat's hull?"

By now Zac had had enough. Setting the mug down, he leaned in and said, "Captain, I don't give a rat's ass what or where the boat's hull is. Topside, backside, upside—sideways—who gives a good shit as long as this damned thing floats. I'm a paying guest. If you want more business from Leon, start treating me with respect." Then he stopped speaking and waited for the explosion that was sure to follow.

The captain wiped his mouth on a paper napkin and stood.

Zac braced himself anticipating the taste of blood as he got socked in the jaw.

Clearing his throat, Captain Tom said, "Didn't mean nothing, I was just funnin' with you. Finish your lunch then go downstairs and take a nap. Forget all this, ain't important nohow." He started up the steps then turned and said, "In case anybody asks, the hull's the outer skin of a boat."

With the saloon to himself, Zac enjoyed what was left of his meal, proud that he'd stood up to the man. Maybe the rest of the trip wouldn't be so bad. First he'd go to his stateroom and check on Jackson, then take a nap.

Chapter 61

Making sure the door was firmly closed, Zac took the key to the trunk from his pocket. For a fleeting second he feared it wouldn't work, that Leon had given him the wrong one.

His hand trembled, making it difficult to insert the small piece of metal into the lock. He jiggled it first one way and then the other. Swearing under his breath, he took it back out, wiped it off on his shirt and tried again. This time the heavy lock popped open with a metallic ping.

Looking up to make certain he was alone, Zac lifted the lid and pushed it back. There, lying on his side, was Jackson, still as unconscious as when they'd placed him in the receptacle hours earlier. To Zac he looked peaceful, if a bit cramped. The small box containing water and breakfast bars had not been disturbed. Reassured that his brother was safe, Zac replaced the lid.

He was tempted to leave it unlocked. After all, this was his room for the duration, what could be the harm? A vision of Jackson waking up and going "topside" flashed before him.

Better lock it. He'd check back every few hours to make sure his brother was all right. Till then, with nothing better to do, he sprawled out on the bed for a nap. The combination of sea air and good food serving as a sedative, he was soon fast asleep.

****

A few hours later, Zac was awakened by what sounded like the approach of angry voices and heavy steps. Before he could get to his feet, the door flew back and a white-uniformed officer walked in, followed by a flustered Captain Tom.

"I told you he's a tourist on his way to Belize."

"That may very well be, but all the same his room's on your boat and we're authorized to search it."

"You sons a bitches harass me all the time and never find a damned thing." The captain's face was beet red.

Zac watched the scene in growing trepidation. What would happen if he opened that trunk?

"Sir, stand aside," the officer said. The determination in his voice said he meant business.

Zac started to follow the captain out the stateroom door, when the naval officer stopped him.

"What's in the trunk?"

Zac swallowed hard and thought fast. "Just a bunch of clothes and old books. I'm taking them to Belize for a friend."

"Don't want to make a liar out of you, but open it and we'll both be satisfied." He stood aside.

Zac considered saying he'd lost the key, but the man didn't appear to be a fool and would only be more determined to get a look. Taking his time, Zac removed the key from his pocket and began to jiggle it back and forth, hoping against hope it wouldn't open.

"What's taking you so long?"

"It's an old lock and hard to open." Zac said and jiggled it a few more times. Just when he thought the man would give up and be on his way, the lock snapped open.

"Good. Now let's have a look."

Zac began to lift the lid as slowly as he dared. A vision of being hauled off in handcuffs danced before him. That's when he realized getting caught might be a good thing. They'd be finished with Leon and the whole freaking mess—except for Izzie, of course.

As the officer stepped over to peer inside, the boat lurched, knocking them both off their feet and slamming the lid shut.

"What the hell was that?"

Zac scrambled to his feet and gave the older man a hand. "I don't know," he said, and surreptitiously gave the trunk lock a push with his knee. "Oops, I think it locked when I fell." He looked at the officer, who appeared several steps beyond aggravated. "Want me to unlock it again?"

"Oh forget it," the man said, his frustration coating each and every syllable.

Zac continued to tremble long after the revving of the boat's engine replaced the man's retreating footsteps.

Chapter 62

His heart still thumping, Zac slumped onto the side of the bed. Sweat ran in rivulets down his face, his back and under his armpits. The thought of a shower crossed his mind. Before he could act on it, Charlie appeared at the door.

"Captain Tom asked if you'd join him in the pilothouse, that is..." a smirk crossed his face, "if it's convenient."

Zac chuckled. "I'll be right there."

"You say something to him?"

"Why?"

"I don't know, he seems to have changed his opinion of you. It's not that he didn't like you, he just has a low opinion of anyone associated with Leon."

"Oh yeah? Why's that?"

Charlie looked as though he'd been caught with his hand in another man's wallet. "Well, er, ah," he seemed to cast about for the right words. "I don't know, maybe I'm wrong. It's just an impression I get whenever we do business with him."

Intrigued at the possibility of finding out more about Leon, Zac tried to press Charlie for details.

"I'm the newest member of Leon's crew and I don't know all that much about his operation. Does he do business with you often?"

Charlie hesitated. "Just once in awhile. Look Captain's waiting topside. Should I tell him you'll be up?"

"No need. I'll be right there." Glancing back at the trunk to reassure himself that Jackson would be all right, Zac wondered what the captain wanted. Only one way to find out.

Opening the door to the pilothouse, Zac found the captain at a control panel, his hands resting on a handsome steering wheel. Leaning back in a comfortable-looking chair, he said, "Well, hey there, Zac."

The windows provided a spectacular view. An L-shaped settee and table took up one corner of the space, which Zac assumed converted into the bunk where Charlie slept.

"So, how'd you make out with that jerk from the Coast Guard?"

"All right, I guess."

"He get a peek inside that trunk?" The captain smirked.

"I unlocked it for him, but just as he was about to search it, the boat lurched and we lost our balance. The trunk 'somehow' got locked again and since it's hard to unlock, he gave up." Zac looked at the captain, who appeared almost giddy. "You did that on purpose, didn't you?"

"Moi? Whatever makes you say such a thing? I was here waiting for him to finish and accidentally lost control. Guess that's what happens when you're harassed by the Yew-nii-ted States Coast Guard." He snickered. "Timed it about right, did I?"

"You really did."

"Wonder what would've happened if I'd been late."

"Guess we'll never know, will we?"

"Your boss, that Leon guy, seems to have a lot of friends in Belize. Always sending stuff to them in trunks."

"I wouldn't know, Captain. I've only been with him a couple weeks."

"Well, you might want to mention what just happened; how I saved his—and your—butts." Stroking the highly polished wheel fondly, he added, "Maybe he should lay low for a while. I'll be damned if I'll lose the Bessie Rose working for the likes of him—even if it does help pay the mortgage on this beauty."

"Should I tell him you said so?"

"No, I'll mention it next time I see him."

"Good idea." Anxious to change the subject, Zac said, "So how fast we going anyhow?"

"Twelve knots." The captain waited for Zac to ask what a knot was, when he didn't, he added, "It's the equivalent of twelve point sixty-six miles per hour."

Zac nodded, distracted by the beauty of the steering wheel. It looked almost like a work of art.

Following his glance, the captain said, "This here's a classic teak yacht wheel. You don't see one a these on every boat, you know. It's handcrafted to the highest standards." Puffing up in obvious pride, he added, "It's got solid teak spokes and felloes secured with stainless fasteners and holly bungs."

Zac realized the captain had deliberately used the terms "felloes" and "holly bungs" knowing he didn't have a clue what they meant. He'd be damned if he'd ask. They were obviously parts of the wheel; he just didn't know which parts.

The captain looked as though he was about to expound when the radio crackled. Zac didn't get it all, but enough. His fear at the outset of the trip would soon be realized: A big storm was headed their way.

Chapter 63

It wasn't long before a dull lead color replaced the sky's cobalt blue. A strong wind picked up and the sea began to churn, causing the trawler to heave. Zac's stomach pitched along with the ever increasing size of the waves. He choked back a surge of vomit.

"Hey, you don't look so good. Probably seasick. Why don't you go ride out the storm in your stateroom? Me and Charlie are used to this. It'll pass in an hour or so. Go on now."

The captain's sudden kindness took Zac by surprise. Maybe he wasn't so bad after all. A sudden downfall flooded the deck. As the boat continued to be tossed in the growing storm, Zac, grasping overhead handrails, made his way down the steps to his stateroom.

Going to the "head" he promptly disposed of the lunch he'd enjoyed a few hours earlier, then retched a few more times. His head hurt; he felt dizzy, his legs were rubbery. He stretched out on the bed hoping a nap would help. That's when the boat's pitching became more violent, sending the trunk sliding across the floor where it crashed into the wall—or as the captain would say, the "bulkhead".

Momentarily forgetting how sick he was, Zac hurried to unlock the trunk, hoping Charlie wouldn't choose this moment to check on him. Wedging himself between the wall and the chest, he pulled up the lid.

Jackson's bewildered look said it all: *Where am I?* Zac helped him out of the trunk; between the boat's pitching and his cramped muscles, he could barely stand. "Wh-what the hell?" His raspy voice was little more than a whisper.

Looking at the door to make sure it remained closed, Zac put a finger to his lips. "Ssh." He motioned Jackson to the bed, then, retrieving the box of rations, opened a bottle of water. "Here, drink this."

As the boat continued to rock back and forth, Zac lost his balance, spilling the water. "Damn." He retrieved the bottle and offered his brother what was left. "

Jackson gulped it down then tossed it aside. "What's going on?"

Zac folded himself onto the bed. "Leon drugged you. We're on our way to Belize to sell you to his connection. I think that's what he did with Izzie too."

Jackson's mouth dropped. "I suspected he was a trafficker, but had no idea it was this bad." He started to say something else when there was a knock on the door followed by the first mate's voice. "Zac. You all right?"

Jackson ducked under a blanket as Zac simultaneously leaned across him. "Uh, yeah, I'm good." He deliberately said it in a voice that made him sound worse than he felt.

Charlie opened the door. "Thought I heard you moan and wanted to make sure you were still with us. Seasickness can be a bitch, that's for sure." He grasped the doorjamb as the boat made like a roller coaster.

"Won't be too much longer; the storm's dying down. Then we'll talk about dinner." He grinned. "Hang in there."

As he left the room, Zac was horrified to realize Jackson's foot had been sticking out from under the covers in the first mate's full view. Whether he'd noticed it or not was anyone's guess.

Chapter 64

The storm finally passed, and Zac awoke the following morning to a calm sea and a growling stomach. He'd eaten so little at supper the previous evening, the first mate had insisted on bringing a tray to his stateroom. Zac gave the bulk of the food to his brother, who'd woofed it down.

Jackson was to remain in the stateroom, hidden from view under a pile of blankets and pillows. Zac stressed the importance of staying inside with the door closed; that their lives and Izzie's could very well depend on it. Faced with the prospect of going back into the steamer trunk for the balance of the trip, he readily agreed.

"I see you're none the worse for having survived your first storm." The captain set his mug on the table as his guest joined him. "Charlie said you were pretty sick last night."

"You can say that again. Could hardly keep a thing down."

"And yet you managed to eat what he sent on that there tray." The captain inclined his head toward the dirty dishes.

Busted. Zac hadn't expected the captain to notice. "Yeah, well, as the night wore on, my stomach settled and I got hungry. It was nice of Charlie to do that."

"Yeah, that it was." The captain stuffed a bite of sausage in his mouth and chewed.

Eager to change the subject, Zac said, "So where are we?"

"Still on the Gulf. Late tonight we pass through the Yucatan Channel." Without waiting for Zac to ask, he added, "It connects the Gulf with the Caribbean."

"Oh," was all Zac could think to say.

"Look, you might as well know where you're headin'. There's an atlas on the shelf." He motioned toward a built-in bookcase. "You should learn something about Belize too, seeing as how you'll be visiting there a few days."

After breakfast, Zac took the captain's advice and pulled out the collection of maps. The passage from the Gulf to the Caribbean was through the Yucatan Channel or Straits of Yucatan, though, as the literature pointed out, it was neither long enough to be a channel nor narrow enough to be a strait. What intrigued him most was that the channel separated Mexico and Cuba. *Damn*, they'd be passing through in the dead of night. Oh well, they'd probably only see water anyway. Still, to be that close and sleep through it gnawed at him.

Anxious to spend time on deck, he grabbed a book on Central America and headed up the steps. From the little he read, Zac learned that Belize was in Central America, bordering the Caribbean Sea, between Guatemala and Mexico. He hadn't realized what a young country it was. It had been a British colony till 1981. Guatemala refused to recognize it as a nation until 1992. With an area slightly smaller than Massachusetts, as of 2011 the country's entire population was only about 321,000. Zac was amazed. Somehow he thought Belize was larger.

He glanced up, relieved to see a sky devoid of clouds and a gently rolling sea. Now that's the way to sail. He prayed there'd be no more storms between now and their arrival the following day. That's when his real work would begin. *How the hell could he keep track of his brother without endangering them both?*

Despite his overwhelming concerns—or perhaps because of them—Zac nodded off only to be awakened half an hour later by the captain. "Ya hungry? I know I am."

Over a lunch of clam chowder, freshly baked bread and salad, the two men fed their faces, ignoring the fact they'd had a sumptuous breakfast only a few hours earlier.

"Sailing stimulates the appetite, that's for damned sure. When you're out here, if you're not careful you'll end up with one of these." Captain Tom patted his ample belly. "No time for exercise on a boat. Seems like all I do is eat, sleep and steer."

His mouth full of the tasty stew, Zac nodded.

"So, what'd you learn about Belize?" The captain pushed away from the table, a mug of beer in his hand.

"Well, let see. For one thing, I was surprised to find out that they speak English and…"

"Yeah," the captain interrupted, "their version is a mix of Kriol and English. It's kinda hard to understand till you get used to it. For example, if you want to say, 'What's your name?' You'd say, 'Weh yu nayhn?' 'Good morning' is 'Gud maanin'.'"

Zac could tell that, as usual, the captain was enjoying himself at his expense. "Know what 'Da how yu di du?' means?"

Zac gave him a blank stare.

"It means 'How are you?'. Oh, here's one you'll need: 'How much does this cost?' say, 'Humoch dis kaas?' He let off one of those explosive laughs Zac detested, then said, "Don't worry, you'll do just fine. What else did you learn?"

"That you can use the dollar, without having to exchange it for local money." Zac continued, "and if you need help, dial 90—that connects you to the police."

"Planning on getting in trouble?" The captain's eyes twinkled. He leaned in and said, "Just watch yourself. Belize has tourist attractions which are amazing, but there are places you want to avoid. Take Belize City, for example, there are gangs and drugs. Most of the murders involve one or both. Now don't get me wrong. There are really nice areas where people with money live. Just don't get mixed up with the others, that's all I'm sayin'. And if you're under the impression the police'll come runnin' to your rescue, you got another think comin'.

"Now, if you're looking for a good time, go to one of them bars in San Pedro Town on Ambergris Caye. By the way, just so you know, it's pronounced *'key'* so don't go calling it *'kay'* and looking all stupid.

"We're dropping you a few miles north of there, so ask any taxi driver. They'll know where to take you." He stood, stretched and yawned, "Gotta get back to the helm." He glanced at Zac, but made no effort to explain the term. "Enjoy your afternoon."

Zac watched as the captain went up the steps to the pilothouse. Glancing around, he took a napkin and wrapped it around several slices of bread then filled his empty bowl with a generous helping of stew. He was about to leave the table when Charlie came bounding down the steps.

"Hey, if you're still hungry, there's more on the stove."

Startled to be discovered pilfering, Zac said, "Naw. I'm going to read awhile in my stateroom and wanted a snack in case I get hungry. Lunch was sure good."

"Help yourself. There's more where that came from." Charlie's face wore an odd expression. "Want me to help with the door?" Before Zac could object, he opened it.

Zac held his breath. How could he explain Jackson's presence and stop him from reporting it to Captain Tom?

Frantically glancing at the bed, expecting to find Jackson smack dab in the middle of it, Zac was surprised to see not only was the room empty, but the bed was neatly made. *What the hell was going on? And where was his brother?*

Charlie stood watching Zac, his hand on the doorknob. "Something wrong?"

"Uh, no," Zac rubbed his forehead. "Just a headache. Guess it takes a while to recover from seasickness."

"I think there's aspirin in the head, let me check." Zac started to say he'd do it himself, when Charlie crossed the room and pushed the door back.

Zac thought his heart would stop beating right then and there. Jackson was probably on the toilet taking care of business. He almost dropped the stew and bread he'd been holding. Stepping over to the chest of drawers, he set the food down, eased onto the bed and waited.

"Yep, there's a whole bottle in the cabinet. I thought I'd left some but wanted to be sure. Take a couple and have yourself a long nap. Headache'll be gone before you know it." Nodding at Zac, he left the room, closing the door behind him.

Chapter 65

With the beat of his heart pounding in his ears, Zac waited a few seconds to make sure the first mate had gone before searching for Jackson. *Where could he be?* The stateroom wasn't big enough to hold many hiding places.

He checked the trunk first. Nope, not there. The only other place he could think of was the shower stall. With the door open, it was almost hidden. That had to be it—he'd plastered himself against the wall. Zac crossed the room and looked inside. All he found was the drip of a leaky showerhead.

That's when panic set in. *Where the hell was he?* He had to be around there somewhere. He was about to search the galley, the captain's stateroom, the saloon—even the engine room, when a cabinet door slowly opened and his brother unfolded onto the floor.

"What the hell?" Zac said, his voice louder than he intended. Then in a stage whisper, he added, "You scared the pants off me."

Jackson gave him a shit-eating grin. "I was on the bed when I heard you guys coming. It was the closest place I could think to hide. Good thing I'm so limber."

Zac nodded. "There's some food. It's probably cold, but better than nothing."

Jackson didn't need to be told a second time. He spooned the stew, sopping up the remnants with chunks of bread. "That guy's a good cook,"

"You're right, but anything would taste good to you about now." Zac watched as his brother finished eating. "Look, we gotta talk. Cover yourself part way in case one of them pokes their nose in."

When Jackson was settled, Zac continued. "Tomorrow around noon, we dock at Ambergris Caye where Leon's contact gets the trunk. After that, it'll be up to me to find you— and Izzie, assuming she's still in Belize." Heaving a heavy sigh, Zac hesitated, then said, "Look, Jackson, why don't we just ditch this whole thing? We could load the trunk with something heavy, and get away before they realize you're gone."

"What about Izzie? Do we just give up on her? Let her rot in some hellhole for the rest of her life? That what you're sayin'?"

"Jackson, I don't know how this is gonna turn out. What if I can't find you? Then what?"

"Then I'll just have to deal with it, won't I?"

Zac noticed Jackson's chin go firm, the way it always did when he'd made up his mind about something. Once that happened, he realized there was nothing he could say or do to change it. He reached in his pocket and handed Jackson the pocketknife his dad had given him when he graduated high school. Since it was the only thing he had from his father, he treasured it and always carried it with him.

"Here, take this—use it then call my cell and I'll come get you. Meantime I'll do everything I can to find you." His voice trembled, he swallowed and lowered his head. "But in case I can't…"

Jackson patted his hand. "It's all right, I know. I love you too. If I don't make it, tell Mom I love her."

Blinking back tears, Zac said, "I'll get you out of this if it's the last thing I do."

With nothing more to say, they hugged for the first time since they were kids. Zac hoped against hope things would turn out all right.

Chapter 66

The following day shortly after noon, Zac tried to control his emotions as two men loaded the steamer trunk into their van. He'd never felt more helpless and alone in his life. What if this went sideways and he never saw his brother again? How could he live with the guilt he'd feel? Or face their mother?

He stuffed the envelope in his pocket as the van drove away. Fifteen-hundred dollars. That's all Jackson's life was worth to them. He'd counted it to make sure. No point discovering after the fact that they'd stiffed Leon. He wondered if he'd gotten more for Izzie.

As the van drove away, Zac tried to get a look at the license plate, but it was covered in mud. He pulled out his cellphone and discovered too late that it was dead. *So much for that plan.*

With a sinking heart, he picked up his belongings and hailed a cab for the drive to San Pedro, the island's only town. His first order of business was to find a place to stay.

****

It took some doing, but Zac found a room he could afford off the beaten track. It was more a hole in the wall than anything. He'd had a hard time convincing the taxi driver he wasn't interested in a fancy resort. The man finally understood and deposited him on

Buccaneer, just off Pescador Drive. The place was run down with peeling wallpaper, filthy curtains and reeked of cigarette smoke. But the price was right and the bed looked, well…it was a bed.

After settling in, Zac decided to look around. It didn't take a genius to see that San Pedro was like many beach towns: there were magnificent places fronting the ocean with lush lawns and palm trees, while a block away ordinary people eked out livings selling everything from souvenirs to daily necessities.

The atmosphere reminded him of a bustling fishing village but with "hot spots" of entertainment. As he wandered about, he noticed wooden houses, some were decorated in Mexican style while others sported a Caribbean flavor. There were gift shops, boutiques, bars, cafes, and restaurants up and down both Barrier Reef and Pescador Drives. Zac could sense the friendliness of the people even though he hadn't walked very far.

Beach attire being the norm, Zac felt right at home in flip-flops and cargo shorts. The aroma of food from street vendors reminded him that he hadn't eaten since breakfast. His initial fear of contracting some kind of tropical bug was quickly replaced by his gnawing hunger.

Every variety of fried meat from recognizable items such as burgers, hot dogs and chicken to the more exotic was available. Zac chose food he was familiar with. No sense taking a chance and getting laid up for the next twenty-four hours puking his guts out.

He had asked the cabbie where to go for a good time. He'd stressed *good time* hoping the man took him to mean *easy sex*. He'd suggested Lil' Mo's over on

Barrier Reef Drive. The cabbie said San Pedro had around ninety ficha bars.

When he asked what the word *ficha* meant the guy shrugged and laughed. Zac wasn't sure, but he thought it meant girls were available and if that was the case, they were widely available on this island of only about 12,000 people. There were prostitutes servicing money-rich tourists, but were they doing it to earn money—or to stay alive?

He didn't know if Izzie and Jackson were destined to work in one of those bars or would be shipped somewhere else, in which case he—and they—were screwed big time. He also didn't know how to go about finding them or where to begin.

Maybe he should start at Lil' Mo's. The cabbie had enthusiastically recommended that place. With some ninety bars to choose from, why had he pushed that particular one? Was he getting a kickback? Zac recalled the man had said to tell the guy at the door that Rollie recommended he go there. That must be it. Mo's was probably no different than any other bar, just more PR savvy.

Back in his room, Zac took a shower and changed clothes. He'd have to look somewhat presentable if he was to have any luck at all. It was a little after nine when he left his room and strolled down the street. Crowds of what he assumed were tourists swarmed the area to spend the evening pursuing what in the way of entertainment local establishments had to offer.

For Zac, the scene was more than a little overwhelming. Not only was he not there in pursuit of pleasure, he wasn't accustomed to nightlife on this scale. Iowa roots and his small-town upbringing hadn't included experiences such as this.

As he stood trying to get the lay of the land, he was drawn to a place that seemed to vibrate with rhythmic drumming and chanting. He let his feet decide for him. Once inside he discovered a cacophony of sound, color and writhing bodies. Everyone seemed taken up with dancing, chanting the refrain, "Tonight's gonna be a good night".

The pulsing beat found its way into his head almost forcing his participation. Lasers and a light show in the semi-darkened room added to the unrelenting celebration. In spite of himself, Zac began to sway in time with the rhythm.

He enjoyed dancing and was tempted to kick back and join in, but he couldn't—not now, not here. Unlike the other bar patrons, he had more important things on his mind. His was a mission that was literally a matter of life or death. He found a spot at the bar and sat down.

"Something to drink?" The bartender, a man of about forty with dark black hair threaded with gray, gave him a friendly smile.

"I'll have a beer."

"Lager or Stout?"

The music was deafening. He had a hard time understanding the man. He finally figured it out and said, "Lager."

A few moments later the bartender slid a bottle of Belikin's Lager across the bar. The label boasted it was "Belikin – the beer of Belize". With a slightly sweet taste and clean finish, Zac found it refreshing.

Fifteen minutes later, noticing the empty bottle the man asked Zac if he wanted another.

Shaking his head no, Zac said, "Where would I go to, uh, you know…?" Unused to seeking the services of prostitutes, he had difficulty getting the words out.

The bartender's expression said he disapproved, making Zac regret having asked. "We're not that kind of place. You need to go down the street for that."

Humiliated, Zac's appetite for the pounding music evaporated. He took his leave, not knowing where his next stop would be. Wandering aimlessly down Pescador, trying not to descend into despair, he wondered where in this seething mass of tourists he could possibly find Jackson and Izzie. And…and even if he did locate them, then what? *How do you rescue a slave?*

The very word sent shivers down his spine. And yet, that's exactly what he was dealing with. Slavery. They'd been sold into slavery and it was up to him to get them out—somehow. Maybe that was the key. If they'd been sold, he'd buy them back.

But how? With what? There was that fifteen hundred dollars the man had given him for Jackson. He could use it to try to buy them back. They would want more and he'd be in deep shit with Leon, but he was in deep shit regardless, so it was worth a try.

He glanced around. The bartender had said to go down the street to find a ficha bar. So that's what he'd do. At least it would be a place to start.

Entering an unremarkable place, Zac felt less intimidated than before. It was as different from the nightclub with its body-to-body dancers as Tampa was from Iowa. He found a table in the back and sat down. A band played with the now-familiar drummers tapping out Caribbean rhythms. Patrons here were more subdued, perhaps they were locals out for an evening. A young woman approached. She wore a provocative outfit and a plastered-on smile.

"What would you like to drink?"

Zac decided to stick with a now-familiar brand. "Belikin's Lager," he said.

When the girl returned with his drink, Zac cleared his throat. "How would I go about, you know, getting the company of a woman for a few hours?" This time he managed to get the question out without feeling embarrassed.

The girl didn't miss a beat. "I can help you with that," she said. "Take your drink and follow me."

She led him halfway down a long hall, stopped and knocked on a closed door. A soft voice inside said, "Come in."

"I believe this is what you're looking for," she said. "Have a good time." Then excusing herself, she left Zac to negotiate the details for himself.

Not knowing what to expect, Zac felt as awkward as an adolescent at his first dance. He'd had sex many times before, but this was different. He always had at least a passing acquaintance with his partner and he'd never had to pay for it. The heat of a blush crawled up his neck and onto his cheeks.

When he entered the room, he was shocked to see that the girl appeared to be only around twelve or thirteen. *Holy crap, she's just a kid.*

Dressed in a flimsy negligee, she reached out her arms and, with a smile that seemed painted on her face, said, "Take off your clothes, I make you happy."

Suddenly Zac was nauseous as he sat on the edge of the bed. The room was dimly lit, making it hard to see. "How much for fifteen minutes?" he said, holding up ten fingers and then five more.

"Twenty dollars, twenty minutes. Take clothes off now."

"No, I want to talk. Will you talk to me?"

"Pay—I do whatever you want."

Zac pulled out a twenty dollar bill. The young girl's face lit up.

"What you want to talk about?"

Not knowing where to start and realizing there was no time to waste for fear he'd be found out, Zac dove right in. "Where do I go to buy a girl—or guy?"

The young girl's forehead wrinkled. "Buy? Like now?"

"No. *Buy.* Take with me." He walked his fingers across the girl's lap.

She thought for a minute, then as if a light bulb went off inside her head, she said, "Oh, you want to keep?"

Zac nodded. "Yes. How do I do that?"

"Mo's. Go there. That's where people go to *buy.*" As she said it, tears welled in her eyes. She blinked them back, hastily wiping away the few that managed to escape.

"Thank you." Zac realized he hadn't asked her name. He pulled out a second twenty and in a low voice, almost a whisper, said, "Keep this for yourself. Don't tell them you have it."

The young girl's face was transformed as she smiled. "You buy *me.* I go with you. *Please?*"

Zac took both her hands into his. "I wish I could, but I can't. I have to find my friends and get them out."

When she gave him an uncomprehending look, he repeated, "You know—friends out?" He put his hand on his heart and then made a fly-away gesture. "Out."

She nodded then said. "Come back for me." And mimicked his heart-gesture. "Get Josie out too. I'm Josie."

He got up to leave but before he reached the door, a rough-looking man stuck his head in and glanced around. "Everything all right in here? She give you a good time?"

Zac wanted to punch the creep and keep hitting him until he was as broken and bloody as he'd no doubt left this child on more than one occasion. Instead, his fists clenched he said, "Yeah, she sure did." He added under his breath, "Bastard."

As he left the bar filled with male patrons his heart sank. Josie had a long, painful night ahead of her. He had visions of grabbing her along with the other young girls in that place and running like hell out of there, but with only fifteen hundred dollars in his pocket and two special people in trouble, he realized there wasn't a thing he could do.

Chapter 67

Following the girl's advice, Zac headed over to Lil' Mo's on Barrier Reef Drive. Like the first club he'd stopped at, the place was hopping. He slipped inside, happy to go unnoticed. Not that anyone would have become aware of him considering that all eyes seemed to be riveted on the floor show.

Girls were on a raised platform and one by one put on a lewd performance. It appeared to be a contest for the loudest applause. He idly wondered what the prize would be.

A light tap on his shoulder told him to order a drink or be on his way. He knew the drill. For want of anything better, he ordered a Belikin—his third of the night. It wasn't bad, just not his favorite alcoholic beverage. But it was cheap and money was tight, so it would have to do.

He scrutinized the dancers, hoping to find Izzie among them and wondering if he'd recognize her if she was. He'd only seen her photograph and on the videotape Jackson had shown him. Considering that most of these girls appeared to be Hispanic, Izzie would likely be easy to spot.

Glancing around the crowded room, he wondered if Jackson was around there somewhere. What would traffickers want with a white man? They'd probably agreed to take him off Leon's hands as a favor. But what would they do with him? He wasn't as controllable as some young girl and he certainly wouldn't become one of their male prostitutes. Then what? Maybe he'd be sold to do forced labor.

His beer arrived along with what Zac thought was a brilliant idea that just might work. As he paid for his drink, he said, "I'm looking to buy a white male to work in construction and heard this is where to go for that. Who do I need to see?"

The server just stared at him as if he didn't comprehend the question. Zac was about to repeat himself, when he said, "Stay here."

Ten minutes went by during which three different young girls had shaken, twirled and writhed suggestively. His beer bottle empty, Zac began to wonder if the server had forgotten about it, when a beefy man motioned him over.

The expression on the man's face said he was not one to be trifled with. Well, Zac wasn't in the business of trifling—he was serious too, so … God, he hoped this worked.

He followed the man to a makeshift office down the hall, well beyond the din of throbbing music and cheers.

"Have a seat," he said, and parked his ample body on a worn swivel chair behind a desk. "Before we get down to business, tell me about yourself." When Zac hesitated, he added, "Yeah, I know, but in this business you can't be too careful. I mean, how do I know you're not some kinda cop?"

Zac gave him what he hoped sounded like a jaded laugh. "Sure as if the cops give a rat's ass about your business as long as they get their cut, right?"

The man nodded. "Understood. But, look, I'm curious. It's clear you're not from around here. If I had to guess, I'd say you're from the States or Canada maybe?"

Zac nodded. "You'd be right."

"So, you're trying to buy cheap labor for your construction business back home?"

"Yep," Zac nodded enthusiastically.

"Mexicans aren't cheap enough?"

"Not as cheap as slaves, I mean, you pay for them and they're yours, right? All I got to do is feed them and keep them out of sight and I'm home free. With immigration clamping down, it's harder to hire illegals and besides you have to pay them, even if it is a lot less. With my profit margin, this is a better way to go."

The man had been scrutinizing Zac as he spoke, looking him up and down and staring him in the face as though trying to detect any hint of deceit.

"What I'm looking for is a white guy. He'd be less noticeable, see what I mean? You have anyone like that?"

The man rubbed his chin as if he was thinking, then said, "Actually I do. Young guy came in just today. I'll let you have him for two thousand American."

Zac's heart sank. That was all the money he had, including what the traffickers had given him for Jackson.

"That's too rich for my blood," he said and stood, hoping his bluff would work. "Thanks anyway."

As he turned to leave, the man said, "Wait, now, don't be in such a hurry. Let's talk about this."

Zac returned to the wobbly chair and sat down.

"What did you have in mind?"

"I dunno. I've never done this before. How's five hundred?" He crossed his fingers. If the man went for it, he'd have more than enough to somehow find Izzie and get them out of the country.

"That's ridiculous. You're not buying a used car, for god's sake. I mean this guy's gonna save you a bundle working for free."

"Yeah but I'm taking a hell of a risk. If I'm caught I go to jail. In the U.S. they don't look kindly on this sort of thing."

"You have a point. Look, the guy we got today's a real pain in the ass. He's gonna be nothing but trouble. I can let you have him at a loss, just to get him outta here. How's a thousand and we call it a day?"

"Not as good as five hundred, but you got yourself a deal. He have papers?"

"Yeah, we got all that covered. Just make yourself comfortable and I'll go get him." The man pushed back from the desk, stood and shook Zac's hand. "Nice doing business with you. By the way, I'm Mo. Come again, you hear?"

After the man left the room, Zac wiped his hand on his jeans trying to obliterate all contact with the monster who obviously had little regard for human life. As he waited, he wondered what he'd do if it turned out Jackson was not the white guy he'd just purchased. What then?

Five minutes later, the door opened and Jackson entered, or rather was shoved inside. Zac was astonished to see how beaten up he'd become in only a few hours. His clothes were torn, his face and arms covered with cuts and bruises. Standing there, his head down, he didn't look up when Mo said, "Gimme the money and he's all yours."

"Whoa, not so fast," Zac saw an opportunity and decided to go for it. "You never mentioned the condition he's in. I mean, look at him. How am I gonna get any work outta him? Looks pretty beat up to me."

"Those're just a few bruises and scratches, nothing serious. He'll be fine."

"I don't know about that. It'll take some time to get him in shape for any kind of construction work."

Mo's eyes widened, his forehead crinkled up. "You sayin' you don't want him? That what you're sayin'?"

"Not for a *thousand*, not in *that* condition. I'm afraid eight hundred's the best I can do. Take it or leave it."

Zac noticed Jackson's head slowly begin to rise, his eyes making contact. *Don't react, bro, don't screw this up.* He prayed and held his breath as the man considered his offer.

"Oh, all right. Take him. Anything to get the sonofabitch outta here. You're getting a real bargain."

"He don't look like much of a bargain to me. I doubt I'll get any work out of him for a while, but since you say he's such a dick I'll take him off your hands." Taking another long look at Jackson, he shrugged and shook his head. "I just hope I get my money's worth."

He stretched out his arm to shake hands with the trafficker. "We'll be on our way. Good doing business with you."

"I almost forgot. Here's his papers." Mo handed Zac the same envelope he himself had given the men who'd picked up the trunk that afternoon. It seemed more like weeks than mere hours had passed since then.

"Oh yeah, thanks." Stuffing the envelope in his pants pocket, he took Jackson firmly by the arm in imitation of what he thought passed for ownership, and they left the club.

****

They were more than a block away before Zac dropped the charade of master and servant. He looked in every direction to make certain they weren't being followed. The people around were obviously tourists intent on having a good time.

"You can drop the act now. We're safe." If Zac expected gratitude from his brother for rescuing him from the slavers, he was sorely disappointed.

"*Eight hundred dollars?* You were going to leave me there if they didn't reduce the price because of my *condition*? What the hell was that about?" He punched Zac in the arm.

Zac laughed. "I was calling their bluff. If they hadn't budged I would have paid the thousand. Look at it this way, now we've got two more hundred to spend."

"*Eight hundred's* all I'm worth?"

"Look, if you want I can sell you to someone else for more."

Jackson punched Zac in the arm again. "No, that's all right *Master*, this works for me."

"They said you were a pain in the ass; couldn't get rid of you fast enough."

"Thank God for that. By the way, you won't be getting your knife back. It nearly got me killed. After they found it on me, they beat me up. When they said that I was sold, I thought I'd be heading to some plantation to pick bananas. Honestly, I never imagined you'd be the one to …" He didn't finish his thought, just grabbed Zac in a bear hug and held on. "Thank you so much. I love you—even if I am adopted."

Zac pulled back. "Adopted? What're you talking about?"

"What you said the last night you were at the apartment. You said I was adopted; that Mom never got around to telling me."

"Oh that. I made it up so you'd get mad and throw me out. I wanted to do the undercover thing without you mucking it up; thought if I got you good and mad, you'd think I took off and leave things alone. I never dreamed you'd stake out the house and get caught. You're lucky Leon didn't kill you."

Jackson nodded. "I know. God, Zac, how're we gonna find Izzie? And if we do find her, how will we ever get her out of here?"

Chapter 68

Izzie repeatedly wiped off tears that kept flooding her face. She had to get control of herself and put on a strong front. If she copped an attitude like some of the low-class women she'd interviewed as a reporter, maybe they'd let her go. The women here seemed so frightened, willing to do whatever they were told—probably to avoid getting beaten. Somehow she'd have to stand up to these monsters, no matter the outcome.

She wished she could press a "restart button" and go back to the point where Jackson warned her to stay away from Leon. If only she'd listened. That was her problem, she never listened; always thought she knew better. Would she ever get out of this mess? Or would she spend the rest of her life as a slave, doing what she was told in order to stay alive?

She'd rather kill herself than submit to the nightly rapes she'd read trafficked women were subjected to. Although at this point she didn't know what their plans for her were, she assumed it wouldn't be pleasant.

The men who "bought" her made her put on a provocative outfit. Her own clothes were torn and smelly, so she was more than willing to oblige despite feeling conspicuous in the scanty apparel. Escorted out the back door of the establishment, she was whisked away in a waiting car. As they drove, she tried to spot landmarks that would help if she managed to escape, but it was too dark out.

The road was narrow, with what looked to Izzie like a tropical forest on either side, replete with enormous potholes. They lurched, swerved and bumped along; she had all she could do to keep from vomiting. From the looks of her captors, they wouldn't take kindly to having their vehicle befouled. She swallowed hard and braced herself for the next sharp curve.

Twenty minutes later, they arrived at their destination. It wasn't at all what she expected. At best, she'd anticipated a shack with machine gun-toting guards and snarling dogs out front. Instead they drove up to a well-lit, gated complex on manicured grounds of lush palm trees and shrubbery. The brick drive curved around past several buildings, some appeared to be individual villas while others were more in the style of a hotel or apartment complex.

This looked nothing like a brothel, or what she assumed a brothel might look like. With the exception of movies or television, she'd never seen a house of prostitution. Maybe they'd had a change of heart and decided to let her go.

The car continued past the elegant entryway around to the back where it stopped and the men got out. They opened the back door and motioned to her. When she hesitated, one of them stooped down and yanked her from the car, wrenching her shoulder. An involuntary cry of pain escaped her lips causing the man to throw her a stern look. Not wanting to invite more rough treatment, Izzie slapped a hand across her mouth and waited for what would come next.

Chapter 69

After stopping at a thrift store to replace the rags Jackson wore, they went to Zac's hotel to clean up.

"I'm starving," Jackson announced and rubbed his stomach. "Haven't had a thing to eat since they took me off the boat."

"Guess they don't treat the 'help' well," Zac said with a grin.

"You got that right. Seems like every time I turned around I got punched. Most of the time I had no idea why."

"They said you were a big pain in the ass. Couldn't wait to get rid of you."

"Then it worked."

"What worked?"

"My plan. I thought the only way I'd survive was by giving them a hard time, so they'd be only too happy to sell me."

"Why didn't you just pretend to cooperate and wait for a chance to get away?"

"It'd never happen. They keep a close watch on the 'help' while they work. And afterward, they're locked up." The sour expression on Jackson's face reflected an unpleasant thought. "They're kept in dungeon-like rooms, crowded to the gills. It's horrible. Think of everything you've ever read about slavery and how blacks were treated worse than animals. It's pretty much the same thing. If I hadn't seen it for myself, I would never believe it was happening. I mean, for god sake, this is the twenty-first century and we're dealing with slavery? *Un-freaking-believable.*"

They'd left the hotel and were headed out for something to eat. Except for a few cuts and bruises, Jackson looked no different than any other tourist. It was late so the bar they found not far from Mo's was fairly quiet with only a few patrons nursing their drinks.

"So, how do we find Izzie?" Zac directed the question more to himself than to his brother and was surprised when Jackson spoke up.

"Maybe you do a repeat of what you did earlier; go to Mo's and say you want a white girl. Act like you're a racist and wouldn't consider having sex with someone who wasn't of the white persuasion."

In between bites of his taco, Zac listened intently. "You know that might work. I just paid eight hundred for a white *boy*—he stressed the word 'boy' and waited for Jackson to react. When he didn't, Zac continued. "It wouldn't be hard to convince them I'm interested in either buying or being serviced by a white woman. Even if Izzie's not there, they might let it slip where she's gone."

After eating, they went their separate ways—Jackson back to the hotel for badly needed rest and Zac to make yet another purchase.

Chapter 70

Zac was sitting at a table drinking a bottle of Belikin's when he felt a light tap on his shoulder. Thinking it was the waitress checking to see if he was ready for another, he prepared to wave her away, then heard a familiar voice.

"Well, hey Zac. How ya' doin'?"

He looked up to see Charlie, the first mate from Captain Tom's yacht, a broad smile spread across his face. Zac stood and gave him a hearty handshake.

"I'll be a son of a bitch. Charlie, what're you doing here?"

"I have a couple days between trips. Can I join you for a drink?"

A niggling voice inside Zac reminded him he had a job to do that didn't include sitting around making small talk. He hesitated a second too long.

"Maybe another time" Charlie said and started to walk away.

"No, wait." Zac called after him. "Pull up a chair. I have some business to attend to, but it can wait." He called the waitress over. "My friend here needs a drink."

Zac liked and respected Charlie and was happy to see him despite the fact they had little in common. "So, how's the captain treating you?"

The merriment left Charlie's face. He shrugged. "What can I say? Captain Tom's a bastard but he pays well, so I shouldn't complain. Besides, who really likes their boss anyhow?"

Zac nodded his agreement.

"You enjoying Ambergris?"

"Haven't seen much yet, but it seems interesting enough." *If he didn't have to rescue his brother's friend from traffickers, it might actually be a nice place for a vacation.*

"Somehow you don't look like you're having a good time," Charlie gave him a penetrating glance. "I know my way around if you need help." When Zac didn't respond, he leaned in and added in a conspiratorial tone, "I don't mean to stick my nose where it doesn't belong, but you seem like you could use a little friendly advice. Belize is a country with two faces; while it's a paradise for tourists, it also has a sordid underbelly. I don't know which you're looking to experience, but if it's the latter you'd best be careful. Around here, people have been known to disappear into the jungle when they get involved with the wrong crowd, if you catch my drift."

Charlie's words took Zac by surprise. While the din of the music and club patrons made hearing difficult, he got the message. He just didn't know how to respond. On the one hand, he could use help rescuing Izzie, especially from someone familiar with the area, but on the other, how much did he actually know about the man? What if he was in cahoots with the traffickers and he confided in him; what then?

"Thanks for the warning, but you needn't worry. I'm just here for a good time, doing my tourist thing before I go back to the States." He took a long pull on his beer.

"Great. Don't miss the Barrier Reef, it's only a quarter mile from Ambergris. It's among the top ten dive destinations in the world." He laughed. "Listen to me, you'd think I was some kinda travel agent the way I'm going on." Charlie glanced at his watch. "Well, I gotta go. Thanks for the drink. Enjoy your stay."

He stood, then hesitated. "If you want to get together, I'm staying at Hotel del Rio over on the beach." When Zac gave him an uncomprehending look, he added, "It's about half a mile north of Central Park. I'll be there till the captain's ready to leave—for a couple days at least." With that, he took his leave.

Zac nursed his beer another twenty minutes, then called the waitress over. "I'm kinda lonely and can use some company. Can you help me out with that?" The girl wasn't the one who'd led him to the back room earlier.

Without registering disapproval, she said, "Follow me." and led him down the same hallway he'd gone down before. When she opened a door and he saw a dark-skinned girl in scanty clothes sitting on the side of a bed, he stopped her and said, "I prefer a *white* girl. You got any?"

She stared at him seeming not to comprehend his request.

Pinching his skin, he said, "*White skin.* I want a girl with white skin."

"This nice girl, clean. Take bath. Skin not dirty,"

Zac had to bite his tongue to keep from laughing when he realized she'd misunderstood his meaning. "I want a *white woman*," he said slowly. "You understand 'white woman'?"

Closing the door, she raised her hand and said, "Wait here."

As Zac stood in the hallway, it occurred to him that she could solve all his problems—or at least a major one—if she came back with Izzie in tow. Could he possibly be that lucky?

Several minutes later she returned, not with Izzie or another woman for that matter, it was Mo who accompanied her.

"Well, look who's back. Good seeing you again so soon." He reached out his hand to shake Zac's. "I hear the girl's not to your liking." He inclined his head toward the closed door. "That's no problem. We'll get you another; we have plenty."

Zac shook Mo's hand, despite the fact it made his skin crawl. "She misunderstood. I prefer sticking with my own kind—if you know what I mean. You got any white women?" He hoped his imitation of a racist was convincing.

Mo scratched his chin, causing his flabby jowls to shake. "Hmmm, ah, yes, I know what you're talking about. Lemme think. We had a white girl come through a couple days ago, but she's already gone."

Zac frowned. "Son of a bitch! Can you tell me where? I haven't had any for awhile, so you know, I can use a little, ah, female companionship."

Mo threw back his head and laughed. "Why don't you just close your eyes and pretend their skin's white, I mean, wouldn't it be easier than going to the trouble of finding a white girl? They're scarce around here, you know."

"I'm finding that out, but you know a man's got his principles after all."

Mo hesitated. "I almost never do this. If my client found out I gave you his information, it wouldn't go well for me."

"Who am I gonna tell? I just want to get laid."

The man slapped him on the back. "Oh, all right. I'll do it as a special favor for a new customer. Wait here and I'll see if I can find out what they did with her."

"What do you mean?"

"Well, you know. Sometimes they take them for personal use; other times, they put them in service where they do business. I don't ask questions; just take the money and pass'em on." He paused to see if Zac had anything more to say, when he didn't, he said, "I'll be right back."

Chapter 71

The following day, Zac and Jackson headed out to the Dias Del Sol Resort about ten miles north of San Pedro. On a pristine stretch of beachfront, Zac was stunned at the beauty of the place. The exterior was pale orange adobe, a perfect fit with its tropical setting.

The registration area spilled into a spacious great room complete with French doors providing access to a veranda. Lounge chairs upholstered in vibrant red and orange prints along with tables and matching umbrellas were more than a little inviting.

He and Jackson were shown to a spacious accommodation with two queen-sized beds, a bath and private veranda with access to the beach. Spectacular views of the Caribbean beckoned from every vantage point.

The brochure in the room bragged that "cable TV, DVD player, a full stock of DVDs, stereo and CDs, wireless Internet, games and books were included along with the use of a freshwater pool, kayaks, bikes and tennis courts."

"Think the services of trafficked women are part of the 'amenities?'" Zac quipped.

"Those'd probably be extra, kinda like when you get something from the minibar." Jackson said and flopped down on the bed. "What now? How do we even know she's here?"

"We don't. But Mo said some guys bought a white girl from him a few days ago. Said he remembers because most of their 'stock' comes from Central or South America, so a white girl from the States really stands out."

When Jackson appeared doubtful, Zac added, "Got a better idea?"

"Not really. All right, if it is her, what then? How're we gonna get her out of the hotel—let alone out of the country?"

"That, my friend, is the million-dollar question." Zac glanced in the mirror, smoothed his hair and said, "Let's get something to eat, I'm starving."

Chapter 72

They had dinner on the veranda overlooking the Caribbean. Zac ordered steak served with garlic mashed potatoes, vegetables and a green salad while Jackson had blackened snapper with white rice and zucchini. They shared a bottle of red wine.

When they were finished, Zac moved to a lounge chair and gazed at the peaceful scene that surrounded them. "Boy, this is the life, isn't it?"

Jackson gave him a look that said, "You kidding me?"

"Yeah, I know, I know. You don't have to remind me, but let me enjoy myself for a few minutes, okay?"

It wasn't that he'd forgotten why they were there; he'd been turning it over and over in his mind trying to decide how to approach the guy. Mo said to ask for Sid, that he'd bought a white girl earlier in the week and that she was "in service" at the resort and would be available as a special favor to him.

If it turned out to be Izzie they were halfway home—halfway because they still had to find a way to get her out of there. It wouldn't be a simple matter of buying her as he had Jackson. According to Mo, a white girl was rare in this area and would be in demand. He'd hated to let her go.

The thought of what she must be going through made Zac sick. Maybe, like Jackson, she'd refused to comply and they would be only too happy to get her off their hands. He doubted it. They'd likely beat her until there was nothing left of the spunky woman Jackson had described.

"So, you just gonna sit there with your eyes closed or what?" Jackson said.

Having made up his mind, Zac opened his eyes and sat up in the lounge chair. "Or what."

"What?"

"Nothing. Look, you stay here. I'm gonna find Sid."

****

Fifteen minutes later, Zac returned sporting something of a smug expression. "She'll be in the room by the time we get there. I told Sid we wanted her services for the rest of the evening. Amazing how we can charge the services of a slave to our room." He shook his head in disgust.

"Let's hope it's Izzie."

"Yeah, I don't know what we'll do if it isn't. Matter of fact, I'm not sure what we'll do if it is."

Chapter 73

They returned to their room more than a little anxious. *Let it be Izzie; let it be Izzie; let it be Izzie* drummed inside Jackson's head with every step. He was almost afraid to see her. *What condition would she be in? Had she been brutalized the way he had?*

She'd been rude to him, refused to listen when he told her to stay away from Leon and had been an all-around pain in the ass from the moment she'd been assigned as his reporter. Still, there was a soft spot in his heart for her that he hadn't recognized until it became clear she was in trouble. Somehow he hadn't been able to let her go. He'd risked his life and most likely lost his job for her and now, hopefully, he'd see her again and somehow get her out of the situation she'd gotten the three of them in.

As they unlocked the door, they saw a woman standing near the window; her head bowed in a submissive posture. At first Jackson didn't think it was her. Her low-cut blouse and miniskirt left nothing to the imagination. Her long blond hair was pinned back with some kind of flowered clasp. What struck him most forcefully was her attitude of total capitulation. She was not the feisty woman he knew. What had they done to break her spirit so completely in such a short time?

"Izzie," he said in a near whisper, not wanting to startle her. When she didn't respond, he said it again. "Izzie, it's me, Jackson."

Slowly lifting her head, she stared at him as if in a trance.

"Izzie," he repeated. When he touched her shoulder she leapt back, as if in fear. "What have they done to you?" he said.

She looked wildly about the room and rested her gaze on Zac.

"That's my brother. We've come to rescue you." He said it softly, hoping to reassure her with the soothing tone of his voice. "You're safe now. We won't hurt you."

Izzie looked from Jackson to Zac and back again. Her blue eyes filled with tears that spilled down her cheeks.

"Jackson," she said. "Is it really you?"

"Yes, Izzie, it's really me." He started to give her a hug when she winced in pain. Dropping his arms, he said, "You're hurt."

"They beat me—over and over," she said, "till I finally promised to do what they wanted." A slight smile appeared, as she added, "You're to be my first."

"Enough with the reunion, we gotta go," Zac no sooner said that when there was a knock at the door. Putting his finger to his lips, he said, "Get on the bed. I'll see what they want."

He opened the door to find a man whose appearance said, "Mess with me and you'll regret it". A scar crawled down his left cheek; his nose appeared to have been broken and healed badly. "Mr. Taylor?"

"That's me."

"Just checking to see if the girl we sent is treating you well."

"We've barely started, if you know what I mean. We get her till eleven; that's what they said when I paid for the room."

"You do, but Sid wanted me to check and make sure you're satisfied. This is her first time out and we want to be sure you get your money's worth. We want our customers to have a good experience at Los Dias so you want to come back."

"Yeah, she's hot. She'll do." Zac assured him.

"Let us know if there's anything else you need. The kitchen's open all night so don't hesitate to order room service."

"Thanks, I'll keep that in mind." Zac hung out the "Do Not Disturb" sign and locked the door. "We gotta get outta here right now."

"We can't." Izzie looked more than a little terrified. "They have people posted everywhere, watching to make sure the girls don't get away." She trembled so hard her voice shook along with her entire body.

Zac nodded. "No one's on the terrace. That leads to the beach and you can get to the parking lot from there. Besides who's going to bother a couple making love in the moonlight?"

"Who? What?" Jackson was momentarily confused, then a light bulb came on and he grinned. "Oh, yeah. Right."

"So this is what we'll do. You two climb over the railing and head for the beach. I'll go out to the car. If anyone asks, I'll say you want to be alone with the girl for awhile. In the meantime you guys make like lovers and meet me, then we'll get the hell outta here. Oh, and double-lock the door after me, that'll make it harder for them to get in. By the time they realize we're gone, we'll be back in San Pedro."

Taking Izzie by the hand, Jackson helped her climb down the incline from the patio leading to the beach. Mindful of her bruises, he gently encircled her waist with his arm and whispered, "lean against me and put your head on my shoulder. In case anyone's watching, we need to appear to be a couple."

Izzie gave him a wan smile. "I can't believe you're here. Jackson, thank you so much."

"You're welcome, Iz, but hang in there. We've a long way to go before we're home free."

Chapter 74

Zac left the room and sauntered past a beefy man reading a magazine. He glanced up. "Good evening, sir. Going out?"

Brilliant observation. What's it look like, asshole? "I need a cigarette." The rooms were strictly no smoking.

"I hear ya, buddy. Wish I could join you but I ..." suddenly seeming to realize he might be revealing too much, he paused, then said, "I'm waiting for my wife. She'll raise all sorts of hell if she comes out and I'm not here."

Sure, and I'm the Easter Bunny. Zac nodded then shook his head. "Women. They're all alike. Catch ya later."

Zac's heart beat wildly as he waited, the car motor purred softly. *What if they can't find me? What if they'd been caught? Do I have a Plan B? Of course not. Fly by the seat of my pants like always. Only this time it won't mean a night in jail or Mom's look of disapproval. This time it's a matter of ...* He heard footsteps and desperately hoped it was his brother and the girl—not thugs coming to beat the crap out of him.

The parking lot wasn't well lit, so he had a hard time seeing who approached. Frozen in place, his hands white-knuckled on the steering wheel, all he could do was wait.

A minute later—a lifetime to Zac—Jackson opened the car door. Izzie climbed in back.

"Quick, get on the floor and cover up with that blanket," Zac said. He put several boxes containing a few articles of clothing and "souvenirs" he'd purchased earlier on top of her, hoping to mask her presence in case they were stopped.

Shifting into "drive" he switched the headlights on, sent up a quick prayer and started their ten-mile journey back to the only town on Ambergris Caye. Each time he hit a pothole, Izzie groaned.

"I'm sorry, I'm sorry," Zac said for what seemed like the one-hundredth time. "It won't be too much longer."

The road was pitch black without a single street light to guide them, making it impossible to avoid craters and ruts that seemed everywhere. He swerved whenever one was caught in the headlights, making the ride even more dangerous as the little car didn't take kindly to evasive action.

Twenty minutes later, as the lights of San Pedro glimmered in the distance, headlights from an automobile approaching rapidly from behind reflected in the rear-view mirror.

"Oh shit," Zac murmured under his breath.

"What's wrong?" Jackson said.

"That must be them. They're coming to get her. Now what do we do?"

The road was narrow, barely wide enough for two cars riding alongside each other.

"I could straddle the middle and prevent them from cutting us off. What do you think?"

Jackson thought a moment too long. The vehicle was now less than three car-lengths back, its headlights nearly blinding them, making it difficult to see the road.

"What's wrong?" Izzie sat up. "Is it them? Are they coming to get me? Please don't let them …" her voice trailed off. "I can't go back, Jackson. I'd rather die than go back there. Please…"

"Get down, get down." Zac was in a panic. Sweat drenched his hands making the steering wheel slippery. *What the hell was he going to do? How could he defend this helpless woman against those thugs?* He didn't have a gun, or a weapon of any kind. All he had was his fists—and his mouth.

He attempted to speed up, but multiple potholes made it impossible. Between swerving and trying to outrun the rapidly approaching auto, Zac feared he'd lose control and the car would roll, crushing them in the process.

As the oncoming vehicle caught up with them and began to pass, Zac braced himself, his foot hovering over the brakes.

"Hold on," he cautioned Jackson. But instead of cutting them off and grabbing Izzie, it kept right on going.

Adrenalin, along with a sense of relief pumped through his body long after the tail lights disappeared in the distance. Zac could hardly believe it, then, glancing at the dashboard clock he realized it was only nine. Idiot! They hadn't discovered Izzie's escape; no one was searching for them—yet.

Chapter 75

They drove into San Pedro unnoticed by a population preoccupied with having a good time. The bars were hopping, the gift shops still open and crowded with tourists. No one took a second glance at the bedraggled trio desperate to escape the island.

Zac drove slowly in contrast to his racing mind: *What now? Where to hide?* How to get outta here before they were discovered and all hell broke loose.

"So, we going back to the hotel?" Jackson said.

When Zac didn't answer, Izzie pleaded, "We've gotta find some place to hide and fast. If those guys catch us, they'll kill you, and beat me again."

"I know," Zac said in the most reassuring tone he could muster. Reassuring? He didn't know what the hell he was going to do. Panic rose inside, his heart drummed in his ears.

"Zac, what are you…" Jackson started to say when Zac interrupted him.

"Shut the hell up, both of you. Let me think." He regretted the words as soon as they flew from his mouth, but it was the truth. How could he figure this out with the two of them ragging on him? He knew only too well what was at stake if they failed to get away. In case they didn't realize it, theirs were not the only lives in jeopardy—his was too.

The car fell silent as he collected his thoughts. Glancing at them both, he could see by their expressions how frightened they were. But knowing that didn't solve anything. He had to find a place to hide until he figured out how to get off this damned island, and he had to do it quick.

As he rummaged around for a solution, Charlie's face flashed before his mind's eye. He remembered the man had said, "If you want to get together, I'm staying at the Hotel del Rio over on the beach, north of Central Park." He said he'd be there a couple days and offered to help if Zac needed him. Well, he needed him. Now if he could locate the place and find Charlie, they just might get out of this alive.

Zach followed Barrier Reef Drive north about three quarters of a mile and easily found the place. With its distinctive thatched-roof design, it would be hard to miss. Driving into the parking lot, he warned Jackson and Izzie to stay put.

"I'll come get you when everything's settled. In the meantime, don't talk to anybody, and—don't under any circumstances go wandering around. Understand?" It'd be just like his brother and that idiot reporter to decide to check things out. It appeared to be a cool place and they were beginning to get their sea legs. Hopefully he'd locate Charlie and they could somehow figure out what to do.

Zac went into the lobby and told the concierge he was trying to find a man named Charlie who was the first mate on a yacht and staying there a few days. At first the guy just stared at him as if he'd lost his mind. There were, after all, countless yachts docked on the island, how could he be expected to remember one guest? But after Zac described Charlie, he became more animated.

"I know who you're looking for. He stays with us whenever his captain has a layover. He really likes it here." He gestured to the spacious surroundings.

"Can't say I blame him," Zac said wanting to hurry the man along without offending him. "So, could you ring his room and see if he's in?"

"No problem." He spoke into the phone, then said, "He wants to know who's asking."

"Tell him it's Zac, the guy who came to Belize with him on the yacht. He'll know."

After a brief conversation, the man nodded and hung up the phone. "He says to come right over. He's staying in the Palms Veranda." He provided directions to the unit and Zac headed out, heartened that his luck was holding. Now if Charlie could help them get outta here, life would be damned near perfect.

Chapter 76

As they waited for Charlie to open the door, Jackson glanced around. "This place's really cool." The units had thatched roofs reminiscent of the primitive structures traditionally used in Belize. Lush tropical foliage camouflaged verandas facing the ocean.

"Yeah," Zac agreed, beginning to feel uneasy. He wondered what was taking Charlie so long. Probably taking a crap. He was about to knock again when the door opened.

"Charlie, my man. Am I ever glad to see you."

Charlie waved them in as Zac introduced him to Jackson and Izzie.

"This here's my brother, Jackson and his... uh, friend, Izzie."

"Good to meet you," Charlie said. "Make yourself at home. Want something to drink? I have soda and beer."

When no one took him up on his offer, he said, "What's this about? By the looks of you, I can tell it's not a social visit."

"You got that right," Zac said. "We're in deep shit and need your help."

"What'd you do, rob a bank?" Charlie said it with a twinkle in his eyes that disappeared when Zac didn't laugh.

"Worse."

"Worse? You kill someone?"

"No, but if we don't get off this island, lives will be lost and I'm pretty sure it's going to be ours."

All hint of amusement left Charlie's face. "You talking about a drug deal gone bad? I warned you to stay away from that crowd, didn't I?"

"You did and that's not it." Zac said. "Remember the trunk on the yacht?"

"What about it?"

"Jackson was inside, being smuggled into the country and sold to traffickers. Same thing happened to Izzie earlier. I managed to buy Jackson back and we just rescued Izzie from the Dias Del Sol, but any minute now the traffickers will realize she's gone and they'll come looking for us. We gotta get out of here before they do."

Listening intently, Charlie looked from Jackson to Izzie and back again. "My God, how awful. You all right?"

"We are at the moment, but if they catch us, we're as good as dead," Jackson said, bruises still visible on his face and arms.

Charlie thought a moment. "I have an idea. Stay here. Don't open the door for anyone. I'll be right back."

Zac heaved a sigh of relief. If anyone could get them out of this, Charlie could. He seemed like the type that would give you the shirt off his back; a real salt of the earth kinda guy. Thank God he'd run into him at Mo's. Funny how things work out.

Half an hour later, there was a tap-tap-tap on the door and a voice quietly announced, "It's me, Charlie."

Jackson opened the door to find Charlie, accompanied by two rough-looking men.

"Zac," one of them said. "Good to see you again."

Zac's heart dropped as Mo walked in. He could scarcely believe his eyes. Charlie, the man he'd trusted with his life, had sold them out. Their last best hope of escape had just evaporated.

"Charlie, why?" he said. "You said you'd help us. I believed you. Why're you doing this?"

"Shut up," Mo said. "You got a lotta nerve saying that after telling me you only sleep with white women." He put his face inches from Zac's, his fists clinched. "I went out on a limb for you with Sid. You got any idea the trouble you caused?" He gave Zac a long, penetrating stare.

Zac almost felt guilty, as though he was being scolded by his dad instead of threatened by a vicious criminal.

"You betrayed me. Well, now you'll pay for it."

"Mo, I'm sorry, I really am. Let us go and I'll give you all my money. Please."

Mo shook a fat finger in Zac's face. "Shoulda thought of that when you decided to steal her from Sid. Bet you're not even a contractor, are you?"

When Zac didn't respond, he said, "So you lied about that too. Who are these people anyhow?"

A glimmer of hope took hold inside Zac. Perhaps this horrible man had retained a spark of humanity somewhere inside. Maybe he'd let them go when he explained who they were.

"This here's my brother, Jackson and that's his friend, Izzie. I've come to rescue them."

"Seriously? How'd they get mixed up in all this?"

"It's a long story but basically they poked their noses in where they didn't belong. So, Mo, how about it? Can you find it in your heart to let us go?" Zac desperately wished he'd managed to connect with whatever heart remained inside this monster.

Mo stared at the three of them for a long moment, rubbed his chin then came to a decision. "Wish I could, but if I caved every time I heard a sob story, I'd be outta business. No, your white asses are mine," he indicated Jackson and Zac.

Inclining his head toward Izzie, he added, "Sid gets his property back."

Izzie began first to whimper and then to cry. "No, please. I can't go back there, please don't make me."

"You, bitch, stop blubbering. I thought you knew your place before I sold you. Do I gotta teach you again?" He raised his hand to strike her, when Charlie interrupted.

"That's not necessary, Mo. I'll take her back and make sure she understands that if she stops rebelling, she can begin to enjoy life. I mean, that resort isn't exactly a slum."

Facing Charlie, Zac shouted, "You goddamned son of a bitch, I trusted you. Thought you were my friend."

"And I thought you were mine," Mo interjected. "Guess we were both wrong. Now, let's get the hell out of here. Charlie, you take the girl and we'll take these two morons." The expression on his face said he meant it.

The brute of a man who'd been silent all this time pulled out a gun and pointed it at Zac and Jackson. As he headed toward the door, Jackson turned and let go a pop to Charlie's nose.

"Ow." Charlie yelped as blood gushed down the front of his pale blue shirt. "Son of a bitch, you broke my nose."

Mo slugged Jackson as the thug with the pistol kept it trained on Zac, preventing him from joining the melee.

"Let's get outta here before someone calls the cops," Mo said, forcing Jackson to his feet. "Let's go," he said, "we don't got all night."

Izzie's screams and the vision of her being dragged from the room reverberated inside Jackson long after pain from the blow subsided. As he and Zac returned to the site from which he'd so recently been rescued, fear for her fate overwhelmed concern for his own—a prospect so bleak that to say it was hopeless would, in truth, be accurate.

Chapter 77

Zac yanked the shackles binding his hands and feet, causing the chain to scrape the cement floor.

"Son of a bitch!"

"Give it a rest, will you?" Jackson said. "You're not going to accomplish anything that way."

"Oh no? Well it's better than just sitting here. At least I'm making an effort to get us outta here. That's more than you're doing."

"And what'll your so-called 'efforts' get us? Huh? Another beating, that's what. You forget I've been through this before."

"So you're giving up, that it?"

"Hell no, but I'd prefer to pick my battles than go off half-cocked. You swearing and rattling those chains will get us exactly nowhere, and possibly annoy Mo to the point he'll put a bullet through our brains."

Zac was exasperated not only with his brother's apparent admission of defeat, but by his own failure to save them. He'd managed to rescue Izzie and Jackson only to put his trust in the wrong person and they'd landed right back where they started from. Only now it was worse. At least before, Jackson and Izzie had someone on the outside fighting to save them. Now there was no one. A paralyzing despair overtook him.

"I'm so sorry, I …"

Jackson interrupted him. "Sorry? For what? You risked everything to rescue me and Izzie—a woman you don't even know. And if it hadn't been for Charlie, you would have succeeded too. Damn, what a *dickhead* he turned out to be. Who woulda thought a guy that appeared so decent would turn out to be no better than those traffickers? You just never know…"

"Man, you got that right. I thought Charlie was a stand-up guy. I mean, he was cool on the yacht, always helping me avoid problems with Captain Tom. God, how could I have been so stupid to trust him like that?" Zac pounded his fist, banging his shackles on the floor.

"Stop. They'll hear you. Zac, I don't want another beating."

"Okay, Okay. I'll be quiet. Let's see if we can grab some shuteye before they decide what to do with us. If you get any bright ideas, let me know."

"You do the same," Jackson said.

The two men twisted and turned trying to find the least uncomfortable position they could and get some badly needed rest. Before long, Jackson began to snore while Zac remained wide awake, trying to plan his next move.

A few hours later, Zac had finally dozed off, his head resting at an odd angle against the concrete-block wall. At the sound of heavy footsteps, he awoke with a start. Forgetting his chained-up condition, he wrenched his shoulder as he jerked awake.

"Jackson, wake up, someone's coming," he said in a loud whisper.

As his brother began to stir, the light came on and Mo entered, trailed by a man Zac had never seen. At about six feet tall, the guy had a boxer's build: thick neck, bald head, and muscles that bulged under his T-shirt. His eyes were reminiscent of a pit bull's—cold, calculating and lifeless.

"Here they are, like I told you—two worthless pieces of shit. The faster someone can take them off my hands, the better."

The man stood eyeing Zac and Jackson as if they were slabs of meat.

Pointing to Jackson, he said, "Stand up."

Zac realized it was a good thing he was in chains. He would have decked the guy but the man's physique told him he'd get the losing end of a fight. Still, Jackson standing there, his head bowed in submission while the guy looked him up and down made his blood run cold.

"I'll take him," the man said.

"What about the other one? I'll let him go real cheap. In fact you can have two for the price of one. Think of it as a fire sale."

The man scratched his head. "I don't know, you seem awful anxious to be rid of him. What'd he do, kill somebody?"

"Naw, nothing like that. He's just a little wild. I'm sure you can break him after a few bouts in the ring with some of your boys. Once you get him trained, he'll work for you real good. I just don't have the time or patience to mess with it, that's all."

"Stand up so I can have a look."

In spite of himself and realizing there'd be a price to pay, Zac stayed put.

"Boy. You hear me? Get on your feet. Do as I say."

Zac raised his chin. "I'm not a boy. I'll get up when I damned well feel like it."

The man looked at Mo and said, "You're not kidding, this one's gonna take some working over." With that he leaned over and yanked Zac to his feet. "You'll do what you're told, if you know what's good for you."

Zac was about to let the man know exactly what he thought of him, but not wanting a blow to the head, he bit his tongue and let his eyes stare holes through the bastard.

The man got in Zac's face. "Better lose the attitude if you know what's good for you. Keep that up and you won't live long enough to have your spirit broken."

Turning to Mo, he said, "Oh all right, I'll take them both.

Chapter 78

Tiny's barking woke Leon from a pleasurable dream, the first he'd had in a long time. He usually had nightmares populated with Seymour's thugs taking him on a one-way trip across the Sunshine Bridge. This one featured Izzie and had something to do with a trip to the beach, the foggy details dredging up feelings he thought he'd finally overcome.

Dragging himself from the soft cocoon of a bed, he glanced at the clock and headed for the door. It was four in the morning. *Damned dog.* He'd let the mutt out when they went to bed a few hours ago. Maybe Tiny was riled up because the product was spending the night. He tried handing the girls off within a few hours of their arrival, preferred it that way—less risk. Tonight had been different. Client couldn't make it, so he'd had to adjust. That's what this business was all about—adjusting.

Tiny barked again, more frantically. Dog'd better *adjust* or he'd do it for him.

As he went down the hall, his bare feet made slapping sounds on the hardwood floor. Tiny's continuous barking morphed into the menacing growls he made when strangers approached. *Odd.* Leon was nearly to the bottom of the stairs and prepared to give the dog what-for, when there was a series of knocks on the door followed by what sounded like a voice on a bullhorn.

"Leon Donatello. Police. Open up."

Before he could move, the door flew back compliments of a battering ram. Leaping down the remaining steps, Leon turned to run out the back, but was stopped by police wielding guns and nightsticks.

Tiny, beside himself with fury, threw his substantial body at the cops—barking, snapping and baring his teeth. Before he could sink his teeth into the fatty part of the closest man's thigh, he was felled by a single shot from a Taser gun.

In the meantime, Leon was ordered to: "Get on the floor. Now. Hands above your head. Spread your legs. Move and we'll shoot."

There were so many orders, so many voices, and so many cops. Tiny, who had begun to recover was put on a leash.

"Where're the girls?" The policeman was hefty; muscles bulged beneath the short sleeves of his uniform. His scalp was visible under what little hair he had, making his stern expression even more threatening.

"Uh, what girls?" Leon lay on his stomach, the man's foot was planted firmly on his back, making speech difficult.

Digging in his heel, the cop said, "This can go down easy or hard, doesn't matter to me. Either way I'll get what I'm after. What's it gonna be?"

"I can't breathe," Leon gasped.

The policeman removed his foot. "Roll over and sit up. Try anything funny, you'll regret it."

As he struggled to get upright, Leon could hear police tramp their way through the house, opening and slamming doors. His hands and feet were bound; there was nothing he could do but wait. *Those fools'll never find the bunker.* Good thing he'd put the product down there for the night. Yeah, they'd have to get up mighty early to outsmart him.

"Okay, start talking, I ain't got all night." The cop pulled Leon to his feet and slammed him onto a dining room chair.

"I don't know what you're talking about. Me and the dog are the only ones here. You don't believe me, go search with the rest. I'll be surprised if you find something, believe me." Leon gave the man his most innocent look—the one he'd spent hours practicing.

The cop put his face inches from Leon's. Wearing an exasperated expression he growled, "Where're those women who came in the back way a few hours ago? Don't say they left because we've been watching the house—front and back. Unless you got a tunnel under …" He stopped and watched Leon's eyes flick from the bookcase to the floor and back. "That's it. You hide them under the house. That's why we can never find them. I'll be damned.

"All right, Leon, how do we get down there?" When Leon just stared at the floor, he bellowed, "Tell me, damn it."

In spite of his efforts at self-control, Leon jumped. He hadn't expected the man to shout so loud.

"Down where? I don't know what the hell you're talking about."

"My ass you don't. You got those girls stashed under the house and you know it. Now you gonna tell me how to get down there or do I have to beat it outta you?" The fury in the man's face said he meant business.

Leon shifted in the chair and tried again. "Pardon me, sir, but you know as well as I do houses in Florida don't have no basements. What makes you think this one's any different?"

The policeman guffawed, then said. "Guess you don't read the paper, dude. Couple years ago a bunker was found over in Drew Park. Guy grew weed down there. Now if he could do that … You see where I'm goin' with this?"

Leon could see clearly where the cop was going and he didn't like it. How'd he manage to figure out the house had a fallout shelter? He didn't appear *that* smart. What should he do now? Come clean and hope for the best? Or keep denying it? Maybe they wouldn't find the entrance and give up. It was, after all, hidden behind that bookcase. Who'd think to look there?

"I'm sorry, officer, I just don't know what you're talking about."

"Have it your way—and call me 'sergeant'." He turned and shouted, "Down here, they're under the house. Tear the place down if you have to."

Heavy boots tramped down the steps in such a rush Leon thought the old staircase might collapse. When the men assembled on the first floor, the sergeant said, "He's got them hidden under the house in some kinda bunker. Question is where's the entrance? He's not talking so I guess we'll have to knock walls down till we find it. Get going."

Leon shuddered. The man meant business. Still doubting he'd be able to find the secret staircase, he held fast. Approximately twenty minutes and multiple plaster holes later, one of the men shouted, "It's behind the bookcase."

Leon's heart sank. Seymour would not be happy.

Chapter 79

Neither Jackson nor Zac made a sound. The men, guns drawn, muscled them into a van conveniently parked outside the unit. The deserted parking lot dashed any hope of the possibility a passerby might intervene. Zac's spirits were lower than they had ever been. Every avenue of escape was now beyond their reach.

They were looking at a life—whatever was left of it—of slavery. The words were foreign to Zac's ears. After all, he was an American. Things like this didn't happen to U.S. citizens. Besides this was the twenty-first century. Slavery? *Him—a slave?* He couldn't get his mind around it. Forced to work for nothing—the rest of his life?

He'd prefer to kill himself than go on like that day after day, year after year. But what about Jackson? If he committed suicide, his brother'd be left to deal with the situation alone. He couldn't do that to him. No, he'd stick it out and somehow they'd eventually get free.

He glanced at his brother who stared at the floor. He leaned over and elbowed him, causing Jackson to let out an involuntary yelp. The gunman, startled at the sudden commotion, pointed his weapon at Jackson's head and said, "Go on, try something."

Regretting his spontaneous and potentially dangerous action, Zac's eyes caught Jackson's in an apologetic glance. His stupid behavior could have gotten them both killed.

He settled with his back to the side of the van, his body bouncing along over endless potholes. His mind went to Izzie, Jackson's reporter friend. It was obvious he cared about her. Look how much he'd risked: his job and now his very life. Was she worth it? Zac had no idea. Jackson apparently thought so. But then he always was softhearted, even as a kid, always sticking up for the underdog and sometimes getting a good beating for his trouble.

He couldn't help but wonder what was happening to Izzie right now. She was, no doubt, being severely punished for attempting to escape. Even if she survived, the life she faced was a horror beyond imagining. And she had no one to keep her going. At least he and Jackson had each other. By the time they escaped—if they managed to—God only knows where she'd be or if she'd even still be alive.

Chapter 80

Twenty minutes later, Zac, who'd dozed off, awoke with a start at a slight blow from the butt-end of a gun. Blinking rapidly, he could see the silhouette of the man yanking Jackson from the van.

"You. Get out." The man who'd ridden with them in the back called to Zac, adding, "He's a snorer."

Zac was about to protest that he'd never snored a day in his life, when the man motioned with the gun and said, "We don't got all day."

The moon through the clouds provided just enough light for Zac to see. They were near water, that much was certain. It sparkled in the moonlight and made lapping sounds as waves hit the shore. Directly in front of them was some kind of planking leading out over water. Suddenly he realized what it was; they were parked beside a pier.

Alarm bells tolled inside as he began to understand what their captors planned: They were being taken out of the country. He panicked. What if they ended up in Eastern Europe or, hell, he didn't know. Russia? Iran? He grabbed Jackson's arm and said, "Let's go." They had only gone about ten steps when the brutish man who'd driven the van knocked him out with a single punch.

Chapter 81

"Time to get up, Sleeping Beauty."

Zac blinked awake. His head ached, his mind was so jumbled he couldn't make sense of anything. *Where was he?* He remembered going to Belize with Jackson in a trunk and rescuing Izzie. But something had gone terribly wrong. Oh yeah, now he remembered. Charlie, his good friend, had ratted them out and Mo sold them to a couple of thugs.

A motor revved; there was a rocking motion. He must be on a boat. His heart sank. Was Jackson all right or had his efforts earned him yet another beating? Someone shook him. He didn't want to open his eyes; didn't want to know what was in store.

"Zac. Zac. Wake up." Someone imitating Jackson slapped his cheeks. "C'mon, bro," the voice pleaded.

That's when the heavens opened along with Zac's eyes. The tableau in front of him was something from a dream. Peering down at him was his brother—not an impostor, but his very own flesh and blood, pain-in-the-ass sibling. And next to him wearing a worried, almost maternal expression, stood Izzie. *Izzie?* Now he *knew* he was hallucinating.

Zac rubbed his aching head and tried to sit up. "What the…" He couldn't make sense of it: First they're betrayed by that son of a bitch Charlie; then they're held in chains and sold off as slaves. He's decked when he tries to escape. And now? Had the guy at the resort decided Izzie was too much trouble and sold her to these bozos? Were all three of them headed to some foreign country? If so, why did Jackson and Izzie look so happy?

"Zac, it's okay." His brother sounded confident, reassuring. Unusual for him. He was a worrier, always thinking about consequences. Zac was the one who flew by the seat of his pants, getting in trouble. *Please God, let it be true. Let this nightmare finally be over.*

And there it was. Izzie and Jackson, eyes brimming with tears, bending over him, hugging him, laughing.

"We did it." Jackson said and gave Izzie a look that said you're more than just my reporter. Much more.

At last Zac found his voice. "You mind telling me what the hell's going on?" He flinched, expecting to be on the receiving end of yet another blow.

"We're on the Bessie Rose," Jackson said and sat down next to him. "Charlie's taking us to Mexico to get help."

"Seriously? Charlie? The rat who sold us out is helping us now?" Zac's eyes bulged in disbelief. "And you believe him? After what he did?" He lunged from the bed, his hands curled into tight fists. "Where's that son of a bitch anyway?" Glancing around he realized they were in what had previously been his stateroom.

"He's upstairs…uh, you know, piloting the boat." Jackson stumbled for the correct nautical term.

"And you believed him when he said he's rescuing us?"

"Yes, he risked his neck to get us out."

"You sure? He's the whole reason Mo got his clutches on us and Izzie taken back to that whorehouse resort. Those guys beat me up pretty good too."

"Not that you deserved it."

When Zac gave him a look, Jackson added, "I'm just sayin'. Charlie said it was all a ruse to get us out of Ambergris without raising suspicions. The men who bought us from Mo think he's a trafficker and that he's delivering us to a buyer in Guatemala."

"And Izzie?"

She'd been uncharacteristically quiet. "Charlie didn't take me to the resort. He brought me here. We've been waiting for you guys. He said we had to get out before they discover I'm gone."

For probably the first time in his life, Zac was speechless. Finally he said, "Well, I'll be damned. And to think you nearly broke his nose."

Jackson laughed. "Yeah, I did that, didn't I? Thank God he doesn't hold grudges."

As the three found their way to the pilothouse, Zac wondered where Charlie was taking them and how they'd ever find their way home.

"There you are," Charlie's voice boomed as they approached. He looked at Zac, "You don't look too much worse for the wear—considering."

"Says you," Zac growled. Jackson poked him in the back. "So I was wrong."

"Wrong?" Charlie gave him a puzzled look. "Wrong about what?"

"About you. I thought you'd sold us to those traffickers."

"I did. In case you didn't notice, Mo had you in chains, or so I've been told." He laughed, then winced and touched his swollen nose. "At least *you* didn't try to break my nose."

At that, all eyes turned to Jackson. "Oh yeah, sorry about that."

"No, that's all right. It made things more believable to anyone who happened to have been watching."

"So, I take it you're one of the good guys," Zac said. "And Captain Tom?"

"What about him?"

"He cool with you taking his precious yacht for a spin in the middle of the night?"

Charlie's eyes went back to the wheel. He mumbled, "I borrowed it. He doesn't know."

"Wait, what?" To this point Zac had been feeling, if not good, at least less panicked. Now the adrenalin of fear snaked its way up his spine again. "You stole his boat?"

"Calm down, Zac. He's out doin' some babe and getting loaded. By the time he sobers up, you'll be safe in Chetumal and the yacht'll be back in its slip. He won't be any the wiser."

"Chetumal? What's that?"

"A port on the Yucatin Peninsula." To Zac's unspoken question, he added, "It's about seven hours from here. A friend of mine'll be waiting and will take you to the American consulate in Cancun."

He sounded so positive everything was going to work out that Zac relaxed in spite of himself. "Okay, then," he said and reaching out, he shook Charlie's hand. "Dude, thanks. We were in a shitload of trouble.

If you hadn't stepped in, I don't even want to think of what might have happened."

"No problem," Charlie said. "Look, why don't you guys fix yourselves something to eat and get some sleep. You have a long night ahead of you even after we get to Mexico."

Heading to the well-stocked galley, the trio didn't have to be told twice.

Chapter 82

Leon leaned over and rested his head on his arms. The cool metal of the table was somehow soothing.

For the past few hours detectives had grilled him nonstop: Who's running the show? How many are involved? C'mon man, you're not smart enough to organize something like this on your own. Give it up and it'll go easier on you.

What should he do? On the one hand, Seymour had been good to him—well, in his own way he had—except for the threats and occasional punches to the gut when something went wrong. But for the most part, he'd let Leon run the show on his own.

On the other hand, the man's head was swollen to the point it resembled one of them oversized balloons. He acted as if he was too good for Leon. Sure he'd managed to rise to the top of the outfit and had more money than God had dirt, but still. Leon remembered when they were both gangbangers scraping and bowing to whoever was in power at the moment.

Look at it this way, if Seymour was in his place, would he protect Leon? *Hell no.* He'd give Leon up in a moment's notice. So why should Leon spend more time in the slammer to protect *him*? Then there was retaliation. Seymour had driven home the point that if Leon *ever* gave him up to the cops, his life wouldn't be worth shit.

Leon started at the sound of the door opening. It was decision time. They weren't going to dick around with him much longer. *What's it going to be?* Protect Seymour and do more time or give him up and look over his shoulder the rest of his life?

"Okay, dirtbag, I've had just about enough. Start talking."

Leon could see by the expression on the detective's face that he meant business. At that moment, he made what may have been the smartest decision of his life. He said, "I want a lawyer."

Chapter 83

After several glasses of cheap wine Zac drifted off to sleep. For the past twenty-four hours he'd been running on pure adrenalin, so when it came to grabbing forty winks he'd found it impossible to slow down. The hum of the boat's engine and a slight rocking motion along with the alcohol finally did the trick.

He dreamt he was back home in Iowa running wild with some buddies. His dad was alive and raising holy hell as his mother, with a pained expression, looked on. For the first time, he was about to stand up to his father and take the consequences, when he was awakened by a jolt which tossed him off the bed and onto the floor.

"What was that?" he said and snapped on the lights.

"We hit something?" Jackson said, sitting up.

Zac shrugged, dragging himself from the floor. "It's probably nothing. Maybe old Charlie fell asleep at the wheel. You guys go back to sleep while I check. If anything's wrong, I'll let you know." Despite his companions' doubtful expressions, they settled down as Zac turned out the light and left the room.

What he found topside was something from a bad movie. Two men had boarded the yacht and were having a heated exchange with Charlie. Zac stayed as far back in the shadows as he could, while still managing to hear snatches of the conversation.

"No, he didn't," the first man said. "He's the one who reported the Bessie Rose stolen."

"We're taking you back to Belize to get this sorted out. Who else is onboard?"

Alarmed, Zac turned to alert his friends—maybe they could hide and somehow go undetected while Charlie got out of this mess. If they towed the yacht back to Ambergris, it was possible they could sneak off the boat and find another way off the island. That was the plan, but like most everything else it fell short when a light came on, and he was discovered on his way back to the stateroom.

"Stop where you are." The man had some kind of nautical uniform on and pointed a gun at him. Zac knew better than to ignore him.

"Yes? Who are you? What're you doing onboard Captain Tom's yacht?" Zac said, figuring a strong offense might do the trick. He was wrong.

"I'll ask the questions. Sit down." The man inclined his gun toward the galley table and chairs. "Who else is onboard?"

Zac started to say no one, when his stupid-ass brother stuck his head out of the stateroom and said, "What's going on?"

That did it. The officer ordered Jackson from the room and pulled the door back to find Izzie sitting up in bed with a puzzled look.

"Get out here and sit next to your friend over there."

Izzie did as she was told, asking Zac with her eyes what in the name of all that was good and holy was going on.

"This yacht was reported stolen by the owner, despite the fact your buddy claims he 'borrowed' it and was taking a few friends for a joy ride. Know anything about that?"

Zac spoke up. "Yes, that's exactly what happened. Charlie's a friend of ours and wanted to take the two lovers here on a romantic moonlight ride before we return to the States."

"Seriously?" The officer gave the bedraggled group a long, hard look. "You don't look much like tourists to me—or lovers for that matter." When no one said anything, he added, "This is what we're going to do."

Chapter 84

Detective Anders was incredulous. He looked from Leon to his lawyer and back again. "You telling me the guy running for mayor of Chicago is the brains behind this whole operation? That he calls the shots?"

"That's exactly what I'm sayin'. Remember you promised if I gave him up you'd put me in witness protection ... that's what you said." Leon looked from the detective to the lawyer. An onlooker might think he resembled a child begging his parents to keep a promise. "Isn't that what he said?" He nudged his lawyer.

"That's what he said all right," the lawyer agreed. "We have it in writing." He waved a sheet of paper like a flag of surrender.

"All right, all right, who's saying any different?" At first the detective seemed to be at a loss for words then came back to himself. "Okay, tell me the whole story. If it checks out, and I can be sure you're not lying then we'll talk about witness protection. Right now all I've got is your cockamamie story about how you're not to blame for all the crimes you committed, that some hotshot in Chicago's the real perpetrator. We've got to have more than your say-so. You understand?"

Leon understood only too well that he was in over his head. Seymour had been careful to cover his tracks, to leave no evidence of his involvement in the operation. He'd limited his contact with Leon, and even then made calls from throw-away cellphones. The few times Leon called him Seymour had pitched a fit, reminding him that he was never, *ever* to contact him at home. They had a go-between who passed messages back and forth, and even then it was rare.

Leon had enjoyed the limited contact with his boss—thought it showed he was trusted, on his way to the top. Now the full impact of that so-called "trust" came crashing down like a hunk of loose cement from a skyscraper. Seymour had set it up so if the operation was exposed, Leon would bear the full brunt of the blame. And Seymour? He'd gotten rich off the sales of the newly enslaved, but had no real skin in the game.

What a fool he'd been. How could Leon *ever* prove Seymour Cottingham, the rich white guy from Chicago's ritzy North Shore was up to his neck in the trafficking of human beings?

For a few minutes there was no sound in the grungy interview room. Leon stared at the wall, noting a place where someone left an imprint of their shoe in the sheetrock. That's what he felt like doing: letting go with some punches or kicks to relieve the growing panic inside. He was facing hard time.

And Seymour? He'd get off and find another sucker to continue his moneymaking. Wasn't that always the way it went? Guys like him were the mules who carried the heavy burdens for little or no reward, while the "brainiacs" at the top got off with a slap on the wrist—if that. Well, not this time. He'd find a way to prove to that detective—and his own lawyer—he was telling the truth. He was merely a flunky carrying out orders and deserved to be set free.

And if that happened, Leon would start over. Find a girl like Izzie and settle down. He saw Izzie's beautiful face in his mind's eye. They'd had a good thing going. If only he'd walked away from the whole mess right then, maybe he'd be with her enjoying the beach instead of sweating it out in a police station and fighting for his freedom. When would he ever learn?

Chapter 85

Never having been taken into custody before Jackson didn't know what to expect. The Coast Guard had turned them over to the police. Now they sat on a bench at the intake room of Belize Central Prison fearing what would happen next. It was well past midnight, and the sergeant at the front desk was none too happy to have his mid-shift lunch interrupted. He listened as the arresting officer explained the situation. Jackson understood only snatches of the mixed English and Kriol.

"They stole a yacht. Coast Guard caught'em red-handed."

Whatever the officer said in response was garbled. Besides Jackson was too busy worrying about the consequences of Charlie's misguided efforts. He couldn't remember exactly who it was, but recalled someone having said to avoid the police at all costs, that they were thoroughly corrupt. Too late for that. To make matters worse, Mo had confiscated their money, so the possibility of a bribe was out of the question.

They were, once again, in the jaws of a dilemma, but this time escape wasn't a possibility. Their only hope was a sympathetic judge. Perhaps once he heard their story, he'd let them go. Even then, without money, how could they make it back home? The all too familiar emotions of panic and fear surged inside. He swallowed hard, took several deep breaths and uttered a silent prayer.

Izzie, who'd been sitting beside him, periodically sniffed and wiped away tears. Then, as if there was no more fight left inside, she slumped and leaned her head on his shoulder.

Squeezing her hand, Jackson said, "Hang in there, Iz. It'll be all right. We got this far. It's only another bump in the road."

"You. Shut up," the desk sergeant growled. He turned to a guard standing nearby, "We can't do anything till morning. Take them to holding."

Jackson had hoped Captain Tom would realize it was Charlie who'd taken the yacht and had only intended to "borrow" it. Now he could see that wasn't going to happen. They'd have to spend at least one night in the clutches of the prison system.

"Put everything in your pockets in this here bag and give it back to me." The guard handed them each a sack. "And don't try hiding anything, 'cause you're gonna be searched anyway, so it won't go well with you if we find stuff." The man was dressed in a khaki army-style uniform complete with combat boots and a thick black weapons belt which held a revolver and nightstick. His black hair was clipped so short, Jackson could see his scalp.

"Get in line while I make sure you done what yore told." As he began to frisk each one, Izzie looked increasingly uncomfortable.

Jackson, noticing Izzie's expression, said, "Sir, is there a female guard who can, you know, search my lady friend?"

The guard gave him a look. "Why shore, we'll get right on it. And is there anything else you'd like? Room service? A pizza or some drinks? How 'bout a private room with a view? You think yore at a damn resort over in San Pedro? If yore lady friend's too embarrassed to be checked over, maybe she shoulda thought twice afore hangin' out with a bunch a thieves." He'd just finished with Zac and said, "Step right up, Miss."

Izzie moved forward, her eyes glued to the floor. "Hands out to the side." He patted her down, slowing visibly at her breast, butt and crotch. Jackson could scarcely contain himself and was about to intervene when the guard looked over and said, "Next."

The holding cell was a grim affair composed of a cement-block wall at the rear and thick bars on the other three sides. A bunk bed and benches were occupied by bodies so close as to appear almost as one in the gloom. More were sprawled on the bare floor, as occupants tried grabbing a few winks in the overcrowded space. The only amenity, if it can be called such, was a toilet consisting of a plastic milk carton cut in half. The stench provided proof it had been used.

Izzie pinched her nose and put her hand over her mouth as if trying to avoid breathing in the foul odor.

"Holy crap, what the hell is this? You expect us to stay here?" Zac had been in jail for disorderly conduct in the past, and most likely had a notion of what prison should be like: clean cells, bunk beds with thin mattresses, blankets, maybe even a pillow, a sink with running water and a toilet in the corner. Belize Central Prison at Mile Two of Burrel Boom Road had none of these. Compared to the sight before him, the jails he'd been in seemed like five-star hotels. "I'm not joining a bunch of low-life's on the floor infested with God only knows what," he declared.

The guard thrust a baton in his face. "Oh no?"

When Zac didn't respond Jackson nudged him forward. The guard gave him a look that seemed to say he was disappointed at being robbed of the chance to demonstrate who was in charge.

Alone in the darkened cell, each of the four carved out a small space on the floor and curled up, intending to get some rest after their ordeal. Snores ricocheting back and forth across the room, the occasional insect bite along with the chill creeping into their bones from the damp cement floor made that nearly impossible. Finally after what seemed like endless hours later, a guard opened the cell door and they were informed breakfast was available—if they were hungry. Morning had arrived at last.

Thinking they'd be offered some kind of cereal, toast and a cup of coffee, Jackson got in line behind his cellmate. Instead of being led to a cafeteria, he was met at the door with a guard handing out sandwiches consisting of two slices of dry bread with a piece of rancid cheese in the middle. And coffee? Their liquid refreshment came from the tap.

As bad as things were, the real horror of their situation came home to roost half an hour later when the men were issued orange jumpsuits, and a guard told Izzie to accompany him to the women's section of the prison.

"I want to stay with them," she protested.

"In case you haven't noticed, nobody gives a shit what you want," the guard said, and gave her a shove. "Now move."

"What about the judge?" Jackson said.

"What about him?" Impatience was woven into the fabric of the man's expression.

"When do we get to see him?"

"In about a month—if you last that long." The surly guard looked pointedly at Zac then threw back his head and laughed.

Chapter 86

Patricia Maxwell was tall for a woman, slim with a rack that made most men drool. She had large brown eyes and thick black hair that reached her shoulders. She was dressed in a business suit that did nothing to hide her voluptuous figure. Her lips were full and just begging to be kissed. The woman was a looker, that's for sure. Even in the dire straits in which he found himself—or perhaps despite them, Leon wasn't above appreciating the sight of a beautiful woman.

"Mr. Donatello? Did you hear what I said?"

Leon's eyes snapped up from where they'd been focused. "Uh, I'm sorry, what?"

"I said we need to face facts. You've been caught in the act. The police discovered those women in your basement. And you were the only one in the house at the time. Considering the circumstances, it'd be ludicrous to tell a judge you were unaware of what was going on."

"But I didn't load them up in that van and drag them into my house. They came willingly." Leon thought he'd made a good point. Maybe Miss Good-looking Attorney sitting across from him in her short skirt with her long legs crossed, would agree.

"But where did they think they were going?" She leaned in to the table and waited for him to respond.

"How do I know? I don't speak their language. I mean, I was just a middle man, providing lodging for the night and passing them on to the next buy…uh, er, person who would take them to their final destination."

"Okay, let's say that's true," Ms. Maxwell said. "Then how do we account for the ledger the police found?"

Unaware that his notebook had been discovered, Leon was shaken. It provided a complete record of the sales that had taken place and was in his handwriting. His mouth parched, he swallowed hard then took a swig from a bottle of water that had been provided.

"How do they know it's mine? Maybe the previous owner left it there." That was a Hail Mary pass, but worth a try.

"Well, we could argue that but then how do we explain your name on the front cover?"

"My name's on it? You sure?" He specifically remembered erasing it. They couldn't possibly know it belonged to him.

"They traced it from the indents the pen made." The attorney's patience was wearing thin.

At this point Leon realized he had no more wiggle room; it was time to start dealing.

Chapter 87

A sea of orange greeted Zac, as he, Jackson and Charlie headed out to the prison courtyard. The baggy jumpsuits encased some of the meanest looking men he'd ever seen. No stranger to barroom brawls, he wanted nothing to do with this bunch. Despite their weapons, the guards were greatly outnumbered and couldn't be counted on for protection, especially since several had taken an obvious disliking to him.

He stood next to Charlie who leaned against the wall and rubbed his temples. "Guys, I'm sorry about all this. I really thought I could make it to Mexico and back undetected. I've done it several times and never had a problem. Guess old Captain Tom decided to take his lady friend for a ride. In case you didn't notice, there was a full moon out last night and it was spectacular."

Zac looked at Charlie as if the man had lost his mind. They had not only been trying to escape from Mo—who considered them one step above dogs—but now they faced felony-theft charges. And the guy who'd taken them from a desperate situation to an impossible one was commenting on the moon? *Seriously?* There were no words. He'd trusted this guy and look where it had gotten him. How long would they be in this hellhole? And would they survive?

Even if they managed to avoid getting beaten to death by that bunch of lunatics, he glanced at a fight in progress, they still had to survive the prison's medieval conditions: polluted drinking water, spoiled food—what there was of it—and getting bit by God only knows what kind of insects.

Maybe he'd manage to stay alive, but what about Jackson, not to mention Izzie. Neither of them had been subjected to the brutality and primitive living conditions they were facing. Zac couldn't do anything to help them—not a single thing.

As he took several steps from the wall, an inmate bumped into him. "Hey, watch yourself."

"You ran into me."

"Say what? You better apologize and be quick about it if you know what's good for you." The man's eyes drilled Zac with an almost maniacal intensity.

Zac rarely ever walked away from a fight, but sizing the guy up he thought this might be the time to start. The man was well over two hundred-fifty pounds and several inches taller than he was. Well-developed biceps bulged from the sleeves of his jumpsuit. Scars, recent cuts and bruises on his face, arms and hands broadcast his willingness to exchange blows.

"My bad. Sorry man, I didn't see you." Zac offered to shake hands but the man refused.

"I'll let it go *this* time," he said. "Don't let it happen again." He walked away without another word.

The other inmates resumed whatever it was they were doing. Zac assumed they felt deprived. Watching an American receive a good beating would have provided a badly needed source of entertainment. Oh well, Zac realized, they knew there'd be another opportunity to revisit the situation—most likely soon.

In the meantime it was around noon and his stomach began to remind him he hadn't eaten since the poor excuse of a breakfast four hours earlier. He approached a scrawny inmate, thinking he could easily defend himself against this one if the need arose.

"Hey Dude. When do we eat?"

The guy gave Zac a puzzled look. "Eat? We already ate. You didn't get anything?"

"Well, yeah, I had a sandwich with cheese for breakfast."

"So?"

"So when do we get lunch? I'm starving."

The man shrugged. "What can I tell you? You shoulda saved one a them pieces of bread to eat later. Supper isn't till six. And don't ask me what time it is now 'cause I don't know." He pointed at the empty place on his arm where the contrast between his dark tan and lighter skin bore witness to the absence of a watch. Then, seeming to notice he'd begun to attract unwanted attention from the yard bullies, he quickly walked away leaving Zac and his rumbling stomach to fend for themselves.

Chapter 88

While her friends were just trying to stay alive, Izzie faced problems of her own. Although not required to don the orange jumpsuits their male counterparts wore, conditions in the women's section were no better and in some respects worse. The guards openly lusted after the more attractive females and were not at all subtle in reminding them that if they wanted to improve their situation they needed to cooperate. Their intentions weren't lost on the women; they knew exactly to what they referred.

Izzie was by turns exhausted, terrified and just plain hungry. The previous night she'd tried to sleep on the cold cement floor. With no blanket to keep out the dampness or stop insects from biting, she had little success.

"So, what 'cha in for?" Her cellmate was an attractive woman Izzie judged to be in her thirties.

"My friend borrowed a boat. Now we're accused of stealing it."

The woman nodded in sympathy. "Oooh, too bad. That'll get you a couple years for sure."

"What? Why? We didn't do anything wrong. Just borrowed a friend's boat to go for a ride."

"Stealing, isn't that what they say you did?"

Izzie nodded.

"Judge doesn't like thieves."

Izzie could feel her heart sink. "We haven't seen a judge yet. Maybe after he hears our story, he'll let us go."

The woman laughed, her face crinkled into a broad smile. "Okay, you hold onto that thought. It'll help get you through the next month."

"Month? Why a month?"

"That's when the judge comes 'round next."

Izzie was so crestfallen, she wanted to curl up in a ball and cry. How could she possibly last in these miserable conditions a whole month? The food was horrible; she'd gotten no-end of bug bites and the guards? How long could she fend them off? The one, she thought his name was Roscoe, had made his intentions very clear: he could make her life easier or impossible. It was up to her.

"How about you? What'd they get you for?"

"Murder."

"*Murder?* Really?"

The woman nodded.

"Who'd you kill?"

"They say I killed my boyfriend, that I stabbed him because he raped my little girl."

"Your little girl? How old is she?"

"Just ten."

"Did you?"

"I found him with her and screamed at him to leave her alone. He came at me with a knife. We struggled and he tripped, cutting himself in the stomach. By the time the ambulance got there, he'd bled to death. I told them what happened, but they didn't believe me."

"What about your daughter? Couldn't she tell them?"

"She did, but they said I coached her. They found me guilty and sentenced me to twenty years, maybe less with good behavior."

"And the guards? Are they after you too?"

She seemed to blush then said, "They were till you got here. You're lucky, you know. They can make things a whole lot better if you give them what they want."

Izzie's stomach clenched; she thought she'd vomit at the thought of what she'd have to do to survive.

Chapter 89

"He ready to spill?" Detective Anders said to Leon's lawyer. He enjoyed doing battle with Patricia Maxwell. They'd dated briefly several years ago, before he settled down and got married. He was faithful to his wife, Beth, always would be. Still, he wasn't above noticing an attractive woman, especially when she sat right across the desk from him.

"Absolutely."

"Gonna give us something we can use?"

"Depends on what he gets in return. You have to understand: the guy he turns over—the operation he exposes—could mean a death sentence. Before he risks his life, he needs assurances that he'll be protected, as in witness protection, and not just some half-assed effort on your part either."

Man, that woman had a mouth on her. Anders leaned back in his swivel chair. "Like I told you before, depends on what he gives us and what he can prove. Just telling us the candidate for the mayor of Chicago is involved with human trafficking isn't enough. We need hard proof. I mean, imagine the explosion his allegations are going to make—not only in Chicago, but across the country. We're going to look like a bunch of fools if what he says doesn't hold water. Know what I mean?"

"I do. Look, talk to him and see what you think."

****

Five minutes later, Anders joined the attorney and her client in the interview room. "Let's get this party started. What've we got?"

Ms. Maxwell looked at Leon. "You're up," she said.

Leon began to talk and the story he told was nothing less than startling to Detective Anders. He claimed he'd known Seymour Cottingham, prominent citizen of Chicago and candidate for mayor, since they were both in a street gang as teens. From there they'd graduated to the mob, but whereas Leon repeatedly ended up in jail for a variety of petty crimes, Seymour kept his nose clean. He had no record whatever—a model citizen that one.

"All right, I get it," Detective Anders looked at his watch. "You claim the guy, who's never been in prison a day in his life, is a big-time trafficker for the mob. That what you want me to believe?"

Leon nodded. With dark circles under his eyes and a troubled expression, he looked exhausted. He'd been held for over twelve hours now with no sleep and little to eat. "That's exactly what I'm saying. He's the one calling the shots."

Anders ran his hand through a head of thick wavy hair. If what Leon was saying was true then this was big. A case like this could make or break a guy's career. He had to handle it right or it'd blow up in his face.

"How did it work? I mean did he call with specific orders or what?"

"Naw, nothing like that. He knew if'n he did that, there'd be a trail and he'd get caught. He had to keep his hands clean so if anything went wrong, nothing could be traced back to him."

"Then how do we know you're telling the truth? You could be making this up to save your own skin."

"But I'm not. Look, this is how it worked." Leon stopped. "Any chance I can get something to drink and maybe a burger? I'm starving."

Anders pressed "pause" on the interview recorder and signaled to the policeman sitting next to him at the table. "He'll get you something. In the meantime, let's proceed." He pressed "record" and nodded at Leon. "You were about to tell us how the operation worked."

"Yes. All right. Seymour, er Mr. Cottingham, set me up in that house in Tampa your guys broke into last night. His contacts in other countries attracted young people, mostly girls but some guys too, telling them and their parents they'd get them into this country and either into schools for an education or good paying jobs so they could send money home. They bought the lie and went willingly. My role was to receive the poor suckers, and sell them to whoever wanted their 'services'."

"That's where that notebook of yours came in?"

"Right. I had to keep a record of some kind, so I'd know if Seymour was cheating me. He wasn't above doing that, you know."

"How did you get paid?"

"Cash only. The asshole," Leon paused and looked at Ms. Maxwell, "Sorry, I mean Seymour covered all his bases."

"So we're right back where we started from then?" Anders' patience was wearing thin. They were going round and round in circles. The bastard was playing him. "We're not getting anywhere. Book him." He signaled to someone behind the two-way mirror.

The door to the interview room opened and the policeman walked in with his food followed by another who appeared ready to do as the detective requested.

"No, wait, I'm not finished," Leon protested. "There's more."

"Well, get to it. Either you can prove Cottingham's involved or you can't. I don't have all day."

Leon opened the bag and dug in. The smell of a hamburger and fries filled the room.

Detective Anders' stomach rumbled, reminding him he hadn't eaten since breakfast. It made him even more eager to finish this and be done with it. He turned the recorder back on.

"How'd you stay in touch?"

"Cottingham called from time to time, but always said I was never to call him. He was clear about that."

"How'd you get paid?"

"He had one of his flunkies drop off an envelope of cash each time we handled a shipment."

Leon's business-like approach surprised Anders. For a run-of-the-mill street thug, he was surprisingly organized. "So you never had occasion to call the guy? Nothing ever went wrong?"

"Well, there was that thing with the girl who killed herself. That was bad."

The hair on Anders' neck prickled; a chill ran down his spine. "What girl?"

"The one that showed up on Clearwater Beach 'bout a month ago. You remember, it was all over the news."

Indeed he did remember. They'd tried everything to identify her. No one claimed the body and they'd finally buried her in a pauper's grave. "You had something to do with that?"

"Whoa, wait a damn minute. I didn't kill her. Lemme be clear on that. I admit she was a 'guest'. Somehow she got hold of my gun and shot herself in the head. I didn't know what to do, so I called Seymour. He freaked out, said I'd jeopardized the whole operation and to get rid of the body. Dumping her on the beach was my idea." Leon seemed proud of that.

"You have a record of who she was?"

"Just what I have in my notebook."

"But you can point that out?"

"Sure. Be hard to forget that one, it caused me so much trouble."

"Okay, we'll get back to that later. Tell me about Zac."

"Zac? What about him?"

"He works for you, right?"

Leon's eyes bulged. "How'd you know about him?"

"Never mind that. Just tell me what he did and where he is now."

"Him? He did odds and ends for me, nothing much. I sent him out of the country to deliver a shipment about ten days ago."

"A shipment? As in a trafficking victim?"

"You could say that."

"I thought your victims were foreigners. You traffic U.S. citizens too?" Good God, this was getting more complicated by the minute.

"Sure. But we usually move them around within the country. I mean when I get a girl from here, I make sure she's sent across the country. That makes the possibility of getting caught a lot less. See what I mean?"

"What made this one different?"

"It was a guy nosing around. I couldn't take any chances."

"So how'd you get him out of the country?"

"In a trunk."

"A trunk? On an airplane?"

"No, by boat. A plane would have been too risky."

Anders began to wonder if that was what happened to the other Taylor. What was his name? Jackson, the news photographer, that was it. He was Zac's brother. He'd been concerned about his reporter friend. Claimed she'd disappeared and wasn't about to let it go.

"So, you took him onboard what? A cruise ship?"

"No, it was a trawler yacht. A friend of Seymour's handles these kinda shipments from time to time."

"Really?" Now they were getting someplace. "And where did he generally take his special cargo?"

"To Belize."

Chapter 90

It was hot—ungodly hot, and there was a constant line at the faucet to get a drink of tepid water. Zac had gone inside to relieve himself and for the moment lost sight of Jackson and Charlie. When he came out, Charlie was in line but Jackson was nowhere to be seen.

"Charlie, where's Jackson?" Zac tapped him on the shoulder.

"I thought he was with you." Charlie looked startled, as if awakened from a dream.

Fearing his worst nightmare—his brother attacked by the gang of vicious thugs that populated the place—may be coming true, Zac frantically eyeballed the courtyard. *Oh God, where was he?*

Numerous groups of orange-clad inmates mulled about, making it nearly impossible to distinguish one from another. Charlie joined him. As they began to search, going from one group to the other, they were more often than not greeted with taunts and hostile stares.

What if Jackson had been cornered in an isolated area of the complex and was fighting for his life. It wasn't unheard of for inmates to be murdered in this place; one had been found beaten to death in the few days they'd been there.

Zac was in full panic mode. *Where the hell was he?* Doubling his fists, his adrenalin pumping, he charged about the yard like a man half-crazed. If they harmed his brother they'd pay for it, that was for damned sure. He'd find out who was responsible and … and… *was that Jackson?* Over there, in the corner of the yard surrounded by a dozen or so men? Were they threatening him? Or about to beat him up? He'd witnessed more than one smack down of that type since they'd been here and shuddered to think of Jackson being on the receiving end.

The closer he got the more befuddled he became. The men were laughing up a storm, almost howling in merriment. What was so damned funny? Were they forcing Jackson to do something obscene? Had they taken his clothes or made him impersonate a woman?

He was close enough now to hear some of the remarks, which only confused him more.

"That's a good one. Tell us another." One voice said. He didn't sound angry or threatening. *What the hell was going on?*

Zac elbowed his way through the tight little group and was astonished at what he saw. Standing there surrounded by some of the toughest men in the yard, Jackson not only didn't appear frightened or under any kind of duress, he seemed to actually be enjoying himself.

"Another time I covered a story about a lady whose legs were cut off in a lawn-mower accident. That was gruesome. Blood everywhere," he said, then noticing Zac, he paused, "This here's my brother. He can tell you a lot of good stories, can't you, Zac?"

Before Zac could respond, the group's reaction left no doubt who they preferred to hear from.

"Tell us how somebody gets to be a news photographer."

"Do you have to have your own camera?"

"Do they provide a car?"

As the questions kept flying, Zac slipped away from the throng. It was obvious Jackson didn't need his help. He was doing just fine on his own.

Chapter 91

It was true Jackson had succeeded in gaining the admiration of the toughest inmates on the yard—unfortunately Zac had no such luck. Despite being the golden boy's brother, for some reason the gang leader had it in for him and lost no opportunity to let him know it. So far, he'd been able to escape with only threats, insults, a few kicks and smacks to the back of the head, but that was all about to change.

The afternoon was one that made the inmates especially surly. The sun beat down unmercifully and the only shade was taken up by the yard's toughest bullies. Zac was fed up with all the bowing and scraping he'd been doing to avoid trouble. Seemed like he'd kissed every ass in the place and was beginning to wonder if it was worth it.

In school he'd stood up to the toughs who roamed the halls intimidating weaker kids, taking their money and knocking armloads of books to the floor. Sure, he'd taken a few beatings in his quest to assert himself, resulting in more than a few suspensions, but in the end he'd earned their grudging respect and they left him—and his brother alone.

Seemed like this was a similar situation, only Jackson wasn't part of the equation. They liked him. Apparently he'd convinced them that if they treated him well, when they got out he'd find them jobs as news cameramen. Zac laughed. *Sure he would.* Well, whatever works. You got to respect him for coming up with the idea. It kept him alive for the time being. Too bad he hadn't been able to include his brother in the deal. That would have been nice. He shrugged. Apparently he'd tried but they weren't buying it. Zac was on his own.

He was about to go outside to get a breath of air when he was hit in the middle of the back with some kind of object. It hurt like a sonofabitch. As he went down, he stole a brief glance at his attacker. It was the same guy who'd baited him from the moment they arrived. Name was Khan, least that's what everyone called him—as in Genghis Khan, the Mongolian warrior of the 13th century. Zac didn't have a clue what the real Khan looked like, but if this dude resembled him in any way, he was pug ugly and fearsome as hell.

He rolled across the floor escaping a second blow then sprang to his feet. Turning slightly sideways he karate-kicked the man, catching him across the jaw. Khan screamed in pain and fell down, holding his face as blood spurted from a split lip.

Thinking he was home-free, that the man got the message and would leave him alone, Zac began to feel good about himself despite the pain in his back. Then he saw them: Khan's henchmen had been standing in the shadows, waiting their turn.

That's when Zac realized he didn't have a chance. There were simply too many of them. He bent over and rolled into a fetal position as blows rained down on him.

The beating seemed to go on forever. On the verge of losing consciousness, his body a mass of pain, Zac was a helpless rag of a man with not an ounce of strength to buoy him. The likelihood of his impending death not only didn't frighten him, he looked forward to it.

Then he heard familiar voices he never thought he'd welcome: it was the prison guards. Zac viewed those guys as toads and bullies, but never saw them beat an inmate—that is, not unless said inmate asked for it. Come to think of it, that's precisely what he had routinely done. Oh God, he just wanted to die—not prolong the agony by getting another whipping courtesy of the guards.

"Go on, get outta here," the guard Zac had mentally named Bulldog yelled at the thugs. As he was pulled to his feet, Zac steeled himself for the next round of pain.

Chapter 92

Bulldog and another guard dragged Zac away from the inmates' quarters to an area of the prison he'd never seen before. It was actually kind of nice, at least compared with where he, Jackson and Charlie were housed.

Having forced him into a bathroom, the guards propped him against a sink and began to clean him up. Zac's brain went on instant alert. He couldn't imagine what they had in mind. Maybe they were going to sell him back to Mo or some other trafficker. Considering that prospect likely, Zac preferred getting beaten to death instead.

A few minutes later, the blood wiped from his face, they gave him a clean jumpsuit and ordered him to put it on.

"What's happening?" Zac couldn't believe he was about to beg these guys to leave him in this hellhole.

"Shut up and do as you're told." The second guard said. "And be quick about it."

"Where's my brother? Is he going with me?"

The guard pulled out his nightstick. "Shut your mouth. I'm not saying it again."

Zac was in so much pain he complied. He changed clothes, leaving the bloody garment on the floor.

"Throw it in the trash, fool. This ain't no pigsty." The guard gestured to the well-kept facility. "We keep it clean in here."

Zac bent over to pick up his old clothing, fully expecting a kick in the rear, but to his surprise that didn't happen.

"Let's go," Bulldog said.

His heart sinking along with any hope for the future, Zac walked alongside his jailers to meet his slave master. They went down a well-lit corridor and stopped before a door labeled "Office of the Warden".

So the warden's in on this. Bet he gets a cut of the sale. It made sense when you thought about it. If Belize was a hotbed of human trafficking, what better place to buy slaves than from an overcrowded prison? Arrest people—then sell them. Who's going to stop it, especially if officials are on the take?

As the door opened, Zac didn't think his future prospects could possibly be worse. There was no hope for rescue, nowhere to turn and apparently he would be leaving his brother, Charlie and Izzie behind. They would, no doubt, assume he'd been beaten to death by the inmates.

He walked in behind the guards whose bodies effectively blocked him from seeing who occupied the room. Not that he cared. Whether it was the warden, Mo or some new slaver, it was all the same to Zac. Why bother giving whoever it was the courtesy of a glance.

"Zac Taylor." An unfamiliar voice said. "Join us at the table."

Zac refused to budge. He just stood there his eyes glued to the floor. They might have possession of his body, could beat him until he could no longer stand, but he'd be damned if he'd be respectful. He'd ignore them—his way of saying, "Go to hell".

"Zac." *Who was that?* It sounded like Jackson. Had they managed to co-opt him? Why? He'd made a place for himself in prison. Sure, they were starving, but he could hang on for a month until they saw the judge. There was no reason for him to go along with this shit.

"Zac," he said again.

He heard footsteps and felt arms encircle him. He glanced up to see his brother staring at him, his eyes blinking back tears. "It's going to be all right. We've been rescued."

Thinking he'd finally lost his mind and that Jackson was a hallucination, he managed a quick look around. The room was fairly well appointed with a large desk and several guest chairs. A ceiling fan spun slowly overhead. Several potted palms squatted next to windows which overlooked the front of the building. A room-size area rug and inspirational wall posters completed the décor.

Zac's brain was so befuddled he couldn't put the sight before him together. There were several men he didn't recognize along with a woman… no—that was Izzie and Charlie. *What the hell was going on? Were they finally getting to see a judge? Is this how they did it in Belize?* No courtroom, just an informal meeting before a judge in the warden's office where he declared they were guilty?

"Zac, did you hear what I said?" Jackson repeated. "Detective Anders came to get us. We're going home."

Jackson's words confused Zac. *Could it possibly be true? Was their nightmare finally over? Detective*

Anders here? Pain from the beating he'd taken engulfed his body making it difficult to breathe. The room began to spin.

"Whoa, get him to a chair. He's about to pass out." The warden, who'd been watching the brothers from behind his desk stood as the guards complied with his order.

Zac recovered quickly but remained baffled as to what was going on. He glanced uncertainly from one person to the next.

"Now that we're all here, let's get started," the warden said. "Zac, of course you know the ones you were with when the Coast Guard caught you stealing that boat."

Detective Anders objected. "That was all a misunderstanding. They didn't…"

The warden put up his hand. "We'll get to that in a moment, Detective. Let me finish." His stern expression told Anders it was *his* prison and *he* was in charge. "So, now, Zac, I believe you also know Captain Tom, the owner of said boat?"

Zac's head was pounding. *Let's get this over with.* The son of a bitch was simply going through the motions. He was going to throw them right back in that poor excuse of a prison where they'd either starve, die of some god-awful tropical disease or get beaten to death. The sad thing was that by the look on Jackson's face the poor sap really believed Anders was about to spring them. *Sure he is.*

He tuned back in to hear the warden saying, "And this is Detective Richard Anders from the Tampa Florida Police Department. I believe you know him as well?"

Zac nodded. Why was the man going through this charade when he had no intention of letting them go?

"So, now, Detective, explain to these good folks exactly what it is you want. And," he tapped his watch, "let's not take all day."

Detective Anders nodded. "Okay. Zac here has been working undercover with the Tampa PD on a human trafficking case back in the States after Jackson and Izzie discovered the operation and got themselves in too deep. The trafficker, rather than kill them, used his connection—in the person of Captain Tom and his trawler yacht—to hold them captive and ship them to Ambergris Caye where they were sold as slaves.

"Zac managed to free them, somehow or other and with the help of the captain's first mate, Charlie, was trying to rescue them by getting them out of Belize. He was in the process of doing that when the Coast Guard arrested them and accused them of stealing the captain's boat. Now the captain here says it was all a big misunderstanding.

"So, Warden, we're asking that you drop the charges and release my friends immediately."

Zac's mouth was so dry he could scarcely swallow as the warden considered the detective's request. *Could it really be true?* Would Captain Tom go along with the detective's account of what happened? *But why should he?* Wouldn't he be subject to prosecution once he got back to the U.S.?

Everyone waited as the warden made a phone call, his voice the only sound in the room aside from the ticking of a wall clock and an occasional outburst from the prison yard. Finally, after what seemed more like years than a few moments, the warden put the receiver back in its cradle.

"I just talked to the prosecutor and he agrees the charges should be dropped."

At first Zac, whose heart drummed in his ears, couldn't understand what he said. Then, seeing Jackson's face break into a smile as he hugged Izzie, he realized what just transpired. Anders' request had been granted. They were going home.

Chapter 93

A gentle breeze wafted over the foursome nursing their drinks on the deck of Crabby Bill's Beach Club. For a few moments they sat quietly taking in the beauty of Old Tampa Bay and watching several dolphins play. Seagulls made a racket as they landed on the railing hoping for a handout.

"Well, that was interesting," Detective Anders said, clearing his throat.

"What? The dolphins?" Izzie said

"No, silly. I'm talking about those people at the cemetery. On the one hand it was sad for them to find out their daughter was dead, but on the other hand, thanks to Zac here—and Leon—they finally have some closure. Now they won't go the rest of their lives wondering. I'm glad you guys showed up. I know they appreciated meeting you and hearing about what you went through."

When no one said anything, he added, "Zac, that number you found on the windowsill made all the difference. Turns out it was part of a phone number. We combined that with the information from Leon's notebook and put two and two together. Now thanks to your tip, Hester's parents can give her a proper burial. Good job."

Zac nodded. "Thanks."

"You're going to make a great detective one day."

"If I make it through the academy."

"Don't sweat it. If you could get away from traffickers and survive the Belize prison, police academy'll be a breeze."

"How long will it be till I get to go after traffickers? That's what I really want to do."

"You have to pay your dues first, of course, become a beat cop for a while. I'll push for you to get transferred to the Human Trafficking Unit as soon as I think you're ready. You just have to be sure to keep your nose clean in the meantime. No screw-ups," he looked at Izzie, "Excuse me, well, you know what I mean."

Izzie laughed. "That's all right, Detective. I've heard worse, especially in the past few weeks." She took a sip of her gin and tonic then glanced at the sparkling waters of the Bay. "Say, what happened to Charlie?"

Anders looked at her for a second. "Oh, that's right, I never told you."

"Told us what?" Jackson perked up, his old news-gathering habit still engrained inside.

"Charlie was working undercover for the FBI. Unbeknownst to the Tampa PD, they'd had Captain Tom under surveillance for some time. They planted Charlie aboard as his first mate to keep an eye on him. He managed to maintain his cover after things went sideways with you guys, but if we hadn't caught that last shipment and arrested Leon, I hate to think how things would've turned out."

"What about Captain Tom? He going to jail?" Zac said.

"No. We gave him immunity in exchange for dropping the complaint against you."

"How'd you manage that?" Jackson chimed in. "I mean he struck me as pretty hardnosed where that boat's concerned."

Detective Anders laughed. "Man, you've got that right. We told him we'd let him keep the boat and wouldn't file charges against him in exchange for telling us everything he knew about Donatello and Cottingham and dropping the complaint against you guys. Luckily he went for it."

"Cottingham? Who's that?" Izzie said.

"Leon's old boss?" Zac said, surreptiously tossing part of a french fry to a seagull trolling for scraps beneath the table.

"Yes, but he was also running for mayor of Chicago," Anders said.

"And the reason for the media frenzy when we got back, right?" Jackson said.

"Sure is. When his connection to organized crime and human trafficking hit the wires, they went bonkers. Add that to the publicity your old boss, Morris Stone, drummed up about your experience and, well I don't need to tell you what happened."

"Yeah, news interviews, requests for talk-show appearances, and get this—we even have book and movie offers." Izzie grew more animated as she related the information.

"Wow, that's great. You taking any of them up on it?"

"At this point we're not sure what we're going to do. We're planning to get an agent and an attorney to handle the details. I mean, there's a lot of money to be made if we do this right." Jackson glanced around the table, "Of course, we'll get you guys involved."

"Dam straight." Zac laughed and took a pull from his bottle of beer. "So, Detective..."

"Rick. Now that you're going to be part of the force, call me Rick."

"All right, Rick it is. What happened to Leon?

"Little shit's tucked away in a place no one—especially not Cottingham's henchmen—will ever find him. At least that's the plan."

"Think he'll stay out of trouble?"

"With him you never know. Maybe he finally learned his lesson." Anders gazed over to the beach where sunbathers and swimmers were enjoying themselves. "But the fact is, without the information he provided, you'd be dead meat. You do realize that, don't you?"

"Yes, but think about this. If it wasn't for him and the crap he was involved in, we wouldn't have gotten in that mess in the first place," Izzie said, her chin firmed up as if ready for a fight.

"Well, now Iz, that's debatable," Jackson said.

"Oh no, not this again," Zac said. He stood and tossed some bills on the table. "I gotta go. See you all later."

Taking that as his cue, Anders also stood. "I better get a move on as well. Stay out of trouble you two."

For a few moments Izzie and Jackson watched as the sun began to slide toward the Bay, leaving vivid golds, reds and purples in its wake. Jackson reached across the table and took Izzie's hand. "Mom said she'd come for the wedding when we get around to setting a date."

"You told her?"

"Well, duh. Of course, why wouldn't I?"

"We haven't told Zac yet. Don't you think we should've said something?"

"We'll do it tonight when he gets home. Okay?"

"Yeah, that'll be fine. So what'd your mom say?"

"That she's happy for us and can't wait to meet you." He leaned over and kissed her, then laughed.

Izzie's forehead sprouted wrinkles. "What?"

"She said she's glad her boys are finally getting along."

Chapter 94

Leon couldn't believe his eyes. *Where were they taking him?* From the back seat of the car, it looked like the surface of the moon. U.S. Marshals had flown him from Tampa to Chicago, then put him on one of their planes, which made him feel mighty important for a few hours.

They continued their journey by car refusing to say where they were headed. Said it was for his protection; that the fewer who knew his destination the better off he'd be. Leon understood their reasoning but thought *he* should be in on it. *For Christ's sake, it was his hide at stake.*

At least they'd let him bring Tiny along. At first they'd balked, but Leon had put his foot down. Said he wouldn't testify against Seymour if Tiny wasn't part of the deal. So they'd caved. Score one for his side.

Now if he could only figure out where they were going. It was somewhere west, he could tell by the sun. Maybe it was California, someplace near the ocean, like San Diego or hell, he didn't know the state; had only read about cities like San Francisco and Los Angeles. Any place like that worked for him.

As he glanced out the window, the landscape seemed just plain weird, like nothing he'd ever seen. *Was this California?* He didn't think so. For one thing, there wasn't a palm tree in sight, for another there was nothing, few cars, and nothing much to see except what looked like rocks that weren't as large as mountains but too big to be considered hills besides which there was no grass on them. *What the hell were they?* Even the flat areas were desolate

"Hey, where're we going?" He leaned up to ask Deputy Marshal Massey upfront.

"You'll see when we get there."

The man hadn't even turned around, just told him to settle down—like he was a goddamned kid. He sat back in the seat and closed his eyes.

Hours later they pulled off the Interstate into a gas station. Leon, who'd dozed off thought they were going to fill up so, still sleepy, he closed his eyes. A few seconds later the car door opened and the federal agent tapped his shoulder and said, "Hey Leon, wake up."

"What?" Leon said. "I don't hafta take a leak." He rubbed his eyes.

Massey laughed. "Get out. This here's your new home."

Leon looked around. This was nothing like the California he'd seen in magazines. Where were the palm trees, the beaches and the beautiful people? For that matter, where was the ocean?

Then he saw it. A sign advertising the "World's Number One Roadside Attraction— where ice water's free for weary travelers and coffee costs only twenty-five cents". It said "Welcome to Wall, South Dakota. Population 850."

AFTERWORD

ESCAPE FROM AMBERGRIS CAYE is a work of fiction that puts a spotlight on a very real and growing problem. While Izzie, Zac and Jackson managed to survive and escape their traffickers, in real life many are not so lucky. It's hard to imagine that in this day and age over 27 million people worldwide are believed to be working as personal and sexual slaves.

Those ensnared in such a life may be as close as your next door neighbor, the server at your favorite restaurant, or the maid in the hotel you stayed at on your last vacation. Help eliminate this scourge by recognizing the signs and reporting suspected trafficking situations to the National Human Trafficking Resource Center hotline at 1-888-373-7888 or text to BeFree (233733). A list of potential red flags and indicators of human trafficking are listed on the Polaris Project website:

http://www.polarisproject.org/human-trafficking/recognizing-the-signs

The Polaris Project is an organization devoted to the fight against human trafficking and modern-day slavery. Knowing the indicators of human trafficking is a key step in identifying its victims. Anyone can become a victim of human trafficking—even you. Join the fight and help rid the world of this unsavory crime by educating yourself about it and supporting federal and local laws designed to prevent and combat it.

ABOUT THE AUTHOR

The author of three previous novels including T*he Waterkeeper's Daughter* (2014), *The Mangled Spoon* (2014) and H*alifax* (2013), Joan Mauch's background ranges from teaching and working for nonprofit organizations advocating for the poor, to a career in marketing and public relations. A resident of Davenport, Iowa, she has a bachelor's degree in chemistry and a master's in urban studies.

Visit her at**: www.joanmauch.com** or on Facebook at **facebook.com/joanmauch.author**.

Made in United States
Orlando, FL
13 September 2023